The Last Mesa

J.D. Cody

Dedication

This book is dedicated to the memory of my grandfather, H.T., who kept his friends and family, including his wife, three daughters, and, later, his seven grandchildren, entertained for many an evening through his gift for captivating and imaginative storytelling. If I have any storytelling ability, I'm sure I got it from him.

J.D. Cody

Table of Contents

Acknowledgments

First and foremost, I would like to thank my high school sweetheart and the love of my life, Missis J.D. Cody. Whose love and support made this book possible. Thank you, Sweetheart!

Also I would like to thank my son for helping me with my computer literacy.

J.D. Cody

The Last Mesa

Prologue

Run For the Border

Rodrigo Reyes Chaveta and Kurtis Owens did not know each other. Nevertheless, they had three things in common. One, they were both wanted in Fort Bend County. Two, they were both fleeing the country to Mexico, and three, fate had brought them both together at Lala's the night it was raided by the Silver City Police Department.

For travelers along Highway 59, Silver City would be the last large city they would pass through on their way to the border. It was another four-hour drive from Silver City to the Mexican border, with only a few small towns scattered along the highway in between, that would offer little in the way of entertainment or merchandise.

I

This made Silver City the last chance stop for travelers to gather any needed supplies with any amount of certainty before entering the vast, uninhabited plains that lay between them and the Mexican border at Nuevo Laredo.

It was also the last chance to take advantage of other diversions offered, more commonly in the larger cities. One of the most popular of these diversions in Silver City was Lala's massage parlor adjacent to La Bonita Cantinita on River Street.

Lala's Massage Parlor's entrance was a facade made up to look like the entrance of a Greek bathhouse, complete with a fake portico supported by large fake fluted marble columns. The girls that worked there had become very bold indeed. Scantily dressed, they would stand in front of the massage parlor's entrance to entice sidewalk pedestrians and the customers leaving the cantina next door. Whenever they saw a police cruiser driving by, they would step behind one of the large fake columns and hide. However, the activities at the massage parlor had become too obvious to be ignored.

The SCPD had been setting up the sting for weeks but had no idea that when they raided the massage parlor for prostitution, they would also capture two high-profile felons in the process. Although the two Felons did not know each other on the night of the raid, they had banded together with the common interest of escape. They had worked well together, not speaking to one another but working in tandem as if they could read one another's thoughts, and they almost got away.

Ultimately, Chaveta and Owens were overwhelmed, arrested, and taken to Silver City Jail. At the Silver City Jail, during booking procedures, the SCPD discovered that both men were wanted in Fort Bend County on previous charges, and they were placed in adjacent cells to await transport back to that county, where they would stand trial.

"What are you wanted for in Fort Bend?" Owens asked Chaveta after learning that they were both wanted in the same county. "Supplying a minor with a controlled substance and kidnapping," he answered. "And you?" Chaveta asked in return.

"Destruction of private property, drug trafficking, driving under the influence, and identity theft. They're getting ready to put me away for a long time. That's why I was running for the border," Owens said. "Well, you stick with me, and we'll make it to Mexico yet," Chaveta said with a smile.

Chaveta had grown up in Houston, Texas, and had spent most of his youth in the city's downtown gyms, training in hopes of having a mixed martial arts career. However, things hadn't gone as he hoped. So, there he was with a set of skills that really couldn't be applied in most jobs.

He tried honest work at first if you can call bouncing at the High-69 Cabaret honest work, but he had a hunger for nice things. The nice things his family had never been able to afford, like expensive clothes, jewelry, cars, and travel. Eventually, his appetite for these things led him into a lifestyle of evil.

On his third day bouncing at the High-69 Cabaret, he had some trouble with a couple of drunk and belligerent bikers who had come in during Happy Hour. He did his job and made short work of them. The dancers on stage and the bar patrons watched in shock, feeling as if they had been transported into the middle of a Hollywood movie. Afterward, Chaveta had been the hero of the hour.

When the bar closed at two that morning, he walked out to his car only to find several bikers standing in front of it. He turned to walk back to the bar only to be flanked by several more. One of the bikers approached him, and Chaveta assumed a fighting stance. The biker stopped and extended his arm toward Chaveta. In his heavily tattooed hand, he held a large manila envelope.

Puzzled, Chaveta took the envelope from the biker's hand and opened it. Inside was a thick stack of one hundred dollar bills. "The boss wants that. You should teach us," The biker said. Chaveta closed the flap on the envelope, placed it in the inside coat pocket of his favorite grey suit, and signaled his agreement to the biker with a single nod.

Within the month, Chaveta was gifted a very nicely rebuilt antique 1941 Harley-Davidson Knucklehead with black paint and lots of chrome. In a word, it was beautiful. He also received the lease to a building in one of the more affluent parts of the city, which housed a new, well-equipped training studio.

IV

From his new dojo, Chaveta began to teach martial arts to his new friends in the Mutt City Mobsters Motorcycle Club. The Mobsters also offered him side jobs as well, and he worked steadily over the next few years. At first, he declined some of the jobs he found distasteful, but slowly, greed chipped away at his moral compass, and he became hardened over time.

During his time with the Mobsters, he went from doing security and bodyguard work to collecting debts on high-interest loans. He then moved on to collecting protection money from small mom-and-pop shop owners, then drug trafficking, and finally, a little wet work.

However, Chaveta eventually developed his own little niche. He now specialized in human trafficking, with an emphasis on the sex slave trade in particular. He would prowl the bars of Houston looking for young men or women who would match the descriptions given to him on his clientele's wish list.

When he found someone that he felt matched a profile specified by one of his clients, he would text them photos for confirmation. If the client confirmed that he approved of the victim, Chaveta would perform the abduction and deliver the poor soul to a prearranged location.

He had met with Traffickers on rural dirt strip runways in the desolate scrub lands of South Texas, where he often had to wait for cocaine shipments to be offloaded from small aircraft before his slaves could be loaded.

They had been Cessnass mostly, except for one red and white Moonie that he had seen often enough that it became recognizable. After the drug shipments were offloaded, the new sex slaves would be forced on, and the small aircraft would fly away.

He had also delivered new slaves to the Ports, where someone would load them into shipping containers destined for third-world countries, where they would become part of some dictator's collection.

Sometimes, he would meet his connections at the boat piers in South Bay, where the abductees would be manhandled onto a yacht, speedboat, or sailboat of some kind and taken away to their new homes.

The charges Chaveta had waiting on him back in Fort Bend County were because a young man had escaped him. If he hadn't, he would have woken up in a very beautiful mansion, completely free to roam the grounds. Of course, had he gone outside the gate, he wouldn't have seen anything in any direction except sand all the way to the horizon.

That's how the Sheik did it. All his young men were free to roam the huge mansion. There were four different swimming pools, tennis courts, gardens, a movie theatre, a fully stocked kitchen large enough to serve a hotel, and everything else you could ever want, except maybe for a telephone or a ride out.

VI

It had been that young party boy's fate to be added to the Sheik's harem of young men, but unknown to Chaveta, this young man had been abusing opioid drugs since adolescence and had developed an extremely high tolerance. Consequently, he regained consciousness in a much shorter amount of time than Chaveta had expected.

When Chaveta had opened the trunk to retrieve his spare tire after acquiring a flat on the freeway, he had not expected the young barfly to be awake. Nor did he expect him to flop out of the trunk and into the middle of traffic right in front of a police cruiser, like a fumbled and dropped fish flopping from the bank and escaping back into the water.

It had been a real mess. The police cruiser had jerked to stop its anti-lock braking system, shuddering to a halt mere feet from the victim, as Chaveta stood there with a look of shock and bewilderment across his face.

The two patrol officers took one look at the victim, gagged with his hands and feet tied, lying on the asphalt of the 610 Loop, and quickly exited their cruiser with their sidearms drawn and ordered Chaveta to the ground. There had been no place to run.

Owens, on the other hand, was a druggie, a con, a grifter, a pickpocket, and a thief. He had been arrested for snatching purses from the backs of chairs in Ausitn's downtown outdoor restaurants, and he had done a lengthy sentence for two counts of grand theft auto.

VII

His specialty the last few years had been identity theft, and that, along with a few other charges, was what he would be standing trial for in Fort Bend County. If he was found guilty of identity theft, it would be his third felony offense in a "three strikes, and you're out" state. In the State of Texas, Owens's sentence for a third-strike felony would be no less than 25 years and could be as much as 99 years.

That's why Owens, like Chaveta, had decided to try to start a new life over the border. Both men out on bail had tried to run. Both men were captured, and now both men would be returned to Fort Bend County, where they both faced lengthy sentences.

However, if Chaveta had his way, they would never reach Fort Bend County. As soon as He and Owens arrived at the Silver City Jail, he used his one phone call to contact William Haski, the head attorney for the Mutt City Mobsters.

Three months later, halfway between Silver City and Fort Bend County, Texas, State Trooper James Corbin had been awake since three a.m. He was called into work after a drunk driver had passed out and veered off the road. The rumble strips at the highway's edge roused the driver just as his truck went into the ditch. The drunk came to, overcorrected, and slid through the ditch. His pick-up doing a 180 had come to rest against a barbed-wire fence where the driver, once again, passed out.

VIII

The accident had been called in by a pizza delivery girl on her way home from work. She had come up behind the drunk just in time to witness his truck go off the road. Thankfully, there were no other vehicles around them. At two-forty-eight in the morning, traffic had been light, and the pizza girl and the drunk had been the only two vehicles on the road.

At the scene, Trooper Corbin had been tasked with helping to detour traffic. A wrecker truck was brought in, and the ranch owner called out. The fence had been damaged, and it wouldn't do to have cattle wandering onto U.S. Senator Lloyd Benson Highway during the fast-approaching morning rush hour.

By the time the fence had been mended and the scene of the accident was cleared, the first grey light of morning began to show. Trooper Corbin checked the time on his dashboard clock. It read six-twenty-three in the morning. He sighed heavily. By the time the accident had been cleared, his shift had begun in earnest. He took solace in the fact that he would be patrolling close to home today and would be able to see his wife and son at lunch.

His wife Linda, a professor at the local university, had taken time off to write a book, and their fifteen-year-old son Hank was out of school for summer vacation. Their schedules had meshed, with Linda writing late into the night while Hank stayed up playing video games. Not wanting to wake them, he had snuck out of the house that morning. He was now feeling a little guilty about not saying goodbye and looked forward to seeing them at lunch.

Sixty-seven miles away in Silver City, Cheveta and Owens were being loaded onto a prisoner transport bus. Before he was escorted onto the bus, a guard paid off by the Mutt City Mobsters' attorney slipped one key into each of Cheveta's socks as he patted him down.

The rest of the plan was simple. He and Owens would wait until an opportune time, release themselves, and overtake the guards. There would be two guards, one driving and one at the back of the bus. Cheveta planned to overtake the driver at the front of the bus, while Owens was to deal with the guard in the back.

A little over an hour into the trip, as they traveled North along Highway 59, Cheveta stared at the prison transport guard at the rear of the bus. The rear guard's face had assumed that glazed-over look that suggested to Cheveta that he had zoned out. Seeing this, Cheveta and Owens used their first key to release their restraints.

As the white prison transport bus began to approach Wharton, Texas. Cheveta leaped out from his seat, sprinting towards the driver. The guard in the back of the bus stared at him dumbfounded, his brain not registering what his eyes were seeing.

By the time the guard's brain caught up to what was happening, Owens had left his seat and punched him square in the face and then proceeded to grab the guard's shotgun with both hands before the guard could raise it. The guard fought back hard, he and Owens falling to the floor of the prison transport bus entangled in a deadly grapple over the shotgun.

X

The driver desperately began to try to pull the bus over to the shoulder of the road while Chaveta worked the second key in the lock of the metal gate that divided them. He succeeded in bringing the bus to a stop and was getting to his feet as Chaveta threw the gate between them open. As the gate flew open, the driver reached for his side arm. His hand fell to the grip of his Glock nine millimeter as Chaveta rushed in and pinned him against the bus's windshield and dash.

Chaveta bladed his right forearm into the driver's throat, with his left hand pinning the driver's right hand down on top of his sidearm, trapping it in the holster. He drove the blade of his right arm hard into the driver's throat, then drew back and threw a hard right elbow to the driver's head, splitting him open just above his left eye, leaving him stunned on his feet with blood running into his eyes.

Chaveta brought his right hand back from the elbow strike and followed up with a bomb of a hammer fist to the guard's slack jaw. Stars briefly exploded in the guard's field of vision before he blacked out, slid down the windshield, and crumpled to the floor of the prison transport bus.

Chaveta reached for the Glock nine millimeter in the guard's holster, but before he could release the retention strap, there was the loud explosion of a shotgun blast. He felt a hot tug as buck-shot grazed his left arm, followed by the sting of debris as it flew all around him.

Owens had lost his battle with the guard in the rear of the bus and had taken a shotgun butt to the head. He was currently out cold on the floor of the bus with the guard standing over him, shotgun aimed in Chaveta's direction, taking aim for a second blast.

Without thinking, Chaveta grabbed the passenger door lever and threw the bus doors open. "You Mother Fucker!" The guard said as he sent another load of number four buckshot flying.

Chaveta dove head first from the bus just in time to avoid the shotgun blast, clearing all of the bus' steps head first with his arms stretched out in front of him. He hit the ground with a forward shoulder roll and popped up to his feet, transferring his momentum from the shoulder roll into a dead-out sprint for a treeline that was across the field from the highway where the driver had managed to stop the bus.

Upon seeing Chaveta exit the bus, the rear guard immediately gave chase, stopping briefly to shake the knocked-out driver as he stepped over him. The driver, regaining consciousness, retrieved a rifle from the locking rack, groggily exited the bus, and joined the rear guard in the pursuit of the escaped inmate.

The inmates chained in their seats had remained fairly quiet throughout the whole ordeal but had gone absolutely ballistic when Chaveta dove from the bus, beginning to scream and howl in excitement as he ran for the tree line.

The screams and howls of the excited inmates brought Owens to his senses. He pushed himself up from the floor onto his knees and rubbed a huge knot on his forehead. Dazed, he looked around until his head began to clear.

Slowly, realization crept over him as he assessed his situation. Head throbbing, he began to stumble to the driver's seat. He did not know what had happened to Chaveta, but if he could, he would escape on his own. He fell into the driver's seat, put the bus in gear, and smashed the accelerator pedal all the way down to the bus's floorboard.

As the bus began to build speed, he looked to his right and saw Chaveta running through the field back towards the highway. He had run into the thicket, lost the guards, doubled back, and was now running to intercept the prison transport bus. The guards exited the thicket just in time to see the bus slow down for Chaveta to jump in.

At a quarter till eleven in the morning, Trooper Corbin was not on his way home for lunch. Instead, he was crouching next to a live oak tree, staring down at the dead brown leaves and other debris that littered the ground in front of him. He stared at the dead grass that was trying to grow in the dry, sunbaked Texas dirt. He studied it all, looking for the clues that would help him to pick up the trail of the two escaped inmates.

The two guards from the prison transport bus had come out of the thicket about a hundred and twenty yards behind Chaveta. When Owens slowed down to let him jump into the bus, the guards aimed at the rear tires and released a hail of gunfire, blowing the back tires out. With the rear tires shot out, Owens only managed to drive the prison transport bus another half mile down the road, where he lost control and crashed over the guard rail on the south side of the Colorado River Bridge.

XIII

Trooper Corbin had been one of the first to respond and had given chase after he saw the two inmates, Kurtis Owens and Rodrigo Reyes Chaveta, disappear into the thick brush and trees of the countryside between the Colorado River and the highway.

He had lost their trail and now sat on his heels under an oak tree as he studied his surroundings. He looked for places where the fallen leaves of the surrounding live oaks might have been disturbed from their natural resting places, where they had fallen to the ground. He looked for any branches, limbs, or twigs that might have been broken by the inmates pushing their way through the underbrush. Slowly, patiently, his eyes continued to scan his surroundings in a grid-like fashion.

It was July, and the ground had been baked hard by the Texas sun, making it difficult to find any prints. Nevertheless, the trooper continued to search and finally detected a faint shoe mark in a bare spot of sandy soil a few meters away from where he was crouched. He cautiously moved closer to the mark in the soil and crouched back down again in an attempt to stay as hidden as possible.

The trooper couldn't determine which way the inmates had traveled from the faint shoe mark. However, he continued to study his surroundings from his new vantage point, and directly, he spied a clump of tall grass laid over in a different direction from the rest, which had all been windswept to the North by the prevalent Southward Coastal winds.

XIV

He stood up to move in the direction of the laid-over grass when his attention was drawn by loud squawking, and the fluttering of wings as a band of Blue Jays took flight from a stand of oaks in the near distance. They had begun jeering loudly in protest of being disturbed by someone or something. The trooper looked from the laid-over grass to the trees where the Blue Jays still flew about in a clamor and took off running as fast as he could in that direction.

The trooper ran as fast as he could until he came upon a thicket where he had to slow down and work his way through. After weaving his way through the thicket, he eventually came to a clearing. The inmate's trail through the Johnson grass that had overtaken the clearing was obvious. The trooper followed the inmate's trail across a clearing and then back into the thicket on the other side that bordered the river.

The closer to the river the trooper got, the more entangled the thicket grew. He fought the underbrush and sticker vines in the sweltering Texas humidity. His sweat ran into the cuts from the sticker vines and into his eyes, making them burn. To his relief, he finally came across an old cow trail that led down to the river.

The inmates had not been so lucky. They had fought the underbrush, sticker vines, and rose of Sharron all the way down to the river. The cow trail that the trooper had found allowed him to pass the inmates up in the brush, reaching the river's edge before them. He came out on a sandbar upriver from them just in time to see the inmates emerge from the tangle of brush at the river's edge.

XV

The Trooper grimaced to himself, not liking what he was seeing. The inmates could not have planned it any better. They had emerged on top of a fifteen-foot washout on the high side of the river bend. Across the river, just downstream, was the low side where sand deposited, creating a sandbar similar to the one the trooper was standing on now. All the inmates would have to do is slide down the washout and then swim downstream with the current to the sandbar on the other side of the river, where the city of Wharton awaited them.

He fired a few rounds at the inmates, and it temporarily drove them back into the wood line, but he would never be able to get to them in time. One of the inmates broke back out of the wood line and made a run for the edge of the washout. Again, the trooper fired several shots as the inmate jumped over the side and started to slide down the washout to the river. The trooper communicated what was happening to the other officers via radio while he watched helplessly as the inmate slid towards the river to freedom.

Three-quarters of the way down, Owens noticed some odd shapes in the water below him. His mind worked out what they were at the same time that his body plunged into the water. He turned in the water, panicking, grabbing, clawing at the steep incline of the washout, trying to climb back up the bank only to come away with handfuls of rotting roots and mud as he slid along the bank desperately fighting the river's current.

XVI

The whole thing took less than twenty seconds. Chaveta watched from the top of the washout as Owens turned in the water like a fish flopping around in the bottom of a boat, and then he watched as Owens tried to claw his way back up the bank in a frenzied panic, unable to purchase any grip coming away with, handful after handful of desperately grabbed mud and debris.

As the river's current dragged Owens down into the water, two of the three huge alligators, whom he had not seen until he had slid better than halfway down the washout, were on him in seconds. His blood-curdling scream was cut short as they ripped him in half.

Chaveta stared as the third gator attacked, and the river water frothed pink and red with blood. Terrified, he turned and fled back down the trail he and Owens had pushed through moments earlier, the wild rose hedge, sticker vines, and underbrush tearing at his face and arms as he bound through the woods horrified.

The trooper had witnessed the whole grisly event. He had also seen the second inmate turn and head back in the opposite direction of the river. *Can't say that I blame him,* the trooper thought. He quickly recomposed himself and began to make his way back up the cow trial in hopes of intercepting the inmate.

At the top of the cow trail, the trooper turned and skirted along the edge of the woods, staying low in the tall grass, trying to avoid detection, but it had done no good. Chaveta had caught sight of the trooper purely by accident as he had pushed out of the brush.

XVII

Chaveta had been scanning the wood line at the opposite side of the clearing, trying to figure out which way to run, when he had gotten lucky and caught a glimpse of movement in the grass. The trooper was less than thirty feet away and had his back turned. Chaveta decided to overpower the trooper and took off in a sprint, running toward him.

As the inmate sprinted through the hot sunbaked clearing, the trooper heard the rustle of the dry, dead Johnson grass as its tiny razors grabbed at the inmate's white prison trousers and turned just in time to intercept the inmate's attempt to tackle him to the ground.

Catching the inmate by the shoulders with his hands and forearms, the trooper blocked him and sprawled. The trooper's feet slid back in the dirt as the inmate drove forward. As the inmate continued driving forward, the trooper, still sprawling, moved his right hand into a C-grip around the base of the inmate's skull and pushed down hard with all of his weight, forcing the inmate face-first to the ground.

The inmate broke his fall by landing on his forearms and knees, then reached up, grabbing for the trooper's sidearm. "Not today, Ass-Hole," the trooper said as he shoved the inmate's head down savagely with his right hand, forcing the inmate back down to his forearms.

The trooper then, keeping his weight on the inmate, shuffled clockwise on his toes until they were hip to hip. This gained him a better position while also moving his sidearm out of the inmate's reach.

XVIII

He then threw his left arm over the inmate's back at his waist to hold him down and brought his left leg under him, crouching on his toes. Leaving his right leg out for stability, he kept pressure on the inmate's back, forcing him to remain on his knees and elbows in the turtle-like position in which he had fallen.

From this position, the trooper slid his right hand from the base of the inmate's skull, over the inmate's right shoulder, and under his chest. He then reached down, grabbed the inmate's left wrist, and pinned it to the ground.

The trooper then pivoted to his right until he was perpendicular to the inmate's side. Once perpendicular, he retracted his outstretched right leg and threw his knee hard into the inmate's right side rib cage. He then brought his right foot down onto the ground into the space his knee had just violently created, bringing his shin tight to the inmate's right hip.

At the same time, on the inmate's left side, the trooper placed the palm of his left hand, the arm of which was still over the inmate's back, holding him in place, on the inside of the inmate's left knee, and forced it out. He then shifted his weight to his right foot, swung his left leg over the inmate's back, and stepped his left foot into the space he had created by holding the inmate's knee out away from his body.

He then hooked the back of his lower left leg into the inmate's upper left thigh between his groin and knee. With his left leg securely hooked over the inmate's left inner thigh, he no longer needed to hold the inmate's left knee open. He was now able to remove his left hand, reach under the inmate's left arm, and grab his own right wrist.

XIX

The trooper had never relinquished the grip of his right hand on the wrist of the inmate's left arm, and now he had two arms working against one. He had essentially created a bandolero around the inmate's upper body with a two-on-one grip controlling the inmate's left arm.

With the strength of both of his arms working against the inmate's one arm, the inmate could not fight it as the trooper pulled his left arm in and pinned it against his own chest. With the inmate's arm pinned, the trooper was able to easily roll forward over his left shoulder, forcing the inmate to roll with him, hooking his right leg over the inmate's right upper thigh in the same fashion as he had done with the left side in mid-roll.

The calculated roll left the trooper on his left side, still glued to the inmate's back. The inmate struggled violently, turning left and right, trying to break free, but the trooper's bandolero grip around the inmate's upper body and his legs hooked over the top of the inmate's upper thighs held the inmate in place.

The trooper held the struggling inmate in this position until he felt him succumb to exhaustion, then transferred the grip of his left hand from his right wrist to the inmate's left forearm, keeping it bent at the elbow and pinned to the inmate's chest. With his right arm now free, the trooper snaked it around the inmate's neck.

XX

Once his right arm was under the inmate's chin and tight around his neck, he released his grip on the inmate's left forearm and placed the palm of his left hand on the back of the inmate's skull while letting his right hand slide down to his left bicep, locking the choke in place. The inmate's field of vision tunneled, stars began to dance around in the small circle at the end of the tunnel, and then, Cheveta's entire world went black.

When he came to, he was face down in hand-cuffs surrounded by thirteen Texas State Troopers. From that point forward, the Texas Department of Criminal Justice took no further chances with Rodrigo Reyes Chaveta. He was confined in heavy chains and transported directly to the O.B. Ellis Unit in Walker County, Texas. Once there, he was placed directly into solitary confinement. However, through their attorney, William Haski, Chaveta was able to get a message to Mutt City Mobsters. The message he sent was…, "I Want Trooper James Corbin Dead!"

Two weeks later, just south of Easley, Texas, Trooper Corbin was parked in a median on Highway 59 monitoring traffic when two bikers passed his patrol unit doing well over the speed limit. The trooper immediately activated his lights and siren as he took off in pursuit of the speeding bikers.

As the trooper crested over the top of an overpass, he caught sight of the bikers and began to close the distance behind them. As the trooper began to close the distance, the two bikers switched on their right-turn blinkers, pulled over to the side of the road, and parked. Trooper Corbin turned off his siren, pulled in behind them, grabbed his ticket book, and exited his patrol unit.

XXI

Ticket book in hand, Trooper Corbin approached the two bikers on the shoulder of the highway. As he walked toward them, a third member of the Mutt City Mobsters hidden in the back of a truck parked across the median found the trooper in the crosshairs of a scope that was mounted to a semi-automatic, large-bore hunting rifle.

As Trooper Corbin stopped in front of the bikers, the Mobster hidden in the back of the truck drew in a deep breath, let half of it out slowly, and held it. Then, with only the tip of his index finger, he slowly squeezed the trigger. Trooper Corbin was struck in the neck and killed instantly.

XXII

Four Years Later…

The Last Mesa

Four Days Later…

Chapter Two

Perdido, Texas

Over 400 miles west by northwest of Corpus Christi, a very desperate Harold Adams, known to his friends as Harry, was walking at a good trot across a sunbaked gravel parking lot in a small west Texas desert town known as Perdido. He was walking as fast as he could, hopefully without drawing attention to himself.

It wasn't even noon on a Thursday yet, but he had already managed to lose twelve thousand dollars at a Derby, or a "Cock Fight," as the people that didn't know any better called them. Whatever you called it, he didn't have the money to pay up. Worse yet, he had taken advantage of an old friend's confidence, and Enrique Ramirez was not a man that you wanted to betray.

The reason Harry had gone to Perdido in the first place was because he had made a couple of bad bets with a bookie back in Corpus Christi. He had thought the bookie was just a bartender, but it turned out that he owned the bar and was some kind of South Texas mobster.

It took three weeks, but the bartender finally tracked Harry down to the trailer park where he lived. He had then sent his two thugs to remind him of his debt. They beat the crap out of him up and warned him too, "Pay up or else!"

Harry had tried raising the money all the next day with no luck. Disgusted, he went home empty-handed. Back at his RV, he grabbed a beer out of his ice-box and flopped down on the couch. It was then that he had noticed his invitation to the Anual Ramirez family barbeque lying on his kitchen table. It had been mixed in with that week's jumble of mail, mostly bills that Harry had been intentionally avoiding.

The Ramirez family barbeque was code for the derby, which was held at their ranch in Perdido every year. It was always held in mid-July, the week of Enrique Ramirez's birthday. The party would commence on the Monday of that week, with the first matches of the derby beginning at ten in the morning and continuing until late evening.

There would be four rings set up under the pavilion of Enrique's Horse Arena, with two roosters fighting to the death in each one. The winners of each match would move forward in the brackets until Saturday, when the last rooster standing would be the ultimate winner of the derby.

The derby was a high-stakes, fast-paced event. At most events, as soon as one match was over, the money would change hands quickly, and a new match would begin. However, at the Ramirez family barbeque, the wagers were often too high for the gamblers to actually carry that much physical cash.

There was always some wild cash from small side wagers, of course, but for the most part, all the wagers were settled at the end of the day. Harry had done very well at the Ramirez family barbeque and derby a few years back and knew how fast the money could stack up. Partially out of fear and partly out of hope, that night, Harry decided to drive for Perdido. Attempting to both avoid his debt collectors and get there in time for the morning matches, he left immediately. As he drove his old caddy onto Interstate 37, he patted the invitation in his breast pocket and prayed for good luck in Perdido.

Perdido, Texas, wasn't really a city. It wasn't even a town. It was what the state of Texas referred to as an unincorporated community. Sometime in the past, the Smith Ranch had traded hands, and portions of it, mostly large swathes of unwanted desert wasteland, had become disordered, lost, or confused during the sale.

The ranch had sprawled out over thousands of acres that stretched over the borders of Piedra and Terlingua County. The problem, or advantage with this, depending on which side of the legal fence you were on, was that Perdido was located in this blurred area of land between the two counties.

When anyone in the Perdido area called one of the Sheriff's Departments, they were told that they lived outside of their jurisdiction and would need to call the Sheriff's Department in the other county. This was because the first county to go out there would legally accept responsibility for that area of land, and the bottom line was that neither of the departments wanted to get stuck patrolling a dangerous wasteland out in the middle of nowhere. For this reason, and the fact that you could see for miles in any direction, Perdido was the perfect place to hold the yearly illegal derby.

Why derbies were illegal, to begin with, Harry couldn't understand. In what he referred to as the good part of his life, before his wife had died and he had started all the boozing and gambling, he had been one of the best salesmen in the state of Texas. He had started out in car sales, moved to oil field equipment, and from there, he landed a job in the sales department of an advertising company. Harry's last job had been with one of the largest advertising firms in Houston.

One of that firm's largest clients had been a large commercial chicken hatchery. While taking a tour of the hatchery, Harry was shocked to learn that, on average, fifty to seventy-five percent of all eggs hatched were males. He had been not only shocked but also disgusted to learn what they did with them.

Since the males make poor meat birds that lay no eggs, and farmers need no more than one to service their entire flock of hens, the poor little fellows are executed minutes after they leave the egg. The truly horrible thing is how it is done.

Every hatchery has a team of experts that sit at rows of tables and sex the chicks as they hatch. Every expert has a vacuum hose mounted to the table beside them. At the end of the vacuum, hoses are chopping blades. As the expert sorts through the chicks, the females are placed into boxes. The little, yellow, fluffy, one-day-old male baby chicks are thrown into the vacuum hose, where they are sucked into the blades and pureed into a liquid that is then flushed down the septic system.

Harry shuttered at the thought and lit a cigarette. He thought about how, in the jungles of South Asia and surrounding islands, the roosters of the wild Red and Grey Junglefowl, from which every chicken on the planet descended, could still be heard crowing every morning. He thought about how any roosters that were close enough to hear each other's crows would travel miles to fight until death.

This had been going on in the jungles for over eight thousand years, but the same thing would happen in a farmer's barnyard with the domesticated descendants of the Junglefowl. It was how nature ensured the welfare of the flock, as far as Harry was concerned.

"At least the roosters fighting in the derbies get a shot at retirement," Harry thought as he made his way across the dry, packed dirt to the area where everyone had parked their vehicles. Most owners would only fight their roosters for a couple of years or for only a certain number of matches. The roosters would then be retired and used only for breeding stock. Some roosters had been known to fight exceptionally well and make their owner enough money to earn their retirement in a single night of battle.

"If I were a rooster, I would pray for battle over vacuum blades," Harry thought as he tossed his cigarette butt to the ground and fished his keys out of his pocket. *"At least then I would have a chance."* That's what he was praying for now. A chance, a chance to get the hell out of Perdido.

Harry stood at the door of his old caddy, "I hope this piece of shit starts," he said under his breath as he rushed to get the key into the door lock. It was more the miles than the years on the Caddy that Harry worried about. As a salesman, he had put a lot of miles on that car.

As Harry inserted the key into the car door's lock, he heard a voice from behind. "Leaving so soon, or do you keep your cash stashed in that Shit-Box?" Harry didn't have to turn around. He knew the voice. It was Alejandro Ramirez, nephew to and enforcer for his uncle, Enrique Rameriz.

Harry turned very slowly to face him, with his hands out away from his body. As he turned to face Alejandro, he saw that his brother Carlos was by his side. "Of course, I don't keep it in the car where someone could steal it. It's at the bank," Harry said, jerking his thumb in the direction of the nearest town, which was over fifty miles away.

"I was just gonna run into town and get the money and come right back," he said. "The rules stipulate that you must settle all debts at the end of the day or before leaving the ranch, you know that. I think my uncle Enrique might want to speak with you," Alejandro said as he folded his arms.

Harry knew that if he resisted, things would end ugly, and opted to go along with Alejandro and Carlos in an obliging manner. Walking between the two brothers in lockstep, he realized that he had made a huge mistake. Instead of improving his situation by coming to Perdido, he had made things remarkably worse.

He was led to a guest room across the courtyard from the main house. Once in the room, he was subjected to a thorough search. His cell phone, car keys, pocket knife, wallet, cigarettes, and lighter were taken. He was then locked in the guest room and left to wait.

Chapter Three

Let's Make a Deal

It was well after dark when Alejandro and Carlos came to fetch Harry for his meeting with Enrique Ramirez. He couldn't be sure of the exact time because they had taken his cell phone, and he had lost the watch his father had left him, shooting dice behind a gas station on the way to Perdido.

The only credit card he hadn't maxed was his Alamo Fuel card, and he was hoping to win some cash to spend at the Dairy Queen. No dice Harry had his dinner from the snack aisle at the gas station. All the same, as they marched across the courtyard to the main house, he could see that the stars were well up.

He looked down from the stars to the other side of the large enclosed courtyard where La Hacienda de Ramirez stood. In front of the large Spanish-style mansion in the center of the courtyard stood a captivating fountain. The fountain featured a nude woman standing seductively with one foot placed upon a large rock.

The woman was made from white cement and was sculpted to look as if she were bathing next to a river bank. Water emanated from a vase that she held over her head. The stream of water poured down, splashing onto her well-defined breast before cascading down her body and then finally pooling into the beautifully tiled basin of the fountain.

The man who sculpted the fountain had illegally crossed the border from Mexico into Texas and had broken his leg while negotiating his way down a bluff. His friends told him they would carry his pack and water and help him walk out. After he handed his pack and water over to them, they left him to die.

While patrolling the perimeter of the ranch, one of Enrique's men noticed buzzards circling next to a small ravine at the bottom of the bluff. He rode closer until, through binoculars, he saw a man seated in a crag in the rocks. He had gone as deep into the crag as he could drag himself and was weakly casting stones at the buzzards on the outside, desperately trying to keep them at bay.

Enrique's man rode in, chasing the buzzards away. He gave the man some water and took him back to Hacienda de Ramirez, where Enrique's family set his leg and nursed him back to health.

Once the man, who was a cement worker and tile mason by trade, was back on his feet, he was so grateful that he built the Ramirez family the beautiful fountain that now stands in their courtyard. In return for the fountain, Enrique gave the mason some cash and smuggled him into Houston, where he would be safe from the border patrol and could find work.

Harry's eyes moved from the serenity of the fountain back to the beautiful, two-story Hacienda de Ramirez. The large two-story white stucco, Spanish-style mansion with its red terracotta roof tiles was beautifully illuminated by the outdoor lighting.

Harry had seen the mansion, which was rumored to have as many as twenty-six rooms, from a distance many times, but only Enrique's special guests were ever invited to stay in the family home during the annual festivities. Harry had always wanted to see the inside of the beautiful Hacienda de Ramirez, but not like this.

The house had been built, in large part, by craftsmen who had crossed the border illegally. Among other activities, the Ramirez family was known to provide safe border crossings for fair prices. For this, the craftsmen were grateful and were happy to pay their debt in labor on the beautiful La Hacienda de Ramirez.

They knew that many who tried the border crossing on their own would die out in the desert from exposure, injuries, snake bites, or being attacked by wild animals. Some would be killed by the cartels that would demand money that they didn't have to cross through their territories, and others would be killed by the people they were crossing with for their food, water, or the money that they carried with them for their start in a new life once they crossed the border.

Alejandro continued to hold Harry by his elbow while Carlos opened two elaborate wrought iron gates. Harry was led through the gates and up to the two hand-carved solid oak entry doors that stood underneath the portico at the mansion's entrance. Carlos opened the large oak doors, and then, with Alejandro holding one arm and him holding the other, Harry was led through the vestibule into the foyer. In the foyer, Harry could hear the muffled thump of loud music.

On the left wall of the foyer was a grand set of stairs that curved up and to the left. To the left of the stair landing, the mezzanine made a half circle back over the vestibule behind them and then ran straight along the right-side foyer, granting access to the upstairs bedrooms on that side of the house. The doors of the bedrooms were visible through the spindles of the mezzanine's hand railing. To the right-hand side of the stair landing was a short mezzanine that led to the large entrance of what he assumed was a hallway that would grant access to the other more private upstairs bedrooms.

Harry's eyes fell back to the ground floor. He could see that there were three exits on the ground floor of the foyer. There was a large set of double doors directly in front of them that led through the back wall of the foyer. He had noticed these doors immediately, as it was these doors from which the loud music emanated. The second exit was a large, open entryway underneath the mezzanine to the left of the grand staircase, which opened up into a large sitting room. The third exit, a closed set of double doors, was to his right underneath the part of the mezzanine that ran in front of the upstairs bedroom doors.

I wonder if they'll pick door number one, two, or three? Harry thought. His question was answered as he was roughly ushered through the double doors at the back of the foyer. As the heavy doors opened, The Talking Head's "Life During Wartime" escaped the room at bone-shaking volume. The large room was filled with music, people, smoke, the clacking of billiard balls, and the clinking of bottles and glasses.

Harry's eyes swept the room. He saw people gambling at roulette and card tables. He saw people seated on stools, pulling at the arms of the slot machines that lined the wall opposite the bar. He saw people yelling at large screen televisions on every wall while they jumped up and down as they wagered on different sporting events.

Others gambled at pool or darts. Some lounged in booths, while the rest were either drinking at the bar, which was illuminated by hundreds of multicolored lights, or they were dancing in the lasers and lights that were reflected from the different disco balls that were suspended from the ceiling in various places above the dance floor.

Alejandro and Carlos whisked Harry across the room through the people crowded around the card, roulette, dice, and pool tables. He was then led through a door at the rear of the illegal underground casino. Once through the door, they proceeded down a hall, leaving most of the noise of the casino behind. With only muffled sounds and the rhythmic thump of the music's bass line persisting.

At the end of the hall, they stopped at a heavy steel door. A security camera pointed at them from above. Alejandro pressed a button on the intercom next to the door, and they waited. Directly, a voice issued from the intercom telling them to "Come in."

Harry recognized the voice as that of Enrique Ramirez. When the door opened, he saw Enrique seated behind a large oak desk. Carlos and Alejandro lifted him by his arms. He was swept across the floor and roughly placed in a high-back chair that stood in front of Enrique's desk.

When the heavy door to the office was closed, Harry heard it mute out what was left of the noise escaping the casino. *This is a room where no one hears you scream,* Harry thought as he repositioned himself from his rough placement in the high-back chair.

Enrique sat with his arms crossed and a genuine look of anger on his face as he stared into Harry's eyes. He took a deep breath and exhaled in a sigh of exasperation. He then unfolded his arms, placed his elbows on his desk, and with his hands together, fingers interlaced, he considered Harry for a few seconds. Then he leaned even further forward and asked in a hushed tone, "You know this is going to end badly, right?"

"Yes, Sir, I do, and I will pay you back, I swear," Harry said. "Shut up! We're past that now. "You've been coming out here for years. You know the rules, and I'm sure you've heard stories about what happens to people out here when they don't pay their debts before leaving," Enrique said.

"Yeah, I heard about what happened to Anthony Fletcher. I heard that he got both his ankles crushed with a two-pound sledgehammer and was dropped off in the desert six miles from a gas station," Harry said. "Help me understand then, why would an intelligent fella such as yourself, knowing what you know, come to Perdido, exploit the trust we've built over the years, and place a wager that he couldn't cover?" Enrique asked as he sat back in his leather office chair and folded his arms.

Harry shifted in his seat nervously under Enrique's gaze, "I'm sorry I took advantage of your trust, but I lost a bet back in Corpus Christi to some thugs. I was going to pay it… Honest, I was, but these assholes grew impatient and started making threats. After they beat the crap out of me, I got scared and fled here. I was hoping to win enough here to save my ass. That's the long and the short of it. I was screwed either way, so I took a chance," Harry said.

"I see, that's very interesting. Tell me, how long did they give you to get the money?" Enrique asked. "They didn't say. They just said that if I didn't get it soon, I would be sorry," Harry said. "How much do you owe them?" Enrique asked. "Ten thousand," Harry said as he looked to the floor.

"Jesus Christ, how the fuck did that happen?" Enrique asked. "Betting baseball," Harry said, "I'd been making a few bets with this guy here and there and had built up some credit with him. I wound up putting five large on the Strhos-Rangers game. The Strhos lost five to six, and I lost five grand. I had the money to pay up, but it was the last of my cash.

"When I paid him off, I made a bet for double or nothing on game two. The Strhos lost three to four, and I wound up owing ten large. I tried to make a bet with him for game three, but he was done with extending me credit," Harry said. "The Strhos won game three, three to one," Enrique said with a smile. "I know," Harry said dejectedly.

"So let me see if I got this straight. You now owe some thugs in Corpus Christi ten large along with the twelve you owe me. Do I have that right?" Enrique asked as he leaned forward once again, resting his elbows on the desk with his fingers interlaced. "That would be correct," Harry answered.

Enrique shifted back in his seat and spoke to Harry calmly, "You mentioned Anthony Fletcher earlier. You know, he was never supposed to crawl out of the desert. I couldn't believe it when I heard the story of how he had crawled all the way to a gas station in Rio Bravo.

"He was passed out when we dumped him off that day. We left him for dead out in the middle of nowhere. When he finally woke up, it was dark. He saw the lights of Rio Bravo about nine and a half miles away and started crawling.

"After two days of dragging himself toward the lights, a summer monsoon came through. After that, he was able to occasionally find water as he made his way through the desert. At some point, he found an old Gain bottle and was able to carry some water with him.

"He crawled across some roads as he made his way, but unfortunately for him, there was never any traffic, so he would continue on. He ate whatever insects crawled across his path, and five and half days later, he arrived at a gas station on the edge of Rio Bravo. His lips were chapped and split. His hands and knees were bloody and mangled. He was sunburnt, dehydrated, and malnourished, but he made it.

"He was smart enough to tell the authorities that he had been out camping and had gotten lost while out on a hike. Do you know what I said when I was told that he had crawled his way out of the desert? I said, "I don't fucking believe it! Now, that's a bet I would have lost!" And as soon as those words left my mouth, I realized that I was on to something there because I'll tell you what keeps me up at night. I wake up in the night very distraught over money that is still owed to me.

"My father taught me that I should look at it as an investment in the business. He said every once in a while, somebody would try to cheat you. He said that you would have to make an example out of them, and then everyone would stay in line for a time, but you know what? When you make an example out of someone by breaking their legs, breaking their hands, killing them, or whatever, you still don't get the money you're owed. Anthony Fletcher crawling out of that desert unexpectedly gave me a great idea. I could still make an example out of someone and not only collect the money owed to me but a whole lot more.

"That's where you come in. My men on both sides of the border have been preparing something special for you since noon today when you became our special guest, and I suppose you saw the crowd in the bar on the way in?" Enrique asked. "Yes, Sir, I did," Harry answered, now somewhat confused about his situation.

"Well, Harry, those are my special guests. They stay with me every year for the celebration. Truth be known, they are some of the wealthiest, most zealous high-stakes gamblers in the world. When they go to Vegas, Monico, or some similar place to gamble, they typically travel by private jet, rent entire floors at the most expensive hotels, and arrive with their own staff and bodyguards.

"They spend and gamble vast amounts of money and are what the casinos refer to as whales. However, to me, they are simply old friends that I have come to know through the years, and as my special guest, they will be given the opportunity to bet on whether or not you will survive "The Desert Gaunlet," Enrique said.

"The Desert Gauntlet, bet on whether or not I survive," Harry muttered under his breath, trying to understand what was happening. "That's right, on whether or not you survive, and other things. For instance, if you don't survive, how many days, miles, or feet will you make it, or how many checkpoints you make? Plus many other scenarios that I have set odds for based on my many years of experience leading people through the wilderness of the Chihuahuan desert. Also, they will be able to bet on any random opportunity that may present itself," Enrique said, then paused to let his statement sink in.

"I'm a fifty-six-year-old man. Just what the hell kind of desert gauntlet are you talking about?" Harry asked. "You're a fifty-six-year-old, out-of-shape alcoholic, smoker to be exact, and that's just how you will be introduced at your weigh-in," Enrique said. "Weigh-in?" Harry asked. "That's right, you'll be weighed in when you're introduced to my special guest.

"At the weigh-in, you will answer any questions my guest may have in full. You will then be given a change of clothes and some hiking boots. Carlos will give you a brief lesson on how to read a compass. I suggest you pay close attention as your life will depend on it. Then, at midnight tonight, you will set out on the course.

"The rest will be explained to you as it is explained to my guest. Do you understand?" Enrique asked. "Yeah, I guess so, but, like you said, I'm in no condition for something like this. I think we both know I'm gonna die out there, and probably very soon," Harry said.

"Two things you need to know. One, I'll make my money back whether you live or die, so I don't give a shit, and two, you haven't heard what's in it for you yet," Enrique said. "In it for me?" Harry asked, confused. "Well, it's like this. A man with something hanging over his head might not have much motivation, and I don't want you checking out too early. I need to put on some kind of show for the gamblers.

"Here's the deal. If you survive, I'll give you ten thousand dollars and a free pass. You can get in your car, drive back to Corpus Christi, pay off your debts, and start over fresh. If you survive, that is," Enrique said, as he turned his palms up and shrugged in a take-it-or-leave-it attitude. "Okay, I guess I'm going along with it. It's not like I have a choice," Harry said. "No, no, you don't," Enrique said.

"Get him stripped down to his underwear and ready to go on stage to be weighed in and introduced to the crowd," Enrique said to Carlos and Alejandro. "Right now? It's the middle of the night, I haven't had much sleep, and I drove through the night to get here," Harry said.

"One, it's not the middle of the night. It is not yet even ten o'clock," Enrique said, motioning to a clock on the office wall. "Two, time is money, so yes, of course right now, and three, I don't give a shit how far you had to drive. Get his ass ready and on the stage now!" Enrique said. Without hesitation, Alejandro and Carlos, one on each side, yanked Harry from the high-back chair by his arms and dragged him through the heavy steel door and back into the hall.

Chapter Four

The Weigh-In

On the other side of Enrique's door, Harry could once again hear the muffled music as it escaped the illegal casino. He was led to a door mid-way down the hall, one that they had previously passed on the way to Enrique's office. Alejandro opened the door, ordered Harry in, and then sent Carlos to make sure the stage was ready before entering the room behind Harry.

As Harry walked through the door, he noticed a guard sitting at a bank of monitors that took up the entire wall to his right. Alejandro noticed him staring at them wide-eyed.
"I had them installed when Uncle Enrique appointed me Head of Security after I received my bachelor's degree in digital communication from Texas A&M University," Alejandro said.

"From this room, not only can we monitor the casino and other areas of Hacienda Ramirez, but we also have a complete three-hundred-and-sixty-degree view of our outer perimeter. This, along with mounted patrols, our drones, and guards posted in critical areas, provides us with fairly adequate security," Alejandro said. He then pointed to a desk and chair on the far wall. "Over there, everything off except your tighty whiteys," he said with a chuckle.

It had been over hours since Harry had a cigarette or a drink. He was starting to feel just a bit touchy, and Alejandro's teasing had angered him, but he was in no position to protest. As he walked toward the desk, he noticed rows of shelving units arranged like isles to his left, loaded with electronic equipment, computer parts, and pieces of drones. "A little hobby of mine," Alejandro said when he saw Harry look at the shelves that lined the walls and stood back to back in neat rows.

Harry approached the desk. On the desktop, he saw a box that contained his cell phone, car keys, wallet, pocket knife, cigarettes, and lighter. He began to reach in for the pack of cigarettes. "No time for that," Alejandro said. "Hurry up, strip down now, and put your shoes and clothes in the box with the rest of your things!" he said.

Harry began to undo his tie in a state of exasperation. The door to the office opened, and the muffled music from the casino spilled into the room. "The stage is set. I took the stripper poles down and set the scale up!" Carlos said from the hallway, having to raise his voice slightly to be heard over the thump of the music. Alejandro nodded, then turned back to Harry. "Time to go," he said.

Hearing this, Harry stood frozen in disbelief, the color drained from his face. Alejandro grabbed his arm and yanked him into motion. He then stepped behind him and shoved him through the door into the hallway, where Carlos immediately caught him and shoved him down the hall in the direction of the casino. Harry caught his balance and started to shuffle on his own accord toward the door, with Alejandro and Carlos falling in behind him, one on each side.

The music was getting louder with each step as Harry approached the door. He felt the brother's hands land on his shoulders. One on each side, and they began to steer him. Alejandro reached forward and opened the door in front of Harry, and he was once again steered through the rowdy casino crowd.

Instead of going between the pool tables as before, Alejandro and Carlos immediately steered Harry to the left, where they walked him along the back wall of the dance floor and up the four steps that led to the left side of the casino's stage. The huge stage was built into the back right-hand corner of the casino and faced out at a 45-degree angle. As Harry cleared the top step, he looked up. In the center of the stage stood a balance scale like the ones used at doctors' offices.

From behind the curtain on the side of the stage, Harry could see that the entire casino was packed. Run DMC's "It's Tricky" filled the room at chest-reverberating volume as most of the people in the casino danced. Harry stood behind the stage curtains. His dread and anxiety were through the roof.

He hadn't had a cigarette or a drink in what seemed like an eternity. He was stressed to his breaking point and about to be humiliated. His head began to swim, and his stomach twisted up painfully. Then he doubled over and retched violently.

"Awe fuck, Alejandro said disgusted, and then he cupped his hands around his mouth and yelled over the music to the bartender, "Hey Esperanza, get someone over here to clean this up!" The bartender made two quick come here motions with her index finger and pointed to stage left. Within seconds, two young ladies appeared with mops and buckets. Stomach empty, Harry sat back and began to shiver with chills. He wanted to cry and scream both at the same time. *I should have just taken what I had coming to me back in Corpus,* he thought for the second time that day.

Enrique mounted the stage from the right. Carlos, who had commandeered the D.J. booth, immediately reached to turn the music off. Seeing this in his peripheral, Enrique took off his hat and swatted him across his face. "Not in the middle of the song. We are not animals here!" Enrique said, scolding his nephew. As the song came to an end, Carlos stealthily turned Enrique's microphone on.

"I trust everyone is having a good time?" Enrique asked the crowd as he walked to the center of the stage. The crowd cheered their approval, many of them holding their drinks up in a salute to Enrique's hospitality. "Good, good, that's what I like to hear!" Enrique said, smiling.

"The reason I have stopped this evening's festivities is that I have an announcement," He said in a solemn tone and then paused for dramatic effect as he hung his head. The crowd quietly murmured amongst themselves, wondering what the bad news could be. "Unfortunately, one of my guests, whom I have considered a friend of the family for many years now, made the decision to take advantage of my hospitality and ignore his obligations to settle his debts at the end of the day," Enrique said.

At this point, the crowd interrupted with hisses and boos. Enrique held his free hand up palm out and made the quiet down gesture as he spoke. "It's okay, my friends, it's okay. He has, shall we say, agreed to make amends in the form of a little desert penance," Enrique said. The crowd began to rumble with excitement as Enrique continued. "He has cheerfully agreed…, well more or less cheerfully agreed to go on a little desert excursion outlined by yours truly, a Desert Gauntlet if you will, in which he may or may not survive," Enrique said.

Hearing this, the crowd cheered enthusiastically with approval. From the roulette table at the front of the casino, Enrique's business associate, as well as fishing and drinking buddy, former Texas crop duster pilot turned cocaine smuggler Ricky "Aces," waved his hat in the air and yelled, "Yee-Haw! Teach him not to fuck with your money Enrique!"

"Don't worry, Mister "Aces," our friend will certainly pay for his contrivance to flee Perdido, Texas, without first squaring his debts. However, you have not yet heard the best part," Enrique paused for dramatic effect, and the crowd fell silent with anticipation.

"My nephew Alejandro here has arranged it so that we will be able to watch the entire event live on the large screen monitors here in the casino, and anyone willing to pay the buy-in fee will be able to make wagers on every facet of his journey along the way!" Enrique said.

The crowd went absolutely ballistic at the aspect of being able to watch and gamble on a man's desperate struggle to survive. "There will be a buy-in of ten thousand dollars each, with 15 percent going to the house. The other 85 percent will be placed into a jackpot and awarded to the gambler that correctly predicts how many checkpoints our participant is able to make it to, with any ties being broken by the gambler that guesses closest to his actual arrival time to the checkpoint.

"Anyone vested in the Desert Gauntlet Jackpot will be allowed to place bets on any other facet of his journey they wish. There will be someone at the bar to take all wagers around the clock until Harry Adams makes it back to the gates of Hacienda Ramirez or dies trying," Enrique said over the uproar of the crowd.

A powerful voice thick with a German accent cut over the din of the crowd with ease, causing the room to fall silent and listen to what he had to say, "And what exactly would this "Desert Gauntlet" Consist of?" The gentleman asked. Enrique recognized the gentleman as Waldwolf Heidler the Third, a fifth-generation Argentinian of German descent and his friend since childhood.

Waldwolf and Enrique's families had done business together since the late nineteen-forties and had remained friends through the years, with the Heidler families often spending their vacations with Enrique's family on the beaches of Mexico. This is where young Enrique spent much of his youth and first met Waldwolf.

Enrique answered his childhood friend in an air reminiscent of a carnival barker, "Well, I'm glad you asked, my good man, I'm glad you asked. Harold here will begin by leaving here tonight from Hacienda Ramirez on foot, his destination, Rattlesnake Cave!"

The crowd gasped, and then from the craps table, the very well-dressed, East Coast mafioso, Film producer, and CEO of the mafia-owned BNJ Studios, Joey "Two Cards" Lombardi, interrupted. "Isn't that the cave fulla snakes on the other side of the border where you guys, uh, you know, "Allegedly," chained up that guy that you caught stealing? What was his name? He had the gold tooth."

"His name was Lester Hunckle, from Montclair, Louisiana," Enrique answered. "And you are correct, my good man. It is the very same cave. It used to serve as one of our drop points before we started using the drones.

"Now, If Harlold here wants to make it back, he will have to hike from the gates of Hacienda Ramirez to the Rio Grande, manage an illegal river crossing, and then hike into Mexico to Rattlesnake Cave. Once at Rattlesnake Cave, he will have to retrieve twenty kilos of pure, Argentinian, pharmaceutical-grade cocaine from within the cave, where it has been safely stashed with the rattlesnakes," Enrique said.

Waldwolf Hiedler III smiled at this. He knew this was one of his regular shipments working its way up from his coca fields in Argentina. Normally, the cocaine would be flown over the river by drone, but Harold here would be doing it the old-fashioned way.

Enrique continued to map out the Desert Gauntlet for the crowd, "He will then have to leave Rattlesnake Cave, hike back to the river, and attempt to illegally cross back into Texas, this time with twenty kilos of cocaine on his back, for my American friends that's about 45 pounds.

"If he makes the river crossing, he will then have to hike to the cocaine drop-off point at the top of Mesa de Angelita, a few miles north from here. If he makes the drop-off at the mesa, he can then proceed to his final destination, the gates of Hacienda Ramirez.

"If he makes it back here to Hacienda Ramirez, he will be paid our standard ten thousand dollar delivery rate, and he will be free to go. All wagering will stop if he makes it as far as the courtyard gates.

"That means, for him to make it out of here, he will have to survive the terrain and temperatures of the Chihuahuan deserts of Mexico and West Texas. He will have to cross over mountains, canyons, and two rivers. He will have to hike through the high desert, survive a den full of Rattlesnakes, and make two illegal border crossings, one with twenty kilos of cocaine on his back.

"Moreover, he will have to do all this while simultaneously dodging the U.S. Border Patrol, rogue Mexican army units, hostile ranch owners, desert banditos, cartel foot soldiers, and the even more dangerous desert wildlife," Enrique said.

"What's so dangerous about the desert wildlife?" Called a voice from the crowd. Enrique looked in the direction of the voice and saw an attractive, scantily dressed young woman standing next to a pool table with a que in her hand. He recognized her as Joy Ride, one of illegal arms dealer Belyy Russkiy's many concubines. Belyy Russkiy, an old friend of Enrique's whom he had provided with all the documents necessary to start a fresh life years ago, never traveled anywhere without his collection of stunning, attractive ladies.

"Well, Miss Ride, speaking from personal experience, I have seen many strange things happen out in the Chihuahuan desert. On my very first trip out as a "Coyote" thirty-two years ago, I saw a mother of three get stung by a scorpion.

"She had an umbrella that she used to block the sun from her youngest, an infant. The scorpion had crawled into the umbrella in the night when we slept, and when she opened it overhead in the heat of the day, it fell to her neck, where it stung her. She made no more than three steps before she died, and her oldest boy ground the scorpion into the sand with his bootheel before I could see it. To this day, I cannot say if it was some extremely toxic wayward species of scorpion or if she had an allergic reaction to the venom.

"Besides scorpions, I have also seen rattlesnake, Black Widow, and Brown Recluse bites that were fatal. I have seen people dragged away by their necks by lions, people torn apart by wild javelinas, and others who were attacked by bears.

"I have seen people taken under the Rio Grande by alligators, crocodiles, pythons, and exotics of all kinds purchased from the black market or from reptile farms in Flordia or elsewhere then dumped into the Rio Grande by overzealous border patrol agents. I'm sure some of you have heard the stories, well I can assure you that they are true.

"I have also seen people attacked by packs of coyotes and feral dogs. I once even saw a man get attacked by a buck mule deer. If we hadn't been there to help, it would have pawed him into the ground.

"I have seen many things. However, the wagers will not be confined by my knowledge of what is out there. Anything can happen, and we intend to take any wager that the participants can imagine. Therefore, we will not only be relying upon my personal experience of over thirty years of illegal border crossings, but we will also be utilizing the latest statistics from the internet to ensure that the odds set on any wagers covered by the house will be as accurate as possible ensuring a fair house advantage," Enrique said.

"I see, and will the "Desert Gauntlet Jackpot" be open to everyone here?" Joy Ride asked. "Yes, It is open to all of my guests, provided they have the buy-in fee," Enrique said. Joy nodded. The last game of pool she had just won before Enrique had come on stage had put her just over ten grand.

In the moment of silence left after Enrique had answered Joy Ride's question, a gentleman seated at a card table stood up and called out, "Excuse me." Enrique looked at the gentleman in the back of the room and recognized him to be Mister Oki Kujira, a successful businessman and accountant for many members of the Yakuza. He also happened to be the financial advisor of the Ramirez family.

"Yes, sir, Mister Kujira, do you have a question that you would like to ask?" Enrique asked. "Yes, you mentioned that we'll be wagering on how many checkpoints of the journey he will complete. Could you further explain?"

"Of course," Enrique said. "There are many trails we use when bringing people or contraband across the border. We use stacked rocks called cairns placed at intervals along the different trails to help orientate ourselves.

"The trail from here to Rattlesnake Cave is no different. There are five cairns between here and the cave. The five cairns, plus the cave, make six checkpoints. The trail from Rattlesnake Cave to the Angelita Mesa drop-off point is marked by six cairns, and the final checkpoint will be the gates of Hacienda Ramirez. That makes a total of thirteen checkpoints. We have a satellite map of the course with all the checkpoints marked, and all participants will be provided with the opportunity to look it over before Harold here leaves the gates," Enrique said.

"Interesting, but how will he find his way from one checkpoint to the other when they are miles apart?" Mister Kujira asked. "He will be given a compass to orientate himself and new coordinates at each checkpoint," Enrique said. "Does he know how to read a compass?" Mister Kujira asked. "I don't know, let's find out. I think it's time you all met our contestant.

"Alejandro, bring Harry out here onto the stage so everyone can get a look. Come on, everyone, let's hear it for Harry, the guy who made this all possible by trying to leave without paying his debts," Enrique said. At that, Alejandro dragged Harry onto the stage amongst the crowd's mixed chorus of whistles, applause, laughter, hisses, and boos.

"Ladies and Gentlemen, may I present to you Harrold Adams," Enrique said as Alejandro forced Harry onto the doctor's scale. Harry swayed back and forth on the scale, but they finally managed to stand him up straight for a moment. Enrique quickly read the scale. "Harry here is a 56-year-old out-of-shape alcoholic smoker standing at five-foot, ten inches tall and weighing in at two-hundred and thirteen pounds," Enrique said.

"Do you know how to read a compass, Harry?" Enrique asked and then stuck the microphone in Harry's face. Harry was disorientated. His head lolled around. Alejandro was holding him up. Enrique slapped him hard across the face.

"I said, do you know how to read a compass?" Enrique asked again. Harry straightened up, "No, no, I don't know how to read a fucking compass," he said. His gut felt like he was trying to digest broken glass. "There's your answer, sir, but he will be given a brief lesson by Carlos before we boot him out the gate," Enrique said to Mister Kujira.

"Ahh, I see," Mister Kujira said and then continued, "Has he ever been physically fit, and if so, how long ago was it?" he asked. Harry stood dumbly until Enrique slapped him for the second time, "Answer," he said. "I-I-I don't know, maybe six or seven years ago before my wife died," Harry managed to stammer out.

He was dizzy, his stomach still felt twisted, he bent slightly at the waist from the pain, and his head felt like it might split open. "What did you do for exercise?" Mister Kujira further inquired.

Harry saw Enrique out of the corner of his eye. He was watching from the side as he held the microphone. Not wanting to get slapped again, he pulled himself together. "I would go to the gym. I ran some and lifted some weights, but I primarily played a lot of basketball," he answered in short breaths.

Mister Kujira seemed to be pondering this information, nodding to himself, the wheels turning in his head when Joey "Two Cards" Lombardi broke in, "So what's it matter? He's obviously outta shape now," he said. "If someone has ever been well conditioned at some point in their life, they may have strength, stamina, and physiological endurance that is not readily apparent to the eye," Mister Kujira said.

"Makes sense to me," Ricky "Aces" yelled out. At that moment, illegal arms dealer Belyy Russkiy, who was seated in a booth with a few of his ladies, called out in his thick Russian accent, "I have question!" "Yes, Sir," Enrique said. "You mention that he is alcoholic, no? I would like to know how much he drinks per one day. He does not look so good, you know," Belyy said.

"Answer the man, Harold," Enrique said. Harry thought about it and answered, "Probably a fifth of whiskey a day with a few beers." *Damn, that's a lot,* he thought after being forced to consider it for the first time.

"I think I would like to make wager that man dies from alcohol withdrawal by day three," Belyy Russkiy said as he held up three fingers. "Now that's what I call being imaginative. Of course, we'll be happy to take that wager if Harold here dies within seventy-two hours after he enters the desert, winner, winner, chicken dinner! Esperanza will figure the odds immediately," Enrique said. The Russian nodded his approval.

"How much does he usually smoke in a day?" Asked Joey "Two Cards" Lombardi, from the other side of the room. "Pack a day," Harry answered. "Jesus Christ," said Joey, "Two Cards." "He's more than thirty pounds overweight, drinks like a school teacher, and smokes a pack a day. That ain't good," He said as Harry looked to his feet.

"Anyone else," Enrique asked. The Australian black market exotic animal dealer Jack Smith, or "Blackjack" as he was known by most, stood at the back of the bar with a handful of darts, spoke up, "Yeah mate, does he have any survival training?"

Harry wondered briefly if the few episodes of the reality survival show "Alone" that he had watched while at the bar counted but decided to keep the joke to himself. Enrique prodded him, impatient for an answer, "Well?" Enrique said as he jabbed him in his side. "No, no, I do not," Harry answered.

Blackjack continued, "Yeah, right, we know he'll hava compass. Will he be given any other provisions, food, water, shelter?" he asked. "He will be given a pair of good hiking boots and one Army combat uniform, or ACUs as they're called, which include a jacket and trousers. He will also be given one Boonie hat, one undershirt, one pair of socks, and one pair of underwear.

"He will not be given any food that is for him to find. We have arranged for there to be water at each checkpoint. However, it will be just enough to get him to the next checkpoint. If he wanders off course, he will more than likely be unable to find water and will die. If he takes too long to reach a checkpoint, he will die."

"Right mate, what about good samaritans? Is he allowed to accept help?" Blackjack asked. "The chances of him running into someone out there in the heat of the mid-summer are slim. The desert is mostly avoided this time of year.

"Most ranchers along the roads no longer stop for people. They got tired of being ambushed. The common practice these days is to drive ahead a safe distance, drop off some water, and call either nine-one-one or the policía, depending on which side of the border he is on. Which will get you tracked down. Right, Harry?" Enrique said, making sure Harry was paying attention. Harry nodded.

"Also, there are bandits out there that will kill him for the nice boots we are going to give him, not to mention the cocaine he will be carrying on the way back. Also, if he is discovered by any cartel members, he will be murdered for trying to cross without paying them first. It will be dangerous for him to show himself to anyone for the most part, but If he does receive help, it will not count against him as long as he finishes the entire course on foot.

"If he leaves the course with or without help before finishing, we will find him, bring him back, and make him finish the course. Only then, he'll do it with two crushed ankles like Anthony Fletcher did." Enrique turned to Harry and poked him in the ribs again, "You get all that, Harry?" he said. Harry nodded. "Good," Enrique said and faced the crowd.

"The window to buy into the "Desert Gaunlet Jackpot" will close at twenty-three-thirty. All participants will be invited to my private smoking room shortly after to view the satellite maps and place their bets for the jackpot before Mister Adams departs from the courtyard gates promptly at zero hundred hours.

"Are there any more questions?" Enrique asked. The casino rumbled with excited chatter. He could see Esperanza was already taking the information of a few gamblers who wanted to buy into the jackpot, but there were no more questions.

"Get him ready," Enrique said to Alejandro as he left the stage. Carlos beckoned to the DJ, and he quickly took his place back in the booth and began to raise the music up slowly as he spoke.

"Okay! Wow!, well That was wild. This has been an interesting turn of events, to say the very least, very exciting, very exciting! Hey, Good luck to all you high rollers out there who buy into the "Desert Gauntlet Jack Pot!" The DJ exclaimed as he turned Lady Gaga's "Poker Face" up to full volume.

Chapter Five

King's Skatepark

Johnny was contemplating all the events of the past few days as he sat in the driver's seat of the white SUV, watching the sunset. He and Stan had followed the girl all day long and had parked back in the same location where they had observed her from the first time. They had been hoping to catch her alone with her guard down, but so far, they hadn't had any luck.

A couple of hours after sunset Johnny was shaken awake to see Stan pointing at the girl. He could barely see her in the moonlight as she walked across the dark empty field from the skatepark to the public restrooms adjacent to the parking lot where he and Stan now sat. "Get ready, this may be our chance," Stan said.

Johnny and Stan watched as the girl crossed the empty field between the skatepark and the public restrooms at the front of the lot where they were parked. After she crossed the field, she entered the ladies' room at the front of the parking lot. When she had gone inside, Johnny quickly pulled the white SUV to the front of the parking lot and backed it into the spot directly in front of the entrance to the Ladies' restroom.

Except for Johnny and Stan, the parking lot was empty. Making sure to leave the rear doors of the SUV unlocked for easy access, Johnny and Stan made their way to the rear of the restrooms, where they would be behind the girl when she exited the restroom and after a few minutes, she came out while answering a text on her phone.

Stan came from behind, threw a bag over the girl's head, and yanked her back toward the ground. Only to his surprise, she didn't go down. Instead, she instinctively lowered her stance and braced herself with her feet shoulder-width apart, knees bent, and bending slightly forward at the waist.

She dropped her phone, brought both hands up, and grabbed the material of the bag that was around her neck. Getting her fingers between the material of the bag and her neck, she pulled down as hard as she could while whipping forward at the waist. Her intentions had been to throw her attacker over her shoulder in a sort of modified hip throw, but Stan had managed to hang on and was only slung around from her back to her left side. However, it did create enough space between the bag and her neck for her to catch a breath while simultaneously succeeding in off-balancing Stan.

Johnny stared in disbelief as the girl that Stan was not supposed to have any problem with slung him around and made repeated attempts to off-balance him. Stan, beginning to lose his grip as the girl continued to struggle, shouted at Johnny. "Stick her, goddammit, she's getting loose!" "I can't. You gotta fuck'in hold her still first!" Johnny said.

At this point, the girl had wriggled free enough to release one of her hands from the bag around her neck and throw a backward elbow strike into Stan's rib cage. Stan gasped and hunched over in pain, barely hanging onto the bag that was still over the girl's head. The girl then stepped her left leg behind Stan's legs and threw a second elbow strike back to his midsection, knocking him backward over her planted left leg.

As Stan fell to the ground, he managed to hold onto the bag around the girl's neck, dragging her down with him. The girl seemed to turn instinctively even as she was falling and had gained a more dominant position over Stan before they ever hit the ground. To Johnny's shock, she had pinned Stan on his back with her left knee in his chest.

Stan was reaching up desperately, trying to hold onto the bag around her neck, while she worked to free herself from the bag, pulling at his hands and forcing her knee deep into his chest while pulling back, slowly prying them apart. Stan's fingers began to slip from the bag. "Help me ... I'm fuck'in losing her, man!" Stan called out to Johnny, desperate for help!

Johnny finally snapped out of his bewilderment, put the syringe between his teeth like some kind of pirate in Chinos, grabbed both of the girl's pants cuffs, and pulled her legs out from under her. With her legs pulled out from under her, the girl landed belly down with Stan still clutching the bag.

As soon as Johnny dragged the girl to her belly, he pounced on her legs and held them together in a bear hug. Stan then rolled to his knees, and while holding her with the bag around her neck, he put all of his weight into the middle of her back with his shoulder.

"Hurry up, man, do it!" he said through clenched teeth as he continued to struggle to hold the girl down. "I'm trying. You gotta hold her better!" Johnny mumbled back as best he could with the syringe in his teeth.

Every time he let go of the girl to reach for the syringe, he could feel her begin to escape. Finally, in a desperate attempt, Johnny let go, grabbed the syringe, and jabbed the needle into the girl's ass. He hadn't wanted to go through the material but had no choice.

When the injection went in, the girl bucked wildly. Johnny had no time to remove the syringe. After making the injection, he had to immediately bear hug her legs again to hold her in place.

"Hold her down! It's gonna take about fifteen or twenty seconds to take effect," he said. Thirty seconds went by, then forty. It began to seem like a lifetime to Johnny as the girl continued to struggle. "It's not working," Stan said. "It's working, just not very well," Johnny said, but then the girl began to struggle a little less.

Johnny reached up, snatched the syringe out, and tossed it aside. "What the fuck is going on here?" He said as he reached up and grabbed the girl's layers of baggy shirts and pulled them up, exposing the girl's muscular back.

Johnny's eyes grew wide at the sight of her back. He reached over, grabbed her ass, and squeezed. He then ran his hand down her leg, squeezing her upper thigh. "Sweet Jesus! She's solid fuck'in muscle!" He said in shock. The girl struggled again briefly, then calmed.

Stan looked at the wallet chain that had been exposed as Johnny lifted the girl's shirts. His eyes followed the chain all the way down to the wallet nestled in the back pocket of her cargo pants. "You won't be needing this where you're going," He said as he ripped it away.

The girl had continued to fade in and out, struggling whenever she came to. The drug had worked somewhat, and Johnny had been very grateful for that. However, he and Stan had fought to the point of exhaustion to get the girl handcuffed and into the SUV.

In the SUV, she passed out, not to regain consciousness until they tried to take her out, where she once again put up a struggle before passing out again. By the time they got her handcuffed to the wall and her photograph sent to their boss, it was close to midnight, and Johnny had started to take account of his mistakes.

For starters, he had judged her height at about five foot two inches tall. Up close, he could see that she stood at least five foot six or seven. That had not been a bad guess, considering the distance from which he had observed her. However, each inch added roughly three pounds to her weight.

Also, her baggy clothes had hidden her muscular body along with ample breasts, buttocks, and hips. Between the attributes hidden by her baggy clothes and Johnny's incorrect guess of her height, he had incorrectly estimated her weight by at least thirty pounds.

Chapter Six

Desert Navigation, 101

As the party in the casino began to rage, Alejandro and Carlos were marching the staggering Harry Adams across the courtyard. Halfway across the courtyard, Harry doubled over, retching and defecating simultaneously. Alejandro and Carlos let him go and backed up at the first sign of his being sick. "Damn, he's got it coming out of both ends," Carlos said.

Harry fell to the dirt, shivering. "Doesn't look like he's ready for Basic Electronics or Land Navigation 101," Alejandro said. They dragged Harry onto the cobblestones next to the guesthouse he had been locked in earlier and sprayed him off with a water hose. His shaking became violent. He was dragged into the guesthouse and thrown into the bathtub with the shower turned on hot. Alejandro threw some clothes on the vanity next to the sink.

"Pull yourself together, get dressed, and be damned quick about it. Any time you waste takes away from the time Carlos has to teach you how to orientate yourself by compass. Fuck that up, and you die," Alejandro said. Harry, still shaking, got out of the shower and shoved his still-wet body into the clothing.

Inside Hacienda Ramirez, Carlos prepared for Harry's desert navigation course while the gamblers who had gathered in Enrique's smoking room looked over the satellite map of the course and placed their bets.

After Harry exited the shower and put on the hiking boots provided, Alejandro set a rucksack next to him on the bed. He then opened it and pulled out a black, plastic, weatherproof box with a two-and-a-half-foot cable coming out of it. The cable was attached to a small camera, which was mounted to a headband.

"It's a small computer that I built with integrated cellphone and camera components. It will broadcast a signal back to the casino using a private digital media platform. All the cellphone and computer functions will be controlled remotely from the central computer here at Hacienda Ramirez.

"If you receive a call, it will be us. So make sure you answer through this," Alejandro said as he pulled an earpiece down from the headband. "To answer the call, you press this button," Alejandro said, depressing the button on the earpiece for Harry to see.

"To change the battery, you undo these two thumbscrews here, remove the water-tight cover, and swap the battery like this," Alejandro said as he removed first the cover and then the battery. "Then you put everything back like this," he said as he reinstalled the battery, put the water-tight cover back in place, and tightened the two thumb screws.

"There is a low battery alarm. When it goes off, change the battery. Each battery will last about sixteen hours. There are twelve batteries here. That's over a week's worth of battery life, which should be more than enough. Make sure you bring the spent batteries back with you.

"If you live long enough to make it to Rattlesnake Cave, transfer the cocaine into the rucksack and pack the camera's computer system on top of it. We already checked, so we know it will fit. However, you will have to put the spare and spent batteries for the camera system in the ruck's outside pockets.

"Along with this point-of-view or POV camera for short, there may be as many as three other cameras on you at one time. There will be people on both sides of the border equipped with cameras following you on horseback, and there will also be camera-equipped drones monitoring your progress from above.

"However, if you want that ten grand to be in your car when you leave, make sure you keep the batteries changed and your point-of-view camera on at all times. Wear it forward when you are awake and prop it up and face it to you when you sleep," Alejandro said as he pointed to the small camera.

After Alejandro finished going over the POV camera with Harry, the computer portion was secured in the rucksack along with the charged batteries, and Harry was told to put the rucksack on. The camera was strapped over the large-brimmed boonie-hat, which was provided to him along with the ACUs he was now wearing.

After Harry had been fitted with the camera and it was powered on, Alejandro escorted him across the courtyard. The gamblers watching the live feed from Harry's POV camera could see that Carlos was now standing next to the gate behind a small table.

On the table sat a compass. Carlos had changed clothes as well. He was now wearing his ACUs, along with his old campaign hat, and he fully intended to enjoy the performance that he was about to put on.

As Harry and Alejandro approached Carlos, the gamblers watched through the lens of Harry's POV camera. Carlos scrutinized the camera perched on the brim at the front of the Boonie-hat. "Camera operational?" he asked. "Hell yeah, we're five by five and live!" Alejandro answered.

"Outstanding, the V.I.P. gamblers are with us then, correct," Carlos said. "That's right, some may still be watching from Enrique's smoking room, but I think most have probably migrated back to the casino by now," Alejandro said as he waved into the camera, smiling.

"Good, good, good, I got it from here," Carlos said. "He's all yours. I'm going in to do a preflight on Rooster One," Alejandro said. Carlos nodded as his younger brother turned on his boot heel and headed inside.

Suddenly, Carlos' whole demeanor changed as he turned his attention back to Harry and began yelling at him in an extremely loud, rapid cadence. A cadence that he had learned at the academy in South Carolina and then later perfected during his three years on the trail in Georgia as a Drill Sergeant.

The loud, fast-paced words hit the already staggering and sick Harry like rocks, knocking him into an even further state of disorientation. The gamblers watched on as Carlos continued his instruction. Some were wide-eyed and slack-jawed. Others were smiling or laughing, but they were all captivated.

"Before I came out here, I met with the participants of this speculative venture in Enrique's smoking room. I went over everything with them that I'm about to go over with you now. Do you know what, ham slice? There is a marginal aggregate of high-rollers in there that think you won't remember a damn thing that I'm about to tell you, and I think that they are 100 percent correct," Carlos said.

The Gamblers watched as Carlos' words hit Harry like machine gun fire. "The rules are as follows. I get to go over everything once. That's one time, no questions, if you don't get it, Oh well, fuck-it, fuck-it, two tears in a bucket, drive on, soldier, drive on! So, pay close attention, or your bones will lay scattered out there in the desert, picked clean by the fuck'in buzzards and bleached white by the Texas sun!

"Fortunately, you will not have to learn how to Identify terrain features, discern distance from, read, or orientate a topographic map, nor will you have to learn about magnetic north, true north, grid north, magnetic declination, or many other things concerning land navigation.

"You will, however, have to learn the concepts of aiming off and handrails, along with how to shoot an azimuth and calculate a back azimuth," Carlos said. *Why is he talking so fast, azimuth? What the fuck is he talking about?* Harry thought as he stood there with his head swimming and his guts twisting up.

Not slowing down, Carlos pressed on. "The compass on the table in front of you is the same lensatic compass used by the United States Army. If you look at the compass, you will see two sets of numbers that go around the outside of the dial. The set of numbers on the very outside of the dial, the ones in black, are the milliradians, or mils for short.

"The mils divided the compass into thousandths and are used to orientate equipment that is capable of precision accuracy over extremely long distances, in other words, artillery. Are you precision artillery? Answer me, goddammit, are you, Fuck no, you're not! You couldn't walk a straight line from here to that fuckin' gate, much less an extremely long distance, so don't use the mils.

"The set of numbers just to the inside of the mils, the ones in RED, divide the compass into three hundred and sixty degrees. The azimuths given to you will be in degrees. If you use mils instead of degrees, you will die, don't fuck up.

"An azimuth is a horizontal angle measured on the compass in a clockwise rotation by degrees that points from the compass to an observed or designated point. A "back-azimuth" is the opposite direction of its azimuth.

"To calculate a back azimuth, you will either add or subtract one half or 180 degrees of the 360 degrees of the compass. If the azimuth is 180 degrees or more of the total 360 degrees of the compass, you will calculate your back azimuth by subtracting 180 degrees.

"If the azimuth is less than 180 degrees of the total 360 degrees of the compass, you will then add 180 degrees to calculate your back azimuth. A back azimuth can be useful in finding your way back to your starting point if needed.

"To shoot an azimuth or back azimuth, you will hold the compass in one of two positions. Position one is used when plotting a course by sighting a reference point in the distance that you can then walk towards, thus staying on the correct azimuth.

"For this operation, you will first move the thumb loop into the downmost position like so," Carlos said as he pushed a hinged metal ring from the top of the compass until it swung all the way underneath. "You will then open the top portion, or case cover, of the compass to a ninety-degree angle like so, thus allowing you to use the sight wire," Carlos said, as he opened the compass' top portion at a ninety-degree angle and pointed to a wire that ran down the center of an oblong peephole.

"You will then lift the eyepiece like so," Carlos said as he swung the eyepiece that had been resting on the compass' face back on its hinge until it stopped. "The eyepiece serves two functions.

"One, the magnifying lens is used to read the numbers along the outside edge of the dial, and two, the sighting groove," Carlos said as he pointed to the groove at the top of the eyepiece. "is used with the sighting wire, like the sights on a rifle, to mark a reference point in the distance such as a large rock formation, ravine, ridgeline, or hilltop. You can then walk toward the noted reference point, thus staying on the correct azimuth. Once you reach your reference point, you can reshoot your azimuth and pick another reference point if necessary.

"After you have moved the eyepiece to the rear, you will insert your thumb into the thumb loop and hold the compass level on the platform created by the back of your thumb and curled index finger, like so. Then, using your other hand for support, you will bring the compass to your cheek.

"With the compass to your cheek and your elbows tight to your body, you will look through the magnification lens. As you look through the lens, you will move the eyepiece forward slowly until the numbers on the compass's dial come into view. Do not move the eyepiece too far forward, as it will lock the dial in place.

"Once the numbers are visible through the eyepiece, you will then turn your body in a circular motion until the desired degree of the azimuth falls under the black index line on the face of the compass here," Carlos said, as he removed the compass from his cheek and pointed to a black line on the dial of the compass.

"The index line on the face of the compass is aligned with the sighting wire. Once the degree of the desired azimuth falls under the index line, you can use your sighting groove and wire to mark a reference point in the distance.

"The second position is used in situations where a reference point in the distance cannot be noted due to the line of sight being blocked by dense foliage, geographic obstructions, or poor weather visibility such as rain or fog. It is also used when it is dark, as it is now, for instance.

"You will notice in the dark that the compass has six tritium markers, one at the top and bottom of the sighting wire, one on the North, East, and West indicators of the dial, one tritium indicator line in the bezel, and finally, there is a tritium bar directly under the black index line. These are here to aid you with nighttime navigation.

"For this method, you will once again move the thumb loop into the downmost position. You will then unfold the case cover one hundred and eighty degrees all the way back until it stops and the compass is flat, like so. Next, you will move the eyepiece back out of the way like so.

"You will then insert your thumb into the thumb loop while placing your index fingers along each side of the compass, holding it level. With the compass close to your body centered in front of you at stomach level, with your elbows tucked in tight by your sides, you will turn your body in a circular motion until the degree of the desired azimuth falls directly under the black index line.

"Next, you will turn the bezel until the tritium indicator line on the bezel is lined up with the north arrow line. This will allow you to hold your course by keeping the north arrow line under the preset bezel indicator line. This method is considered safer than trying to remember the degree number, which could lead to confusion. The larger north arrow is also more easily referenced in the dark than the small numbers on the dial.

"The trail you will be navigating is one of many my family has used through the years when aiding migrants to cross the Chihuahuan desert into Texas. It was also used to traffic contraband before we started flying it over in the pack drones. It is well marked by cairns every few miles, using highways, roads, and trails as catch features.

"A catch feature is an obvious landmark beyond your target location. The purpose of a catch feature is to alert you if you have traveled past your target location. There will be a catch feature given for every checkpoint. This eliminates the need for keeping a pace count. Each canteen you find will have the description of the next catch feature or the location of where the next cairn can be found.

"When you shoot your azimuth, you will need to deliberately set a heading that you know is to the right or left of your target location. A compass will get you close, but it is not exact. If you try to use dead reckoning, you will not know if your target is to your left or right. This will lead to confusion.

"By deliberately aiming off to one side, you can then use the highway, road, river, or whatever catch feature was given as a handrail to lead you to the cairn. Each degree you alter your heading will move your final destination point approximately 100 feet per mile. Most of your checkpoints are three to five miles apart.

"Lastly, you will notice that there is a cord forming a loop attached to the compass by a metal ring. This is called a lanyard or, in your case, a dummy cord. I highly suggest that you put it around your neck because if you lose that compass, you're fucked.

"This concludes your block of instruction on basic desert land navigation," Carlos said and then paused to briefly look at his watch. "You have four minutes to familiarize yourself with the lensatic compass. At zero hundred hours, you will be led outside the gates of Hacienda Ramírez, at which point you will shoot your first azimuth."

Harry stood bent at the waist, stomach cramping. His head was pounding. He had been dumbfounded by Carlos' instructions and had only been able to understand small snippets of them. The pain in his stomach spiked, and his head began to spin violently. He dropped to his knees, vomited, and passed out.

Chapter Seven

252 Degrees

Harry came to shortly before midnight when he felt Carlos and Alejandro pull him to his feet. Carlos hung the compass around Harry's neck, and they dragged him through the gates of Hacienda Ramirez.

"This is the point from which you'll shoot your first heading at a 252-degree azimuth. Don't fuck-up and forget your first heading. It's 252 degrees," Carlos said loudly, slapping him on the back with every syllable.

"Your first cairn will be on this side of the river, marking the trail down to where you will need to cross. Your next coordinates will be written on the side of your next canteen. At each checkpoint, a canteen will be buried about three feet to the west of the cairn.

"Each canteen will contain just enough water to get you to your next checkpoint. Our sister Maria, the family doctor, will make sure of that," Carlos said. With that, Carlos and Alejandro let Harry's arms go, and he slunk back to his knees outside the gates of the west wall of the courtyard.

Harry knelt in the sand and gravel with his eyes closed and his tears drying on his face. The gamblers watched from inside as the minutes passed. He was afraid to open his eyes. His head still ached, and he was scared Carlos would be standing there waiting to yell at him again. *252 degrees,* he thought. He had been repeating the number in his mind for the last few minutes, trying not to forget it.

His stomach cramps only came in waves now and were in a lull at the moment. He thought of his wife. The pain of her loss was still there. The six years she had been gone had done little mending. The day's events and blunt questioning he had received from the crowd of gamblers in the casino had led him to consider the life choices he had made over the last few years that led to his current situation.

He had done okay the first couple of years after his wife had passed. He had held it together for his daughter, but somewhere along the way, he began to falter, and eventually, his daughter had to move out on her own. The tears began to roll down his face afresh as he thought about her.

252 degrees, the numbers echoed in his mind. "I could still try to do right by her," Harry said in a whisper. He had little hope of making it out of the Chihuahuan desert alive, but he could try. He owed it to his daughter to at least try. His hand ran down his chest, tracing the length of the lanyard until it stopped at the compass.

252 degrees, the numbers reverberated through Harry's mind in Carlos's drill sergeant cadence. He opened his eyes and began to look at the compass. "Let's see here, I think he said you have to open it flat at night," Harry said to himself as he began to open the compass flat, but he began to feel nauseous and started dry-heaving. After a few minutes, he recovered and opened the compass.

Still on his knees, he could see that they had taken him to a trailhead just outside the gates and that he was facing in roughly the right direction, which made sense. Weak-kneed and trembling, he made it to his feet and held the compass, mimicking the way Carlos had shown him. Teary-eyed and without his glasses, he struggled to read the tiny numbers as he turned his body. *Now I understand what Carlos had meant about presetting the bezel,* Harry thought, thankful he had understood that part of Carlos' instructions.

He stared at the dial of the compass. His head was foggy, but being a former salesman, he had a head for numbers, and in time, he worked out that each tic mark on the dial was five degrees. Thus, he concluded that the spaces in between each tic mark would be valued at two and a half degrees. After he had figured this out, he slowly turned his body until the black index line was over the space between the 250-degree mark and the 255-degree mark.

Technically, that would be two-hundred and fifty-two-point-five degrees, Harry thought as he spun the bezel until its tritium marker line clicked into place over the dial's north arrow. "Close enough," he said under his breath.

He looked up from his compass to the newly waxing crescent moon and shook his head in disappointment. *That's no good,* he thought. The tiny sliver of the moon, barely visible, gave almost no light, leaving the desert landscape and the direction in which he would be traveling shrouded in darkness.

The night was clear and cool, a welcome reprieve from the heat of the day. Harry guessed that the temperature was somewhere in the low 70s and found it hard to believe that It had reached a high of 111 degrees that day.

The heat had been so unbearable that the bulk of Enrique's guests had preferred to stay either in the casino or under the cover of the arena. *I better take advantage of the cool night air,* he thought. He consulted the compass and took his first steps through the darkness toward the Rio Grande.

Inside the casino behind the bar, which also served as the casino's cashier's cage, Esperanza, Enrique's little sister, who was one of four turf agents in the family, had already been busy setting odds and taking wagers. The desert gauntlet gamblers had begun making wagers immediately.

They wagered if Harold would leave or not, and they wagered on what hour he would depart if he did. They wagered over whether or not he would make it as far as the river and, if not, what would be the cause of him not making it. Esperanza took all wagers, everything from snakebites before dawn to a broken leg before the first cairn is reached, all with odds in the house's favor, of course.

When Harry took his first step towards the Rio Grande, cheers and boos emanated from the gamblers vested in the desert gauntlet. Cheers from those that had wagered that he would leave within the first hour and boos from those who had wagered otherwise.

Harry's first steps into the darkness renewed the interest of a few of the gamblers who had sauntered off bored after he had remained kneeling and inactive for several minutes. They now rejoined the others in watching Harry's progress from one of the three large screen monitors in the bar that carried Harry's live feed. The other four were currently featuring different sporting events for the amusement of the other guests.

Harry moved forward slowly in the darkness, concentrating on the compass. His hands began to tremble. He paused, took a few deep breaths, and the trembling subsided. He was sweating in sheets, and his clothes were soaked through. He wiped the sweat from his eyes, steadied the compass, took his bearing, and pushed forward another thirty yards before the trembling in his hands recommenced.

This time, the trembling was more pronounced. *Fuck, I'm getting the fucking withdrawal shakes,* He thought, as the sweat ran down his face and burned his eyes. He pushed forward through the darkness, trying to control the trembling in his hands, and then he was falling.

In the darkness, concentrating on the compass, his eyes bleary with sweat and tears, Harry had walked off a twenty-foot cliff face. Inside the casino, the desert gauntlet gamblers watched transfixed, then erupted in gasps of oohs and ahhs as the screen violently tumbled from sky to ground and then went black.

There had also been a mixture of cheers and boos as Harry fell. Cheers from the gamblers that had bet Harry would not see the cliff and boos from those who wagered that he would avoid it. With the night vision supplied by Harry's camera, the desert gauntlet gamblers had an advantage he did not.

They had seen the cliff's drop-off well in advance and had scrambled to make their bets on whether or not he would walk over the edge and, if he did, what his damage would be. Esperanza had set odds for him walking over, plus everything from a broken pinkie toe to death, and he had indeed walked over the edge. Now, all that remained was to assess his damage.

In the control room, Alejandro sat behind the panel, staring at a dark screen as he dialed Harry's earpiece for the third time. There was no answer. His next call was to Carlos. "Yes, Sir," Carlos answered before the second ring. "Harry got off-trail and walked over the cliff face just west of here. His camera has gone dark, and he is not answering his comms link. You and a couple of the hands will have to go down there by horseback to find him."

"I'll send someone with a camera immediately. I want to get something on the screen for our patrons to watch as soon as possible," Alejandro said. "Understood. I'll have Felipe head to the stables to get the horses ready," Carlos said.

Inside the casino, the vested gamblers discussed the situation. "I think he is dead," Belyy Russkiy said. "That would be most unfortunate since I have wagered a large sum on him dying in the vast stretch of desert between the third and fourth cairn," said Mister Kijura.

At that moment, the gamblers heard a loud gasp as Harry fought for his breath, followed by the raspy scraping of gravel and sand. Then, the image of the desert's night sky, brilliant with stars, bordered by the cliff face, was illuminated on the screen in the green tint of the night vision camera.

"His' moving his' still alive! He will live to die of alcohol withdrawal later!" Belyy Russkiy said. Mister Oki Kujira smiled and nodded his approval. Ricky "Aces" cursed aloud while others held their breath to see if their wagers on a broken arm or leg would pay off.

In the control room, Alejandro called Carlos to halt his mission, "Carlos, stand-by looks like he's starting to move," He said as he stared at the stars on the screen. Just then, the screen whipped around as Harry grabbed the Boonie-hat and camera and slowly pushed himself to his knees.

Harry had tumbled down the cliff face and had gotten the wind knocked out of him after falling flat on his back at the bottom of a dry creek bed below the cliff. Now, on his knees, he felt extremely nauseous. His headache was unbearable. His hands were shaking too badly to hold the compass, and every muscle in his body cramped and burned.

He struggled to peer through the darkness at his surroundings. Up the bluff to the left of where he knelt was a small rock overhang barely visible under the new moon's light. In the casino, the gamblers watched the screen whip back and forth once more as Harry struggled to his feet and scrambled through the scree up the bluff to the small rock overhang.

There, he slipped his rucksack off and placed it on the ground. His hands were trembling as he struggled to position the camera, but he finally succeeded. Inside the casino, the gamblers watched as Harry crawled under the rock overhang, curled up in a ball, and began to shake and sob.

"No broken bones," Esperanza said from behind the bar. "And I'm off duty until tomorrow evening. Francisco here will be taking your bets until eight a.m. Goodnight, lady and gentlemen gamblers, and good luck!" Esperanza said as she excused herself from the bar.

As Franciso introduced himself to the gamblers inside the casino, outside under the rock overhang, Harry lay curled up in a ball shaking, eyes closed tightly, passing in and out of a fragmented sleep, vexed with fits and nightmares. When awake, he thought of pushing forward, but he still felt sick and was no longer willing to walk in the dark.

Chapter Eight

King's Beach

Hank Corbin had taken the day off. He had intended to try to sleep in for once, but unfortunately, he had too much on his mind. Unable to sleep, he had decided to take a drive to think things over and ended up on King's Beach, listening to the waves break on the shoreline in the darkness as he sipped his morning coffee.

Except for a couple of people who, unlike Hank, were taking a stroll at the end of a late evening, rather than beginning their day, and a couple of night anglers out wade fishing in the darkness, he had the beach all to himself.

Today was the day that he became a responsible adult. He had finally been able to save enough of his paycheck to pay for car insurance. His mission for the day was to get the Impala inspected and registered before the weekend.

Hank's new attitude was mostly due to him having a close call about three weeks prior. He was coming home from work when he zoned out and ran a red light right in front of a city cop. When he looked down at the speedometer, as usual, he was doing well over the speed limit.

Luckily, he knew the Officer. Not only did he know him, but he was friendly with him as well. Officer Jacob Stallard didn't even approach his car, and Hank knew it was because he was trying not to see anything that he would have to act on, like Hank's expired inspection sticker, for instance.

Instead, Officer Stallard just stood outside his patrol car door and gave Hank the "I'm only gonna look the other way just this once because I like you, but you better get your shit together" speech… Just a slight ass-chewing. Hank knew he had caught a break.

Officer Jake had been coming into Sal's Doughnuts, where Hank worked for his pre-shift coffee, even before Hank had ever started working there. He had always been friendly, and most of the time, Hank comped his coffee. His father had worked in law enforcement, and he respected law officers. His father's path to law enforcement had been through the Army. He had been on active duty, only enlisting in the National Guard when he became a Texas State Trooper.

Hank had thought about joining the military like his father. This had been the reason for his moving back to Texas. "If you're gonna enlist, you might as well do it out of Texas," His Uncle Dan had said, reasoning that Texas had excellent veteran education benefits that Hank could take advantage of once he got out.

Hank's Uncle Dan had also served in the Army, but unlike his brother, he wasn't a career soldier. He had been a good soldier and felt that every American should serve their country somehow, but he had often said that he was a four-and-out-the-door type of guy.

"It was one of those square peg, round hole type of situations," Dan told Hank many times. He would always laugh after he said that, but then again, Dan was always laughing. He was an easy-going, jovial type of fellow. He never pushed Hank to do anything and never said anything about his putting off the military to work at Sal's.

Hank didn't set out to work at a doughnut shop. He had only taken the job because it fell in his lap. Upon moving to Corpus Christi, he befriended one of his uncle's coworkers' sons. His name was Walter Wade Danville, but everyone called him Tinker because, besides working at a doughnut shop, that's all he did. Whether it be on cars, motorcycles, or computers, there wasn't anything he couldn't work on.

Tinker's father, Walt Senior, had been a boat mechanic before he went out to work the rigs on the maintenance crew, and he had every tool imaginable in his garage. Tinker had grown up working in the garage, but his father was always quick to point out that this was not how Tinker had learned his skills. Tinker's father had told Hank, "The boy was just born like that. He took the lawnmower apart and put it back together when he was five years old because he didn't like the way it was running."

Tinker had always kept an eye on Uncle Dan's house as well as his father's when they were out on the rigs, splitting his time between the two homes. When Hank showed up, they made fast friends, having much in common, and they soon learned to depend on one another a great deal when Walt Senior and Uncle Dan were gone.

Tinker had arranged for Hank to interview for a job at Sal's, where he worked. Then, when Hank got the job, Tinker talked him into taking it. Hank agreed to it, figuring he'd just work there until he figured out what it was that he really wanted to do, but he wound up doing nothing, and before he knew it, he had been giving Officer Jake his morning coffee for a little over a year.

Sal's was a decent enough job, and he liked most of the customers, but he knew he needed to find something that fit him better. Getting his car sorted out was only the first step. If he wanted to make his family proud, he needed to sort out the rest of his life as well.

Hank thought of his mother. He and his mother had moved back to her home state of California when his father had been killed to stay with her family. The loss of his father had been extremely hard on both of them, and they needed to have family around for support. His mother was still in California Teaching at Berkeley, but she called Hank often. Hank's thoughts then turned to his father. Even though his father was no longer with him, he still thought of him often.

Hank's father had known that photographic memory was a trait that ran in their family. He had also known that it was necessary to exercise it to bring it to its full potential and tested Hanks's memory almost daily, either with a list of words to remember or to see how many details he could recall from a photo in a book. Hank was always rewarded for any details he could recall.

One of the things Hank's father would often do when Hank was very young was to hold out a handful of change in front of him in the morning before he left for work, only letting Hank have a glimpse before quickly closing his hand and placing the coins in his pocket.

In the afternoons, when he would return from work, Hank would get to keep any of the coins that he could remember the denomination and year of. Consequently, Hank's memory had become quite astounding by the time he was only ten years of age.

Hank's father also taught him how to read people's body language. How to pay attention to detail and to notice when things were out of place. He also taught him much in the way of martial arts, some through formal lessons, but mostly, he disguised it as horseplay, which made learning it fun.

His father also taught him how to drive in the Impala. Hank would always be thankful to his father for all his lessons, but the memories of his Dad connected to the Impala always made him smile the most.

Hank's mind then began to wander to his Uncle Dan. Uncle Dan was a gracious host, but Hank didn't want to continue taking advantage of his uncle forever. His uncle worked offshore and made good money and would never accept any offers of rent or any other forms of compensation when Hank would offer. He would just always say that he appreciated having someone around to look after the place when he was offshore. Hank could see that, yet he still felt like he should be out on his own.

All these thoughts going through Hank's mind became too much. He gave up and decided to give himself another week to find a job. He would pick up a newspaper on the way home to see if he could find anything in the classifieds and that tomorrow after work, he would go by the unemployment agency, but if he hadn't found a job that fit within the next week, he would join the Navy.

With that decided, Hank watched as the sun's first light began to rise over the bay's horizon. It first began to cast dazzling hues of pinkish-orange over the dark water with breathtaking purples in the skies over the bay, and then stunning oranges, pinks, and purples began to mix in with shades of blue in the sky.

Chapter Nine

280 Degrees

Over four hundred miles west of King's Beach at Hacienda Ramirez, Joy Ride watched Harry's live feed as he awoke from a nightmare in a state of terror. In his nightmare, he had been set adrift at sea in a raft and was propped up at one end with his eyes closed, seasick, dying of thirst. When he opened his eyes, opposite from him in the raft was his wife's corpse staring back at him. He watched as the flies played around her nostrils and eyes as the raft rocked up and down.

Harry, heart racing and nauseous, rolled to his knees, dry heaving. There was nothing left to come up. Slowly, he realized where he was and sat in the early morning twilight, trying to console himself. Along with his headache, nausea, and occasional tremble, he was now also dehydrated.

Harry thought about the canteen at the first checkpoint and knew that he needed to get his ruck on and get to it before his dehydration became too severe. He could now partially make out the horizon and some of the desert's features in the early morning twilight and wondered how far he had gotten off course after falling down the cliff face.

He reasoned that he must have fallen straight down for the most part. Slowly, he got up, put on the rucksack along with the POV camera, and began to make his way down the bluff. Being careful not to slip in the scree that littered the bottom, he slowly descended into the dry creekbed where he had landed after walking over the cliff face the night before.

As he prepared to reshoot the 252-degree azimuth, it dawned on him that he had forgotten to use the aiming-off technique, advised by Carlos. He decided he would use the aiming-off technique to shoot an azimuth well to the north of the first checkpoint.

He decided this for two reasons. One, this would ensure that he would reach the river well to one side of the checkpoint, ensuring that while he might have to walk further, at least he would know he was walking in the right direction, and two, he might have to drink from the Rio Grande.

Drinking from the Rio Grande was a risky proposition. At the very least, he could acquire dysentery. Dysentery, along with his already dehydrated condition, would add up to a death sentence, but if he went much longer without water, he would die anyway.

Even so, before he drank from the river, he wanted to walk a good distance from upstream. The very least he could do was check for dead animals or any other visible contaminants in the river on his way to the first checkpoint. He had made a joke to himself while on stage about learning his survival skills from watching "Alone," but he had watched an episode on a T.V. above a bar one night where a contestant had made that very mistake.

He would attempt to make it to the first checkpoint and drink only the water left for him by Enrique's men. He would then refill the canteen from the river and try to make it to the second checkpoint, only drinking the river water if he absolutely had to.

However, if they did not leave him enough water at the first checkpoint, he intended to drink his fill of the Rio Grande and refill his canteen as well. This was providing, of course, he had not seen anything upriver to dissuade him.

Harry heard a buzzing sound and watched as Alejandro's camera drone, Rooster-One, flew overhead. Alejandro switched from Harry's POV feed to the drone's, and the gamblers watched as Harry used the sighting method Carlos had shown him to mark a 280-degree heading.

He marked the heading by a very distinct rock formation on a mountaintop in the distance. He had chosen that particular rock formation mostly because it was roughly in the direction he estimated he needed to go in but also because it reminded him vaguely of the rock formation that The Lone Ranger's horse Silver would rear up next to in the openings of all those old Lone Ranger re-runs. He had loved to watch that show as a kid and knew he wouldn't confuse that rock formation with a different one.

Harry was not sure how far he was from the river, but Carlos had mentioned that the cairns were placed every few miles. He had also said that a one-degree alteration would move your arrival point one hundred feet per mile. Harry's brain was muddled, but being a former salesman, he had a head for numbers and soon estimated that a thirty-degree alteration should land him roughly about a half mile upriver from the first checkpoint.

On the other side of the creek bed, the bank rose sharply into a tall rocky ridgeline scattered with scrub-brush and cactus. He found a ravine and worked his way up to the top of the ridgeline. Once at the top of the ridgeline, he could see the mountain with his rock formation in the distance, framed by two other larger mountain peaks. Between him and his rock formation lay an expanse of sandy, rocky desert, which then gave way to the foothills of the mountains.

Harry had no idea how long he walked before finally reaching his first reference point. It couldn't have been much over half a mile, but fighting his way over the foothills and scrambling up the bluffs and ravines of the Chiso Mountains in his condition had been no easy task.

He had been forced to stop several times while he waited for tremors, nausea, or both to pass while he rested. Also, his weakened condition obliged him to walk around some of the higher, rougher terrain and foothills. As a consequence, it was now already approaching mid-morning in the Chihauhaun Desert.

Harry had made his way up the small mountain and was now sitting on the west side in the shadow of his rock formation. From there, Harry reshot his two-hundred-and-eighty-degree azimuth. The sights fell directly in the middle of a large mesa that looked to be a little over a mile away. Like Harry's Lone Ranger rock formation, the mesa was also very distinctive and would serve well as his next reference point.

At present, there was shade to be found beside large boulders, rock formations, and other terrain features. Some of the desert plant life even offered some sparse shade. Be that as it may, Harry knew that within a couple of hours, the shade would be gone, and the temperatures would soar. He did not have any way of knowing what the temperature would rise to that day, but he knew that on the day of his arrival, it had reached a high of a hundred and eleven degrees, which was a fairly normal high for the Chihuahuan Desert in July.

Harry stared at the mesa in the distance and wondered if he could make it before the sun rose too high. In his condition, he would probably die if he didn't either make it to the trees, along the river or find some other shelter from the sun before midday.

Weak and sick as he was, Harry's thirst drove him to his feet. Rooster-One, which had been recording from a stationary position atop a large boulder, roared to life, lifted into the air, and hovered overhead. Harry could not see the operators, but he had heard their horses and knew that they were somewhere close by.

As the drone gained altitude, Harry started for the mesa. If he didn't make the first checkpoint and get some water soon, he would be in trouble. He would have to worry about finding shelter from the sun later.

Chapter Ten

Lost and Found

After watching the sunrise, Hank walked up the shoreline to the trashcans next to the public restrooms up the beach from where he had parked. He finished off the last of his coffee and tossed the empty into the trashcan. As he tossed the empty, something on the very top of the trash caught his eye. It appeared to be some dude's wallet. It was the type that snapped shut and was attached to a long chain, the type a biker or a skater would carry.

Hank figured It was probably stolen, and he was sure it had been looted of any cash or cards, but perhaps they left their identification card or their driver's license. Sure that the poor fella would be happy to get at least that back, he fished it out of the trash, thinking that if there were any identification in the wallet, he would drop it off in a mailbox somewhere close by.

The snaps were already unfastened. He opened the wallet and checked the cash pocket first. "Empty. No surprise there," He said as he turned his attention to the rest of the wallet. "What do we have here," He said as he stuck two fingers in an inside pocket and slid out a driver's license belonging to one Miss Abigale Reese Adams.

Hank looked at the driver's license photo. *The categories of people who carry this type of wallet are Bikers, Skaters, and posers. Miss Adams appears to fit into the skater category,* he thought. The photo on the license showed a young girl with a nose ring and multicolored hair with pinks, purples, blues, and oranges that reminded Hank very much of the sunrise he had just witnessed.

He tried not to make snap judgments. However, King's skate park was only about fifty feet away on the beach, and the address given on her license was also not far away. He was fairly confident in his deduction of her being a skater.

Normally, he would have just found a post office box to toss the wallet into. However, he decided that since her address was close, he would just try to drop the wallet off personally. The fact that she was close to his age and attractive and that the height and weight on her license added up well in his mind played a part in this decision as well.

With wallet in hand, Hank began the trek back down the beach to the parking lot where he had parked the Impala. After unlocking the Impala's driver's side door, he tossed Miss Adam's wallet onto the dash, slid into the front seat, stuck his key in the ignition, and turned it only to hear his engine give a futile half-crank followed by that dreaded click-click sound that always let you know that you are completely screwed. *Well, at least I have a set of jumper cables. If I can just get lucky enough to find someone to help me out,* he thought as he opened the door and stepped out.

Hank locked the door, put his keys in his pocket, turned around, and came face to face with two men. One was standing slightly behind the other. "Hey buddy," The one in front, obviously the leader, said. "Do you have a phone I could use? I haven't spoke to my family for a while, and I'd like to let them know I'm okay."

"I tell you what," Hank said as he fished his phone from his back pocket. "You give me the number, I'll dial it and let you talk to them on the speaker, but I'm not giving you my phone. No offense, but I've heard of too many people getting robbed that way."

Hank barely got the words out of his mouth when the head dirtbag produced a knife from under a green t-shirt, which looked to Hank as if it had missed about three months of laundry days. Dirty Shirt's buddy stood behind him, grinning like an idiot, showing a mouth full of missing teeth. The remains of which he did have were yellow and broken. He was obviously scared as he kept his position behind his partner, preferring to let him handle the situation.

"There is a way you're gonna give me that phone. It's called at knifepoint, and I'll be taking your wallet too," Dirty Shirt said. "Okay, man," Hank said as he turned slightly, setting his phone on the car's roof. "Just take it easy. You can have both, no problem, but I'll have to unlock the door. My wallet is on the dash," He said as he stepped to his left and gestured with his right thumb toward the car door window behind him.

Dirty Shirt tilted his head and looked past Hank to see Miss Adam's wallet still lying where Hank had left it. Hank drew his right foot back waist-high, loading his leg up like a giant spring, and while Dirty Shirt stared at the wallet on the dash, Hank stomped the arm he was holding the knife with hard into his ribs, knocking the wind completely out of him. The knife clattered to the ground as Dirty Shirt flew back, crashing into his yellow gap-toothed cohort, sending them both down hard, landing in a tangled mess on the parking lot asphalt.

Hank thought briefly of engaging them, but they were both filthy and looked as if they had pissed themselves, and he didn't want to touch either one of them. Plus, there were two of them. He quickly retrieved the knife, but before he could decide what to do next, the would-be muggers found their feet and ran away, leaving Hank shaken but okay.

It was after nine in the morning before Hank finished answering all of the police officers' questions. He had hoped they would send Officer Jake, but they did not, so the interview was almost as nerve-wracking as the mugging, and by the time it was done, he was spent.

The only good thing to come out of it was the officer was nice enough to give him a jump. After getting back into the Impala, he noticed Miss Adam's wallet on the dash. He still had that to do, but he needed to go home first. He wanted to collect himself, and Tinker would be home from work by now. He would ask him to look at the Impala before he risked getting stuck somewhere again.

Four and a half miles South of King's Beach, Abbie woke up on a restroom floor handcuffed to the handrail in a wheelchair-accessible stall. The drugs they had given her made her groggy, and she had spent the night drifting in and out of consciousness.

She was still mad at herself for letting her phone distract her. She had known better. They had come from behind, first putting a bag over her head and then restraining her. She fought, but there were at least two, maybe three of them, and they had pinned her to the ground. Then came the injection.

The last thing she remembered before going out was one of her attackers taking her wallet. He had noticed the wallet chain hanging by her side. "You won't be needing this where you're going," He had said, laughing as he ripped her wallet away. *What an asshole!* Abbie had thought as she lost consciousness.

When she came to, she was in a vehicle with no memory of getting in or how long they had been driving. By the time they stopped and dragged her out, she was starting to feel a bit more herself. Although still a little off-balance, she tried to fight, even succeeding in knocking one of her kidnappers to the ground for a second time, even though she still had a hood over her head and her hands were still handcuffed behind her back.

Her kidnappers must not have appreciated that too much because things got a little rough after that. She was manhandled into the wheelchair-accessible stall. The cuff was taken from her right hand and locked around the handrail, and there she was left on the floor next to the toilet.

Chapter Eleven

The Rio Grande

The hike to the mesa had been brutal. The gamblers had been watching as Harry was forced to stop multiple times, either because of the shakes or sickness or because he had been too fatigued to move forward. It had taken him at least two hours to cover the distance between the rock formation and the mesa. Money had been lost and won each time he had picked himself back up out of the sand.

It was now late morning as he looked down from the West side of the mesa top to the Rio Grande that lay about half a mile away. The shade was becoming sparse, the temperature had risen considerably, and while his nausea had somewhat subsided, his tremors and dehydration were getting worse. Although he felt sick and exhausted, the rising temperature and his thirst spurred him into shooting the 280-degree azimuth.

He mentally noted two new reference points in the distance. One was a distinctive part of a ridgeline on a mountaintop that was two or maybe three miles in the distance. The second was a much smaller mesa than the one he was currently standing on. It was two or three hundred feet north of where the river came around the mountains and made an aggressive ninety-degree bend to the south.

From the mesa top where Harry currently stood, he could see that in the short distance to the river, he would have to go through some foothills and cross over a road that was cut through the bottom of a rock pass. The ridgeline on the mountain top in the distance would be tall enough to guide him whether he be at the bottom of that rock cut or in the draws of the foothills.

When the small mesa next to the river came into view, he would make straight for it, and then, passing to the south of it, he would come to the river just past where it made the big bend.

The river continued to run south of the big bend in a southern direction for what looked like a couple of miles. Harry was sure that his first checkpoint was a mile or so south of the big bend there was a long, straight section of the river.

He made his way down the large mesa and started walking to his reference point in the ridgeline. The sun was already beating down, and midday was fast approaching. Although his tremors were now coming harder and more frequently, and his hands kept cramping shut, his bouts of dry heaving now came less frequently, and despite his nausea being a constant companion, he now thought of nothing but water.

He remembered his father as a young man digging post holes for fences in the hot Texas sun. Harry had helped him stretch barbwire in the summers when he was off from school. "When a man is truly thirsty, he won't want anything but water," his father had said many times as they labored.

Harry had found that to be true for most of his life, but it had been a long time since water had been high on his list of liquids. In truth, he had even begun to find it detestable. However, he was now consumed with the thought of it. The thought of wet, cool, clear, pure, fresh, life-giving water.

He heard the rapids of the Rio Grande long before he saw it. The drone flew high to give the gamblers a bird's eye view. Harry's view of the river was blocked by small trees, scrub brush cacti, and tall grass. Instead of passing to the south of the small mesa as he had intended, he was forced to climb to the top of it for a better view.

From the top of the small mesa, he could see that the river bank was heavily choked with scrub brush for miles. There was no way that he would ever be able to fight his way through all those thorns. He would have to give up on his plan to check the river for contaminants as he walked the bank.

Down river from the mesa, Harry spotted a sand bar with a trail that worked its way up the bank. He decided to check from there, but first, he scanned the river from the top of the small mesa, looking up and down for contaminants. Then, he looked upstream in the distance. Shielding his eyes from the sun, he strained to see if he could detect anything large in the river, such as a dead deer or cow, but he saw nothing.

After he was satisfied, he scrambled down the little mesa to a trail he had spotted from above. Whether it was a game trail or an old cow trail, he did not know. *It could be a people trail for all I know,* he thought.

He walked the trail for about two hundred yards, then made his way down to the sandbar, removed his rucksack, positioned the POV Camera, and waded into the river, submerging himself under the water. He held his mouth shut tight, and it had been all he could do to keep himself from drinking while he cooled himself down.

After the quick plunge, Harry had hurried back to the sandbar, partially because he needed to get to the water at the first checkpoint and partially out of fear. While he had been in the water, all of Enrique's talk about alligators and pythons had crept into his thoughts, and he could have sworn he saw something moving like a shadow under the water. The gamblers had watched in excited anticipation but had been disappointed.

He surveyed the river and its banks as he stood on the sandbar while he put on the ruck and POV camera. Less than two hundred yards downriver, he spotted another much larger sandbar. Beyond that sandbar, he could see the water breaking over rocks in large sections all the way across the river, making it where someone could easily walk across to the other side.

While Harry had thought the river crossing would be further downstream, he realized that this was probably the site of the first checkpoint, but like before, the thorny scrub brush made the river bank impassable. He thought momentarily about abandoning the river bank and swimming downriver the rest of the way, but then Enrique's talk of monster pythons and alligators came to his mind once again, and then he thought about the shadow moving under his feet in the water and decided against it.

He started back up the bank. His wet clothes hung to his body, helping to cool him down, but he was still dehydrated. His right hand cramped shut in pain. He used his left hand to pry it open as he trudged forward on heavy legs.

He followed the trail in a daze as it meandered through the scrub brush and cacti. He was beginning to feel light-headed when the large trail he was on intersected with a much smaller one. He could not believe his eyes. Right in front of the large trail stood a rock cairn at least three feet tall.

Joy Ride cheered when she saw the cairn on the monitor through Harry's POV and then jumped up and down with excitement as Alejandro switched the screen to an overhead aerial drone shot of Harry standing at the first checkpoint, hands raised over his head in celebration.

The small trail had been Harry's intended path, and the cairn had been placed in front of the large trail where he would have seen it easily. About three feet to the west of the cairn lay a large flat stone. He dropped to his knees and prayed as he lifted the stone. Underneath the stone was a thirty-two-ounce green military-style canteen.

He unscrewed the top of the canteen and drank the entire contents in seconds. He had told himself on the trail that he would not do that. He had told himself that he would ration the water. He had even repeated to himself over and over that he would ration the water, but that had not mattered.

His stomach began to cramp in unbearable pain. He had drank way too much water way too fast. The pain in his stomach intensified and then was washed over by a wave of nausea. He clamped his mouth shut and began to swallow repeatedly, fighting his stomach's convulsions to regurgitate the water. Some of the water regurgitated into his mouth. He swallowed it back down, knowing that he could not afford to lose a single drop, and then he stayed there on his knees for several minutes, waiting for his nausea to pass.

While he was waiting for his nausea to pass, he broke out in a cold sweat. *"Sweat,"* he thought. He felt like crap but knew that sweat was a good sign. The wave of nausea passed, leaving him feeling a little better but still a bit woozy. He looked at the empty canteen. On the side, written in permanent marker, were the words dry creek bed. Below that were the coordinates 250 degrees. "Dry creek bed," He said in a whisper.

Carlos had said that the trail was marked by cairns every few miles, but he had no way of knowing exactly how far away the dry creek bed or next checkpoint might be. It was now close to midday, the heat was becoming unbearable, and he needed to find shelter soon.

As he tried to unfold the compass to shoot the new azimuth, his hands cramped painfully shut, requiring him to stop and physically force his hands open by stretching the thumbs and fingers apart by pressing them open on the sides of his legs. He then had to ignore the pain in his hands as they cramped shut around the compass.

He brought the compass to his cheek, but before he could shoot the azimuth, he began to shake violently. He waited for the shaking to stop and tried again. Again, he began to shake before he could use the compass, the shaking starting in his hands and then violently working its way up his arms to his chest. However, on his third attempt, he was able to pick out a tall mountain peak in the far distance that corresponded with the new azimuth.

He then looked at the mountains that were just across the river, about a mile up from the bank. He scanned them from their foothills to their ridgeline, looking for shelter from the midday sun. He could see no rock formations or anything else that might provide shelter. Past the opposite river bank, there was nothing but rocky undulating sand and ankle-high creosote bush all the way up into the mountains.

On his way to the river, he had seen some rock formations that would offer shelter, but they were too far back to retreat to now. Although he dreaded it, he decided that he would have to shelter by the river. He walked less than a hundred feet back up the bank, not far from where he had stumbled across the first cairn to a small mott of mesquite trees. There, he walked around the trees until he found a spot in some shade that was free of prickly pear.

Harry took off his rucksack and set it on the ground. He then positioned his camera on top so that it was facing under the mesquite trees where he intended to lay. He had been mindful of the camera so far. If he survived this hell, he wanted his money.

Harry carefully spread his ACU jacket over the gnarled limbs of one of the mesquite trees for extra shade, using its thorns to hold it in place. With his shelter set up, Harry put his boots in the sun to dry and lay down in the sand. Rooster-One made a final pass and then returned to its cameramen for a fresh battery. As Harry pulled his boonie hat down over his eyes, he prayed none of the river monsters Enrique spoke of were near.

Chapter Twelve

The Plot Thickens

Hank had made it back home and was filling Tinker in on the morning's excitement. He listened, mystified, as he fiddled with the battery connections under the *Imapla's* hood. After Hank finished his story Tinker let out a slow whistle in astonishment, "Shit, that was close. You did good, though. What made you think to try that kick? I'd of just handed everything over," he said.

"I should've. That would've been the smart thing to do, but those guys looked pretty rough. They weren't very steady on their feet and were kind of swaying like they didn't have any balance. It looked to me like they had been up all night tweakin' and were starting to crash. I guess I figured my odds of winning were pretty good, so I took a chance," Hank said.

"Well, I guess it would've been different if they had a gun. You read the situation well enough. Try the ignition," Tinker said. Hank slid behind the wheel and turned the key. The Impala turned over but did not start.

"The corrosion on your battery terminals probably caused the battery not to charge properly. I guess we'll have to jump her off, but the battery should charge fine after that now that I've cleaned the terminals," Tinker said as he opened the Impala's trunk to retrieve the jumper cables.

He began shifting items from one side of the Impala's cavernous trunk to the other as he dug in search of jumper cables. "Really, Hank, do you need to carry all this stuff around?" he said. "It doesn't hurt anything, and if I took it out, it would just be in the way somewhere else. Besides, you never know it may come in handy," Hank said.

His statement sounded good and was true. However, the real reason Hank didn't clean out the Impala's trunk was that almost everything in it was right where his father had left it after their last camping trip, and he just didn't want to.

The most Hank ever did was maintain the equipment, and that he did standing at the Impala's trunk. He would remove whatever was to be maintained or cleaned. This could be anything from one of the fishing poles whose reels needed oiling to a machete whose edge needs a quick touch-up. Whatever it was, he would clean it, check it over, and put it back in its place.

"Oh, yeah, like these fishing poles, we better keep these in here. You never know when a fish might just jump right out in front of us unexpectedly," Tinker said. "You never know," Hank said, laughing it off. Besides the fishing poles, Tinker also removed a tent, two sleeping bags, and other camping gear.

After digging even further down in the trunk, Tinker was finally able to pull the jumper cables free from their hiding place.

He then walked back to the front of the Impala and hooked one end of the jumper cables to the battery of Hank's uncle's fishing boat, which Dan kept on a battery charger in the driveway, and the other end to the Impala's battery. "Try it now," he said after a few minutes. Hank turned the key over, and the 454 turbojet roared to life! "Thanks, Tink, I owe you," Hank said.

"No worries, buddy. You don't owe me anything. You're just gonna have to learn to clean the corrosion from your battery terminals every once in a while," Tinker said. "Nope, That's what I got you for! Now, how about you ride with me to drop off this wallet? Just in case I run into any more trouble, car or otherwise... I've had enough for today," Hank said. "Sure, I don't have anything else going on. Let's take a ride," Tinker said as he climbed into the passenger seat.

They made a quick stop at the gas station. Hank topped the Impala off with fuel, and Tinker purchased a Moonpie, a small bag of peanuts, and a Coke. Hank got behind the wheel as Tinker slid into the passenger seat. Once in, Tinker ripped open the bag of peanuts and dumped them into his Coke. Within a few minutes, they were pulling up and parking on the street in front of the small garage apartment bearing the address found on Miss Adam's driver's license.

As the Impala rolled to a stop, Hank's eye caught a coffee cup from Sal's Doughnut Shop lying just off the curb across the street. This irritated him. He had always disliked litterbugs. He wondered which one of his customers had been low-class enough to toss it and made a mental note to pick it up on his way back.

Hank looked at Tinker sitting in the passenger seat. "Wait here. I'm going to go knock on the door and see if anyone's at home," He said as he stepped one foot out onto the pavement. "Ten-Four Good-Buddy," Tinker said as he took a swig of his Coke and happily chewed on the peanuts that had washed up.

Hank got out, walked around the Impala, crossed the sidewalk to the driveway in front of the three-car garage, and made his way to a staircase on the side of the building that led up to a small balcony porch. He climbed the staircase to the balcony and knocked on the apartment door. There was no answer. After a minute, he tried again, still with no answer.

After knocking a third time, Hank was beginning to feel like it was a wasted trip. Finally, he went back to the Impala and had Tinker retrieve a pen and paper from the glove box. He would have to settle for leaving a note. He placed the note on the door and then walked across the street to retrieve the discarded coffee cup.

As Hank walked up to the coffee cup, he noticed cigarette butts lying all around the cup. Hank found it a bit odd that somebody had sat there long enough to go through that many cigarettes. He probably wouldn't have noticed the cup at all, except the logo from Sal's Doughnut Shop jumped out at him like a beacon. He had been working there too long. He took the lid off of the coffee cup and used it to sweep the cigarette butts into the cup.

He walked back to a trashcan that stood next to the fence at the end of the garage apartment's driveway, opened the lid, tossed the whole mess in, and then walked back to the Impala. Tinker was sitting in the passenger seat in the midst of destroying a Moonpie. Hank got in, started the engine, and drove away. Only he didn't make it very far.

About a block from the garage apartment, his phone began to ring. "Hello," he said. "Please come back if you can. I need to talk to you," said the voice on the other end of the line. "Is this Miss Adams?" Hank asked. "No, I'm her roommate, but please come back. I'm worried that Abbie is in trouble," the voice said. "Okay, okay, no problem, just hang tight, and I'll be right there," Hank said as he turned the Impala around in the next convenient driveway and began to backtrack to the garage apartment.

"What's up?" Tinker asked, noticing the look on Hank's face. "I'm not too sure, but I think the young lady that owns this wallet may be in some kind of trouble. That was her roommate on the phone, and she sounded pretty worried," he said. "Well, if you're not having a hell of a day!" Tinker said. "Tell me about it. What have I got myself into now?"

Hank stopped the Impala on the street in front of the garage apartment, this time parking on the opposite side of the street from where the coffee cup had been lying. "Stay in the car?" Tinker asked as Hank parked. "No, buddy. I think maybe you better come with me this time, just in case," he said. Tinker nodded, and they both got out of the Impala and approached the staircase together.

At the top of the staircase, Hank knocked at the door. Directly, a female who looked to be in her early twenties opened the main door. Leaving the storm door locked, she peered through the glass, "You have Abbie's wallet?" she asked. "Sure do, right here," Hank answered, holding the wallet up so she could see it.

"I'm Hank, and you are?" Hank asked to prompt the young lady behind the glass to introduce herself. "Oh, I'm so sorry. Please excuse my manners. I guess I'm just a little shaken up. I'm Abbie's roommate, Liz," she said. "No worries, Liz, I can understand that. Now you said Abbie might be in some kind of trouble?" Hank asked through the storm door glass.

"Yes, I think so. Yesterday, there was a white SUV parked across the street for a long time. They left right behind Abbie after she passed them on her way to the park. It made me a little nervous, but I thought that I was just being paranoid, only when Abbie didn't come home last night... Well, I just knew that they had something to do with it. That's why I didn't answer when you first knocked. I thought that they had come back, but then I saw your note," she said.

"Have you called the police?" Hank asked. "Yes, I called this morning and let them know that she has been missing since last night," she said. "I see. Now, when you say she was going to the park, I assume that would be the skatepark at King's Beach, right?" Hank said. "Yes, that's right, but how did you know..." Liz answered with a puzzled look on her face and started to ask Hank how he knew which park Abbie had gone to but was cut off.

"And, you say it was a white SUV? Were you able to get a plate number?" he asked. "No, I didn't think I needed it, and they were parked too far away," Liz answered. "How about the make or year model?" Hank asked. "I think it might have been either a late 90's or early 2000's Chevy," Liz answered.

"Could you see the driver or passenger?" Hank asked. "I could see that there was a driver and someone in the passenger seat, but I couldn't make them out through their window tint," Liz answered, "By their silhouettes, they appeared to be males, medium build, with short hair," she said, and then asked Hank, "How did you know Abbie had gone to King's skate park?"

"Well, I first suspected that she may have been at King's Skate Park based on the type of wallet that she was carrying, the way she looked in her driver's license photo, and the fact that I found her wallet not far from the skate park in the trashcan next to the public restrooms at Kings Beach.

"My suspicions were later reinforced when I made the first trip up your stairs. On the way up, I noticed that your staircase railing showed a lot of wear from someone doing multiple rail slides down it, and there was also the Grinder Street Skateboard Company sticker on the surfboard leaning in the corner of your porch," Hank said. Liz stared at him in disbelief for a second and then nodded her head, "Yeah, that makes sense. That restroom was on her way home," she said.

Hank held the wallet up again, "Do you mind if I hold on to this?" he asked. I may use her ID to make some missing posters," he said. "You go ahead. I won't be around to give it to her if she comes back anyhow. I'm not staying here by myself. My brother is on his way to pick me up right now. I'm going to stay with him until all this gets sorted out. You have my number. Save it and call me if you hear anything. If I hear from Abbie or the police, I'll call you," Liz said.

"Well, now what?" Tinker asked as he stared through the Impala's windshield. "Well, you're not gonna believe this, but I think I have a clue," Hank said. "The hell you say! You're not thinking about looking for this girl all on your own, are you?" Tinker asked. "No way, buddy," Hank said smiling, "You're gonna help me."

"That's what I figured," Tinker said, "So what's this clue you got?" he asked. "Well, you remember that coffee cup I picked up?" Hank said. Tinker nodded his head in affirmation. "Yeah, sure do, So?" He said with a shrug. "Well, there were cigarette butts all around it," Hank said. "So," Tinker said, still not quite following Hank's logic.

"So, it probably belonged to whoever was in the white SUV that Liz spotted. She said it was there for a while. It would take someone a while to work their way through that many cigarettes, and there is a good chance that whoever tossed the cigarette butts also tossed the coffee cup."

Tinker's face lit up as he realized what Hank was driving at. "So that means they came through Sal's Doughnut Shop!" he said. "Yep, and if they came through Sal's Doughnut Shop, then we have," at that point, Tinker cut Hank off and finished his thought, "We have them on security video!" he said.

"Exactly, and not only that but there is a chance that they may come back, so we'll have to keep an eye out for them," Hank said. "Awe, man, do you think they might really come back?" Tinker asked nervously. "Best coffee in town, I wouldn't doubt it," Hank said, shrugging his shoulders.

"Well, I know this much," Tinker said, "Whether they come back or not, you'd better be there. Salvatore Bombalone Fornaio is a good guy, but you already missed a day's work, and if you're not there tomorrow, he'll skin you alive." Hank's thoughts turned to Sal. He was a good man, for sure, but if Hank missed another morning, Tinker was right. He would skin him alive.

Sal treated Hank and Tinker very well. Nevertheless, anytime one of them couldn't work the morning shift, Sal would have to come in early to cover for them, and anytime Sal didn't make it to surf the morning tides or dawn patrol, as he called it, he would be cross all day.

"Yes, Sir," Hank said, "You're right about that one, but we have a little time. Tell you what, let's go home, scan Miss Adams's driver's license photo, make some missing posters, and try to post a few before it gets too late.

"In the morning, I'll cover the counter while you review the security video. You're better on the computer than I am. Sound like a plan?" Hank asked. "Sounds good to me, but we better get moving. There's a lot we gotta get done before work, and we better be there at Three-thirty a.m. sharp, or Sal will be on us all day!" Tinker said. Hank nodded as he threw the Impala into gear, and they were off.

Chapter Thirteen

Water

Abbie's body was stiff and sore. She seemed to be losing track of time and felt like she had been stuck there forever. Because she was handcuffed to the stall's handrail, No matter how she tried, there were only three positions she was able to get into.

She was forced to alternate between sitting on the floor, either holding her left arm up to keep the handcuff from digging in or relaxing it, in which case it did, standing in one spot, or sitting uncomfortably on the very edge of the toilet, which had no lid. No matter which position she chose, she would begin to ache after a certain amount of time, and the amount of time she could spend in each of the three positions seemed to be getting shorter.

The soreness in Abbie's wrist had also been intensified by her spending most of the morning trying to squeeze her hand through the cuff with no success. Her shoulders and arms had also taken a beating because, when she gave up on trying to slip her hand through the cuff, she gave breaking the handrail off a try, but it was no use. It was solid. Her only conciliation was at least there was a toilet.

They had offered her no food or water, but she routinely fasted and was used to going without, especially in a circumstance where she was remaining inactive. However, she was stressed, and she knew that stress alone could burn significant calories. More worrisome than that, she felt dehydration coming on, and this was no good because if given the chance, she fully intended to fight. This time, she would not be drugged, and they would not be sneaking up on her from behind.

Abbie had considered drinking the water from the toilet bowl but had been putting it off just in case they decided to give her some. However, she was beginning to think that they were denying her on purpose, to keep her weak so that she wouldn't fight so much.

About to give in and drink the "bowl water," she flushed the toilet and waited for the tank on the back to fill up. She wanted to flush a few times before she drank. *The water in the tank is clean!* She thought as she stood there listening to the tank fill.

Relieved, she yanked the lid off and drank the clean water from the tank, but not too much. If given the chance, she wanted to be able to move quickly, and too much water would slow her down. *Why hadn't I thought of that sooner,* she thought, as she quietly replaced the lid and sat back down on the floor.

Meanwhile, up the bank from the Rio Grande, under the mott of Mesquite trees, Harry lay drifting in and out of sleep, sometimes hearing voices and wondering if they were real or if he was dreaming.

His body felt like lead. The alarm clock on his wife's nightstand began beeping to a hellish disconcert. *She must've gotten up early and gone for a run without turning it off,* Harry thought. He rolled over and groaned in his sleep. She was always doing that.

"Awe, Jesus!" He said, cursing as the alarm as it finally roused him from his sleep. Then, as he awoke, he realized where he was and sat up, still somewhat confused. "What the fuck is that beeping," he said. As he sat there, his mental faculties slowly started coming back to him, and he realized that the beeping was his POV camera's low-battery alarm.

The battery had picked a good time to start going dead. Harry had passed out at some point that afternoon, out cold. Fortunately, the low-battery alarm had woken him up in time to get moving before he lost too much light.

After replacing the camera's battery, Harry put on his rucksack and POV Camera before walking back down to the river. There were several shoe and boot prints in the sand on the trail that led down to the river bank. Apparently, others had crossed the river, passing right by him as he slept under the mesquite trees. Either they did not see him or chose to ignore him.

At the river bank, the camera drone flew over Harry as he knelt on both knees to fill the empty canteen from the river. He looked back up the bank, and in the distance, he could see the cameramen. One held their horses while one flew the drone, and the other operated a still camera mounted on a tripod.

Harry placed the canteen in his rucksack. Next, he saturated his Boonie-hat, t-shirt, and ACU jacket before putting them on. He then put on his rucksack and repositioned the camera over his Boonie-hat before crossing the river.

Keeping his POV camera and spare batteries dry had not been a problem. Harry could see why they chose to cross the river here. This section of the river ran over a large rock bed that, when the river was low, could be easily crossed.

Harry walked through calf-deep water for about 15 feet from the river bank to a patch of dry rock bed in the middle of the river. The bank and river bottom there had been mostly comprised of little flat stones that looked to Harry to be some type of flagstone.

The little flat stones provided good footing and made the crossing to the dry rock bed in the center of the river easier. From there, he walked a little less than the distance of a football field across the dry rock bed. Occasionally, he came to areas where he would have to walk through water. However, it was never more than ankle-deep until he had to cross from the edge of the rock bed to the river bank on the Mexican side of the border.

From the edge of the rock bed to the river bank on the Mexican side was less than thirty feet away. In the middle, the deepest part of the river had only been up to Harry's lower thigh, and his rucksack had remained well above the waterline.

The water there had been fast-moving, and Harry slipped once or twice on some of the larger stones that were slick with algae, but for the most part, the small, flat pieces of flagstones that littered the trail and the river bottom once again provided decent footing.

On the other side of the river, Harry made his way up the bank, keeping his new reference point in sight. He continued to walk for about another 300 yards at a slight uphill grade through the sand rocks and calf-high creosote until he came to the edge of a dry creek bed.

This must be the one, He thought as he scanned the banks of the dry creek. The creek appeared to be fed by three ravines during the wet season. The ravines were about half a mile apart, one close to where the creek joined with the Rio Grande, a second one halfway upstream, and the largest at the head of the creek in the west.

The ravine at the head of the creek in the west was bordered by spurs coming down from the mountains on each side. The spur bordering the west side of the ravine ran down into the foothills, creating a natural dam. The spur bordering the east side terminated as a fifteen-foot cliff face that bordered about two hundred yards of the creek's west bank.

Harry decided to walk west to the head of the creek first and work his way down to the river as he searched for the checkpoint. However, he stumbled upon the cairn after only walking about halfway. Again there was only one canteen. Written on the side in black marker was "195 degrees, follow ravine to the mountain pass. 3rd checkpoint at a curve in dirt road on the other side."

Harry drank some of the water from the canteen, only this time more slowly. Although his shaking fits seemed to be getting much worse, his dehydration cramps were slightly better, and he thought it best to continue to hydrate as much as his nauseated stomach would allow.

After a few sips from the canteen, Harry set up his compass so that in between his shaking fits, he could try to shoot the new azimuth. On his third attempt, he was finally able to stop shaking long enough to successfully identify the larger ravine in the west as the correct reference point.

Harry walked up the bank and stood across the dry creek bed from the mouth of the large ravine. He followed the ravine up the mountain with his eyes, picking out as much of a trail as he could, but it was mostly obscured by rock formations at the higher elevations. He looked from the rock formations to the saddle between the two mountains, stared at it momentarily, and then crossed the dry creek bed to the mouth of the ravine.

While winding his way up the ravine trail, He spotted a lizard sunning himself on a flat rock. He stood high on his front limbs, holding his body upright almost at a 45-degree angle with his back legs spread apart and bent at the knees, allowing only the bottoms of his hands and feet and the middle portion of the underside of his tail to come into contact with the extreme heat of the sunbaked rock. The lizard bobbed up and down on his forearms as Harry looked him over, somewhat astonished by his beautiful coloration.

At his waist, the lizard wore a sash of two prominent black bands bordered in yellow. His head, forearms, rear legs from the knees down, and his tail were a bright blue. From the yellow and black sash at his waist up to his neck and as far as his elbows, he was bright red in color. From the sash to the base of his tail and down to his knees, he was lime green in color, giving him the overall appearance of a blue lizard wearing a red shirt and green pants with a black and yellow sash.

Maybe I should try to catch it for food, Harry thought briefly, but the idea of eating it made him nauseous, and his stomach began to convulse. *It's hard enough just to keep the water down right now, plus he's too pretty to eat anyhow,* Harry thought. Then, in a flash, the lizard scampered away into a pile of rocks, and Harry realized that in his weakened condition, he would not have been able to catch him anyway.

After having to take several breaks, he finally made it to the top of the mountain pass, in the saddle between the two mountains. The last part of the trail took him along a ledge. As he stood on the ledge, he looked down and could see the dirt road running east to west just south of the mountains' foothills.

He could also make out another mountain range far away in the distance. Between the faraway mountain range and the dirt road was nothing but miles of high desert in every direction. He could easily follow the trail down the mountain with his eyes to where it terminated at a distinctive curve in the dirt road and knew he would find the third checkpoint close by.

As he traveled down the trail, a little more than halfway down, a huge rock overhang caught his eye. *I don't need shelter right now, but it might come in handy on the way back,* he thought.

Its entrance had been blocked by falling scree and loose rocks from above that would have to be cleared, but that would not take him long. He made a mental note of its location as he continued down the mountain to the dirt road.

He didn't have to hide from traffic on the dirt road. There had been none. He had spotted the third cairn easily as he came down the mountain trail. There had been nothing to obstruct his view, and he had walked almost straight to it. Buried three feet to the west of the cairn was a full canteen with instructions that read, "243 degrees, Two-lane blacktop CHIH-76."

Harry shot the azimuth per the new coordinates. The mountain range was too far away to see any distinctive features. Nonetheless, he was able to select a large hill in the distance as his reference point.

The hill had a distinctive rock outcrop that pinnacled straight up from its top in a column, making it very discernable from the other hills around it. With his new reference point established, he proceeded to cross the dirt road into the rolling desert in search of the two-lane, black-top Chihuahua Interstate Highway 76.

Nightfall found Harry another half a canteen of water lighter and not yet at his hilltop reference point. It had grown too dark to see. He considered moving forward using the compass to orientate himself in the dark, but his body ached, and he felt exhausted. He also worried about getting off course and walking past his reference point in the dark. Instead, he opted to wait for daybreak, but having found no shelter, he was forced to lay out in the open under the stars.

In the distance, he heard a horse neigh and knew it was the cameramen. He wished he could take comfort in having someone close by, but he knew they would be of no help. They would run the cameras and never interfere, no matter what horrible thing was happening to him. *They're like fuck'in National Geographic,* Harry thought as he lay there in the sand.

Chapter Fourteen

Time to Make the Doughnuts

Two in the morning came too damn early, as far as Tinker was concerned, yet there it was. "Time to make to make the doughnuts," he said as he shook Hank a little more roughly than he had the first time.

"Come on, buddy, we gotta get moving. We've got a big day," He said as he further urged Hank to wake up. They had stayed up a little later than usual the evening before, intending to get as many of Abbie's missing posters up around town as possible, saving a few to take to Sal's to put out on the counter.

Tinker finally heard Hank begin to move around. He knew it was him because the first thing he did upon rolling out of bed was to trip over a pile of books that he had stacked on the floor, then stumble into his dresser, knocking over an array of objects he had piled on the top.

Tinker laughed when he heard the crash. "He doesn't throw away anything," he said under his breath. Then he heard Hank begin to stumble around. *He won't be worth a damn until I get him to Sal's and get some coffee dumped down his neck,* he thought.

They hardly ever had coffee at home for three reasons: one, they were always running late. That would be Hank's fault. Two, they had to make it once they were at work anyway, and three, which was the biggest. At work, it was free.

Tinker located the keys, went to the driveway, and started the Impala so that he could warm it up while he waited on Hank. So far, Tinker was the only other person Hank had ever allowed to drive the Impala, except for his mother. This was because he knew that any harm that came to it while Tinker was driving he would repair, the same as he did for Hank as far as that was concerned.

Still not completely awake, Hank opened the Impala's passenger side door and fell into the seat. The door closed with a heavy, satisfying thunk. Hank smiled. He loved that sound. You just didn't get that with the newer lightweight cars. It was like a pleasant memory from the past. Tinker placed the car in reverse and backed out of the driveway.

In the desert, Harry was off to an early start as well. Laying under the stars that night, there had been little rest and no sleep. His muscles cramped painfully through the night, and his shaking fits had been so bad that he sometimes had to shove his shirt in his mouth to keep from chipping a tooth as he shook. When he didn't have the shakes, he would break out in cold sweats. Then, feeling chilled to the bone, he would shiver violently.

He had spent that whole night in misery. Consequently, he was up early in the quiet, still darkness before the morning light. Rucked up and camera on, he watched the horizon take shape from the darkness in the early morning's first light.

Once there was enough light for Harry to begin to see his hill with the rock outcrop, he verified it with the compass. With his reference point established, he wasted no time starting out for it. Not only was he already up anyway, but his water supply was also dwindling. Hence, he needed to get to the next checkpoint. Furthermore, he wanted to be sure to have enough time to find shelter from the midday sun later on.

Off to his right, Harry heard the familiar buzz of the cartel's camera drone once again. True to their word, the camera drone had buzzed him at regular intervals, and he had also caught glimpses of men on horseback following him at a distance. The drone buzzed around him a few more times in the early morning darkness, then gained altitude and began to track him from above.

Back in the casino, the live feed from the drone showed Harry bright as day as he made his way through the desert under Rooster-One's night vision-equipped camera. However, most of the gamblers were either asleep, had lost interest, or had gone back to indulging in their more favored diversions, only checking in occasionally to see what checkpoint Harry was at.

Nevertheless, a few of the gamblers had stayed rather captivated by Harry's plight, the most captivated being Miss Joy Ride. Joy had watched Harry's live feed nonstop through the night and was still unable to take her eyes off the screen as Harry slowly trudged through the desert sand.

As Harry trudged through the desert sand, Officer Jake Stallard was reluctantly making his way down Bakner Steet in Corpus Christi. Although he was sick of working a rotating shift, he was happy enough to be back on the day shift. Although it would take a couple of days for him to adjust, once he did, he would begin to feel normal, at least for a little while. Then, it would be time to rotate to the third shift, which he could never seem to get used to.

It was easier when he was younger, but now that he was in his mid-thirties, it was starting to get a little bit tougher. Ideally, he should have been promoted by now to a position where he would be on straight days or, at the very least, have a set schedule with his pick of off days. However, Officer Stallard had suffered a few setbacks in his career.

For starters, he had learned that most supervisors don't like it when you kick the shit out of another cop. *Even if they are low-life dirtbags, he thought.* If there was one thing he didn't like, it was a crooked cop.

Officer Stallard also seemed to have a bad habit of wrecking patrol cars, which supervisors also seemed to frown upon, even if it was done in the process of catching the bad guys. Furthermore, they also frowned upon a police officer beating a detainee senseless, even if said detainee is a known rapist that keeps getting out of jail only because of his political connections.

That last one had cost him. *That low-life had connections way up the ladder,* Jake thought. He had almost gotten fired for that one. Fortunately, he was a good cop, and for that reason alone, he had enough people looking out for him to pull the necessary strings, and he had been able to hold onto his job. However, now he was on thin ice with no hope for future promotions.

He tried not to think about all that right now. It would be for the best if he concentrated on the positives. He was on the day shift for now and was scheduled for two weeks' vacation at the end of his rotation. Plus, he was making his way to Sal's, where he thoroughly intended to get a Super large coffee, a couple of Boston creams, and a newspaper. Then, he was going to park somewhere off the grid and pretend to monitor traffic. *Not a bad day,* The officer thought.

He pulled into the doughnut shop parking lot and parked right in front. He liked to be able to have the patrol unit within eyesight. He didn't think it would be a good idea to lose another one.

He had to laugh at himself as he walked to the door. You couldn't get any more cliche than a cop in a doughnut shop, but he didn't give a damn. Sal had the best coffee in town. He opened the door and walked toward the counter.

"Good morning, Officer Jake!" Hank said, greeting Officer Stallard upon sight. After the officer had gotten to know Hank a little better, he had told him that it was okay to call him by his first name, but Hank never dropped the officer part. Now, he always referred to him as Officer Jake.

"Good morning, Mister Hank, but I thought I told you that just plain Jake would be fine," he said. He had responded using mister in front of Hank's name to drive the point home. "Yes sir, Officer Jake," Hank responded with a smart-ass grin on his face. Jake smiled back, shook his head, and sighed dramatically.

"The usual, right?" Hank asked. "Yes, sir, and some quarters for the newspaper machine," Jake said. "Newspaper machine, they still make those?" Hank shot back and laughed. "Hey, buddy, if I wanted this kind of abuse, I could have stayed at the precinct!" Jake said. "Alright, Alright, I'll stop," Hank said in a relinquishing tone while putting his hands up in a gesture of surrender.

"Bout time, Kid," Jake said and flipped a twenty on the counter. As he did so, his eyes fell on the stack of missing posters. He picked one up, "What's this all about?" he asked. "Well, Jake, I was hoping to talk to you about that, but it's sort of a long story," Hank said. "No worries, I've got plenty of time," Jake said. "Okay, let me grab Tinker from the back so that he can watch the counter. He's still going over the security video but hasn't found anything yet," Hank said. "Security video, found anything? What the hell is going on around here?" Jake asked. "That's part of it. Let me get Tinker up here, then I can explain."

Hank brought Jake's order to the booth where he had sat and handed it to him. He then took a seat across the booth from Jake and gave him the whole story. Starting with finding Abbie's wallet in the trashcan and ending with Jake's arrival at Sal's that morning.

Jake had begun to stare down into his coffee cup, deep in thought, as Hank had finished his story. After a few seconds, he picked up Abigail's missing poster, stared at it for a while, folded it up, and stuck it into the breast pocket of his uniform shirt. Then he looked at Hank over his cup as he took a sip of coffee.

"Listen…Usually, I'd tell someone not to be poking around and let the police handle the situation, but I know you, and I know you won't listen. However, you should know that there are all kinds of reasons people go missing. It's even possible she doesn't want to be found. It's also possible that there could be some bad people behind this.

"Either way, you and Tinker should be extremely careful. If you see or hear anything, you will call me immediately before you move a muscle. Got it?" Jake asked as he slid his card across the table. Hank nodded his head affirmatively as he picked it up and looked at Jake's contact information.

Seeing this, Jake continued. "Okay, good. In the meantime, I'll make some calls, find out whose desk this landed on, and see if any progress has been made. I'll also do some poking around to see if I can come up with anything on my own. If I find anything out, I'll let you know," he said. Finishing his statement, he slid from the booth and stood. Seeing this, Hank followed suit. The two shook hands, and Officer Stallard left with a new mission for the day.

Chapter Fifteen

A Mourning Run

Harry was moving a little slow this morning, but he smiled as he watched his wife run ahead of him in her tight little yoga pants. He loved those yoga pants. She was just ahead of him in the distance and making good time this morning. She turned back, giving him that smile that always made his heart race a bit, and waved for him to catch up. He knew he could catch her if he really wanted to, but for some reason, this morning, he felt a little tired.

In fact, he was feeling completely exhausted. His legs were heavy, and he felt cold. His body began to shake violently as he stared at his wife in the distance. She was beginning to leave him behind.

"No, Lucy, No… Don't leave me!" Harry said, pleading as he gasped for air, trudging forward through the sand. Tears streamed from his eyes as he pumped his legs harder, trying to keep up. "Don't leave me," He said, gasping before passing out and falling headlong into the sand.

On the floor next to the toilet, Abbie's head began to clear as she woke up. The more her head cleared, the more she realized where she was and that she must have passed out again. She had been sitting on the floor with her arm resting on her knee. She had figured out that she could do that to help keep the handcuff from digging into her wrist.

She was thirsty again. She listened carefully, making sure she didn't hear anyone in the hall. She didn't want to get caught taking a drink for fear they might move her someplace where she wouldn't be able to get access to water.

After listening intently for a minute or so and not hearing anything, she quietly removed the lid from the back of the tank, set it down, and began to drink. While she was drinking, she noticed a long, thin chain that went from the flush lever to the flapper at the bottom of the tank. It was connected to the lever with a little thin, flat metal snap hook.

Abbie's heart began to pound with excitement! She began trying to disconnect it, but it was extremely difficult. She could only reach the hook with one hand, and her fingers began to ache as she struggled to manipulate the stiff, flat, slippery metal hook.

She continued to work at the hook until she heard voices. At the sound of the voices, she immediately gave up on the hook, quietly put the tank's lid back in place, and sat on the floor just as the lavatory door opened.

Abbie sat on the floor as still as possible as someone walked in. She could just see their shoes and pants legs from under the stall's partition. Holding the door open, the shoes stepped in and kicked the garbage can from the corner to in between the door and doorjamb. There, the shoes left the garbage can, holding the door open.

The shoes belonged to Johnny Merle. Johnny turned, walked back to the office down the hall from the lavatories, and stepped in where his partner Stan was sitting in an old office chair. His feet were propped up on a desk that was covered in a thick layer of dust. Johnny and Stan had been the first ones to use the abandoned desk and chairs since the furniture store had gone out of business.

Stan shifted in the chair, faced Johnny, and asked, "Everything under control?" "For now," Johnny answered. "I'm going to go get us some more coffee. I checked on the girl earlier. She was quiet, but I could have sworn I heard her moving around again in there. I propped her door open with the trash can so you can keep an ear out while I'm gone," he said. "Mmmmm. Good deal. I'll keep my ears open," Stan said.

At that same time, less than a mile south of where Abbie was being held captive, Tinker was going through the doughnut shop' fast-motion security video. He had watched it all morning until his eyes had begun to blur. Nevertheless, he persevered, and by eight that morning, he had found two SUVs with occupants that fit the loose description given to them by Abbie's roommate.

He had even managed to get a license plate number from one of them. It had been captured by one of the doughnut shop's better cameras as the SUV went through the doughnut shop's drive-through.

At that point, he and Hank decided to give the security video over to the police. They called them and were told that the detective working Abbie's case would be stopping by shortly. Feeling that It was now out of their hands, Tinker began to relax and settle into his work.

At thirty minutes after eight, a white sports utility vehicle pulled in and parked. Hank and Tinker had looked up from their work to see the driver just as he was grabbing the handle to the entrance door. Hank walked behind the register and stood facing the door. Tinker had no time to react. He had been sweeping when the guy came in, so he continued to do so as inconspicuously as possible, stopping only occasionally to nonchalantly wipe down a tabletop while trying not to draw any attention to himself.

The driver and sole occupant of the white sports utility vehicle, one Johnny Merle, walked straight up to the counter. "What can I get for you, sir," Hank asked. "I would like two large black coffees and a dozen assorted," Johnny said.

Breakfast for two, Hank thought. He could see Tinker over the customer's shoulder, trying to stealthily send a text message. Johnny's eyes fell on Abigail Adam's missing posters next to the register, and Hank could see that the man was visibly shaken.

The driver shuffled his feet and began to turn towards the door where Tinker was still trying to send what Hank was sure was a text to Jake. "Sure you don't want an extra or a Super large? The Super is only sixty-five cents more," He asked, hoping to distract the driver of the white SUV while Tinker completed the text. "Yeah, sure, that's fine," Johnny answered, turning back to face Hank. *That was close,* Hank thought.

He tried twice more to stall for time, trying to entice Johnny into some semblance of a conversation, and both times was hit with the same deadpan expression. When Hank asked for his doughnut preference, Johnny answered him in a frustrated tone, "I'm kind of in a hurry. Just grab a couple each and throw them in. It doesn't matter which. That's why I said assorted!" Hank could tell he was starting to get testy. He boxed the doughnuts without any more questions. Then Johnny paid in cash and left.

Jake received Tinker's text message on the other side of town and drove like hell to get there. He made a few circles around Sal's Doughnut Shop but had been too late. The white SUV had been long gone by the time Jake had arrived.

Hank had also grabbed his keys and tried to follow as well. However, by the time he got to the Impala parked in the back alley, the white SUV was already out of sight. He had tried a few streets with no results before he gave up and drove back to Sal's, where Jake and Tinker waited outside in the parking lot.

"Guess they got away," Hank said as he stepped out from the Impala's driver's side door and closed it behind him. "Sorry, fellas, I was on the other side of town," Jake said apologetically. "No worries, Jake, you got here as fast as you could," Tinker said, chiming in, but that had been little consolation to Jake. He remained outside while he called the license plate number of the white SUV into the detective in charge of the case and then went into Sal's for some coffee.

"So, did you give them the plate number?" Tinker asked Jake as the door closed behind him. "I did," Jake answered. He then ordered a coffee from Hank and continued, "They said they would look into it, but those guys are way understaffed, so I think it's best if I keep poking around a little," he said.

Hank set Jake's coffee in front of him, "I think that was one of them for sure," he said, "He ordered coffee for two, and Liz said she saw two guys. Also, when he noticed the missing posters, I saw him turn white as a sheet and start looking around. I would start by looking around here close to Sal's. If they are coming here for their morning coffee, they can't be too far away." Jake nodded in agreement.

Hank was more right than he knew. Less than a mile away, Johnny was standing in the warehouse, where he and Stan were holding the girl hostage. He stood watching the warehouse door slowly close to the ground, shutting off the outside world. Jake and Hank each had narrowly missed running into Johnny on his way back to the warehouse that once had served as a furniture store.

Johnny had decided to fuel up and grab a couple of lotto tickets before returning to the stresses of the warehouse. "God," he prayed, "Please let me win." If he did win, he would walk away from all this.

He didn't mind working at the bar, but his boss, Luke, liked to supplement his income by covering illegal wagers. He primarily dealt with his regular customers, and everything usually stayed friendly, but things could get ugly occasionally.

Luke covered bets on all sports wagers, including college and high school sports. He also covered bets on illegal street racing, wet t-shirt contests, underground fights, and derbies.

He sometimes covered underground fights and derbies that were held on the same day. They would fight the roosters first, and then the men would fight after in the same sand pit as the roosters had. Anything you could think of to bet on, Luke would cover it.

The gamblers that Luke dealt with usually paid up very promptly. Even though most of them were customers at the bar and were familiar with Luke's friendly side, they also knew that Luke Harrison was only a friendly man until he was not.

They knew that he had enforcers and that there would be retribution for unpaid debt. Johnny and Stan had been called upon a few times when Luke's patience had finally worn thin, and bad news had a way of traveling fast in Corpus Christi.

The warehouse door finally made its slow descent all the way down to its threshold. When it closed, Johnny slid the bolt in place and locked it. He then went to the passenger side of the SUV, opened the door, and retrieved the coffee and doughnuts from the passenger seat. Coffee in one hand, doughnuts in the other, he struggled to close the SUV's door with his foot.

Just as he succeeded in closing the SUV's door and was about to walk away, his phone rang. "Oh fuck'n great!" He grumbled under his breath. "How do they always know when your hands are full," He said as he walked to the front of the SUV, set the doughnuts down on the hood, and fished his phone from his pocket. It was his boss, Luke.

Abbie had been sitting quietly while the lavatory door was propped open. She had wanted to work on freeing the hook but was afraid that with the door propped open, the thug left on guard would hear her moving. After some time had passed, she reasoned that she would just have to be extremely quiet. She was about to get up and try for the hook when Johnny came busting through the door at the end of the hallway.

She could smell the exhaust fumes that wafted in with him as he entered the hallway and deduced that there was a garage entrance of some kind. She listened quietly as he walked hurriedly past the lavatory door, saying something to his cohort.

Johnny walked into the office and set the coffee and doughnuts down on the desk in front of Stan. "Luke just called," he said. Stan put his finger to his mouth, "Shhhh! Watch it with the names. You still got the door propped open. She may be able to hear!" he said.

Johnny felt stupid. He had walked right past the lavatory door and had seen that it was still open. In his hurry to relay Luke's message, he had not thought anything about it. He walked back down the hall, kicked the garbage can back into the corner, and the door closed slowly on its overhead hydraulic arm.

When the lavatory door closed, Abbie stood up, removed the tank's lid, set it down as quietly as possible, and, once again, began trying to retrieve the hook. This time, she was more successful than with her last attempt, and she managed to retrieve the hook within only a couple of minutes of trying.

She stuffed the hook into her sock, drank some water from the tank, replaced the lid, and sat back down on the floor. Once seated back on the floor, Abbie removed the hook from her sock and inspected it. It was a thin and flat piece of metal. *It just might work,* she thought as she began trying to bend it into shape.

In the office, Johnny was relaying what Luke had said to Stan. "It's like this. Luke sent the pictures we took of the girl handcuffed to her old man in a text, and there was no response. So, he sent a second text, saying that if he didn't bring the money to the bar by close of business Friday, he would never see his daughter again."

"Yeah, so what happened?" Stan asked. "There was no response to this text either. So, Luke tried to call him, but it wouldn't go through, and he's been calling him repeatedly for over twenty-four hours now, still with no answer."

"It's like he's got his phone turned off, or something, and the boss has no idea if he's turned it on long enough to receive the text or not. Plus, the guy has disappeared. He's like a ghost. Luke can't find him at the RV park or anywhere else.

"Anyway, the boss is starting to get pissed. He figures the girl isn't any good to us anymore, and he wants to ditch her before she becomes a liability. Said he'll meet us here at noon to fill us in on the new plan," Johnny said and then sighed loudly as he sat down. *I hope it's a good one,* he thought as he pushed the plastic tab on his coffee cup's lid open.

Chapter Sixteen

The Windmill

Harry awoke confused in the middle of the high desert with the late morning sun beating down on him. He could hear the buzz of one of Alejandro's camera drones circling overhead and the annoying beep of the low-battery alarm. He pushed himself up to his knees, his Boonie hat hung by his side, still caught in the headband of his POV camera. He took off his ruck and let the whole mess slide to the ground in front of him.

He then took out his canteen and drank the last of his clean water. It had gone down fast. He knew he should be rationing but had not been able to stop himself. *Worse comes to worse, I'll drink the river water.* He thought as he pulled Alejandro's electronic contraption from the rucksack and began to perform the battery swap.

He surveyed his surroundings as he finished securing the battery compartment door. He could still see the far-off mountain range in the west but had lost sight of the dirt road and his hilltop reference point. *I must have zoned out, strayed off course, and passed out,* He thought.

As he stood there pondering what had happened, his thoughts were interrupted by a different yet equally annoying beeping sound. This time, it was his earpiece. He had no sooner secured the battery compartment door when it started beeping.

He reached into the tangled mess, retrieved the earpiece, hooked it over his ear, inserted the speaker, and pressed the answer button. It was Alejandro. "Fix the fucking camera already, Harold," He yelled through the earpiece before disconnecting. Harry groaned, staggered to his feet, and sorted his POV camera out.

In an attempt to locate his reference point, he opened his compass and turned his body until he faced 243 degrees. However, as he had suspected, because he had wandered off course, the hilltop was no longer in line with the azimuth. There were hilltops in the distance scattered sparsely from north to south, but if any of them were his reference point, he could not tell.

The only way out Harry could see was to head back east until he ran into the dirt road, find the third checkpoint, reshoot the azimuth, and start over again. The only problem was that he only had the canteen of river water left, and this time when he got to the third checkpoint, there would be no replenishments.

He didn't want to drink the river at all, but even if he did manage to drink it without getting sick, there was still no way he could cover that much distance with that little water.

In a state of panic, Harry made a last attempt to locate his lost reference point. Slowly, he began to turn in a circle, examining each of the hilltops in the distance one by one, desperately searching for the one with the rock outcrop.

As he gravely scanned the horizon from hilltop to hilltop, he identified something unusual in the distance. As his mind snapped to what it was, Harry's sunburnt, wind-chapped lips cracked as they parted into a painful smile. There, in the distance, was a windmill.

There had been windmills on the cattle ranches all around Alice, Texas, where he grew up, and he knew they ranged in size. This made it difficult for him to estimate how far away the windmill was. However, what he did know was that at the bottom of that windmill, there would more than likely be a huge stock tank full of water for someone's cattle. There, he could quench his thirst and refill his canteens before making the trek back to the dirt road checkpoint to reshoot his azimuth.

The sun was almost directly overhead as Harry approached the windmill. The camera drone was hovering above him, just off his right shoulder. Alejandro had given up on Harry's POV camera for the time being, considering that for the last mile, Harry had staggered from side to side so severely as he walked that some of the gamblers couldn't watch his feed without getting motion-sick.

The gamblers preoccupied at the card tables had started watching when they heard a scream coming from a booth in the corner. It had been Joy Ride screaming at the monitor when Harry had suddenly bolted into the desert like a madman. After that, Esperanza's runners spread the word of Harry's new predicament to the other gamblers regardless of where they were, and they all flocked to the casino and joined Joy and the others as they watched the drone's live feed.

When Harry passed out, they had gambled on whether or not he was dead. When he got up, they gambled on which direction he would go in. When they figured out that he was headed for the windmill, they gambled on whether or not he would make it, how long it would take him if he did, and just how far he would make it if he didn't.

Alejandro noticed that as Harry approached the windmill, he started to walk straight, and his head no longer lolled from side to side. His gaze was now transfixed on the large galvanized stock tank at the bottom of the windmill. From the control room, Alejandro turned the live feed for Harry's point-of-view camera back on. The gamblers now watched from Harry's point of view with anticipation as staggered toward the stock tank.

Harry could think of nothing but the cool fresh water in that tank as shuffled toward it like a zombie. The trek there through the sand and creosote in the hot desert sun had been long and arduous. The intense heat, coupled with the dead calm, had been unbearable. The heat was still unbearable, the sun continued to beat down mercilessly, and there still had not been a single breath of breeze.

Sunburnt, wind-chapped, and parched, Harry dropped to his knees at the side of the galvanized stock tank. Grasping the rounded lip of the tank with both hands, he took a deep breath in preparation to thrust his head into the cool, clear water and stopped short. There, floating in the middle of the tank, was the partially decomposed body of a huge brown rat. The gamblers stared at the monitor in shock and disgust.

Harry looked at the decomposing rat in disbelief as it hung suspended just below the water's surface. The rat's back was arched. Its head and all four feet hung down in the rat's dying pose of complete exhaustion.

He turned away and sat in the sand with his back against the stock tank. The windmill offered very little shade. Nonetheless, he wedged himself between the stock tank and the windmill as best as he could to get in it and then began to consider his situation.

There was a pipe that went from the windmill to the stock tank. It went over the top edge of the stock tank and ran horizontally over the water for almost two feet. When the wind turned the windmill's blades and engaged the water pump, the water would flow through the pipe and into the stock tank. Harry speculated that the rat must have slipped off the pipe when it crawled out to drink the residual water that collected at the open end.

It was in this train of thought, while he was contemplating the workings of the windmill, that he realized that if the wind would just pick up enough to turn the windmill's blades, he could fill his canteens with fresh water directly from the pipe.

He removed his rucksack, took out his three canteens, and unscrewed the lids of the two empty ones in preparation. He wanted to be ready to catch any little trickle of water that even a slight breeze might generate. Then, after positioning his camera on what little shade he could find at the bottom of the windmill, Harry squeezed into it and sat down.

As he sat there, he stared at the canteen of river water next to him. He was beyond thirsty but resolved to try to wait for the afternoon winds to pick up.

Chapter Seventeen

The Boss Arrives

At a quarter till one, Johnny's phone rang. It was Luke, "Yeah, I'm here. Open the warehouse," he said. He was over forty-five minutes late and had just pulled into the back alley. Johnny got up to go to take the padlock off the bolt on the overhead door. Stan, who had just sat down to a meatball sub, didn't bother getting up. He had been going to wait until Luke had left to eat it but had grown hungry and impatient.

Once in the warehouse, Johnny removed the padlock, slid the bolt, and pushed the button that raised the overhead door. After the door's slow ascent, Luke pulled into the warehouse of the former furniture store. He was currently leasing the old building with the hopes of franchising his bar and grill in the very near future.

Luke had noticed the huge *For Lease* sign was still up. He assumed the realtor hadn't had the chance to come by and take it down. He had a million things to do but was currently in the middle of a mess that he wanted out of as quickly as possible. The other stuff would have to wait, but as for the *For Lease* sign, it needed to come down now.

"Johnny, you and Stan go take that *For Lease* sign down, quick! All I need is for that realtor to come by to take it down and start poking around. Y'all go roll it up and bring it back here and put it in the back of my car. I'll go by the realtors and drop it off after we're done discussing how we're gonna clean up this mess," he said. "Yes, sir boss, I'm on it," Johnny answered. He hadn't thought of that, but then again, he was a bartender, not a professional kidnapper.

He walked back to the office and found Stan still at his meatball sub. "Come on, Stan, boss says we gotta go take the sign down from the window out front." Johnny watched as Stan's face got all screwed up. He was not happy about having to leave his already late lunch.

"Why the hell we gotta do that?" he asked. "Boss said he didn't want to chance the realtor coming by to get it and start poke'n around with the girl here. There's an extension ladder in the warehouse. Come on and help me carry it around to the front," Johnny said. Stan set his sub down and sighed begrudgingly. "Alright, alright, let's go," He said as he got up.

Abbie had worked on the hook for what seemed to her like forever, bending it this way and that, trying different angles. She had seen handcuff keys before and had sort of reasoned out how they worked.

126

However, she was no locksmith, so it would be all about trial and error. After many attempts twisting the flat piece of bent metal this way and that, she was about to give up when, to her surprise, the handcuff fell open.

She sprang up, went to the lavatory door, stood behind it, and listened... She didn't hear anything. She opened the door just a crack and peeked out. She didn't see any movement or hear anyone. Slowly, she opened the door a bit more and peered out into the hallway.

To Abbie's immediate right was the men's lavatory, then the hallway terminated at a metal door with a sign that read warehouse. Across from the men's lavatory was what she thought might once have been an employee break room, which was now filled with old shelving, furniture, and other odds and ends. To the left of that was the hallway entrance. Across and down the hall to her left was what appeared to be an open office door.

Abbie still didn't see or hear anyone around, so she cautiously stepped into the hallway and walked toward the metal door at the end with a sign that read warehouse. Slowly, cautiously, she cracked the door open. Peering in through the crack, she saw three men in the midst of a discussion that sounded mildly heated.

Stan and Johnny had grabbed the extension ladder and were headed for the double doors that led from the warehouse to what used to be the showroom floor. Luke shook his head, "Just where do you two think you're going?" he asked. They stopped dead in their tracks.

"You'll have hell getting that ladder around that SUV. It's parked right in the fucking way, and the front doors are locked and broken any damn way. You'd have to shove them open.

"Just carry the damn thing around the outside of the building, for Christ's Sake!" Luke said. He felt like he was about to have a nervous breakdown. "Damn," He said under his breath, "Do I gotta hold their fuck'in hands?"

Abbie let the door close slowly and hoped they had not noticed. Heart racing, she stood and listened at the door for a moment. Luckily, they hadn't. She could hear them still arguing over the ladder. *That was close,* she thought.

She turned on her heel and went down the hall in the opposite direction, away from the warehouse door. She passed the abandoned clutter-filled break room and made a right turn. The right turn led Abbie into an adjacent shorter hall. To her left was a second office that stood empty and dark. The other end of the short hallway led into what looked like an old, empty showroom floor.

She looked across the empty showroom and saw the storefront. She could see that it was mostly glass. It had the typical glass double doors surrounded by the big glass windows that would be found on almost any storefront.

The glass was tinted, and the largest window was mostly covered by a huge sign, making the room dark. She ran to the glass entrance doors in the front of the showroom only to find them locked and chained together. "Fuck," she whispered. She scanned the room, looking for something to either break the glass or the padlock with. Unfortunately, the showroom floor was bare.

She cupped her hands to the dirty, tinted glass of one of the doors and peered out desperately, but there was no one to call to. The parking lot was empty, and even if someone had been closer, they probably wouldn't be able to see her past the sign or through the dirty, tinted glass.

She knew she didn't have much time. Her mind raced as she tried to think of a plan. She decided to go back and try to find something to break the storefront window with, either in the office or the old breakroom. She ran back across the dark showroom floor to the hallway, barely missing Stan and Johnny as they came around to the front of the building, carrying the extension ladder.

As Johnny and Stan set the ladder up outside, Abbie was entering their office. The first thing that caught her attention was the smell of food. She was starving and starting to feel a little weak. On the desk, she spied a partially eaten meatball sub, a large soda, a box of doughnuts, and her skateboard.

She went directly to the sub and took a huge bite. She then washed it down with a couple of gulps from the unattended soda while her eyes scanned the office, looking for something to break the glass with.

The office was empty except for the desk and two chairs. She grabbed one of the chairs and considered it. It was very light, mostly plastic, with very thin metal legs. She was afraid it might not be heavy enough to break the glass.

She worried that if she tried to break the glass and failed, the noise would alert her captors. That would be game over, so she decided to look for something heavier. *A fire extinguisher would be heavy enough for sure, or maybe I could find something in the clutter of that old break room,* she thought.

She took two more huge bites of the sub, set it back down in its place, and helped herself to more of the soda. She then grabbed four of the doughnuts from the box on the desk, wadded them up into a tight little ball, and shoved them into her pocket before stepping into the hall to continue her search for something to break the glass with.

As she stepped into the hall, she caught a movement in her peripheral vision. It was the warehouse door beginning to open. Her heart jumped in her chest as she dove for the Ladies' room door and ran back to her corner next to the toilet. There, she quickly sat down and slipped the cuff over her wrist, making sure to leave it loose enough that she could easily slip it off later.

The lavatory door opened, and there was another pair of shoes below the stall's partition yet again. However, this time, it was a different pair. She knew they belonged to one of the three men she had seen in the warehouse, but she didn't know which.

The shoes continued to pause behind the stall's partition for a few seconds. Her abductors had always been careful to stand on the other side of the partition so that she could not see their faces. *Too late,* she thought as the door opened and the shoes walked back out.

When the shoes left, she breathed a sigh of relief. It had been Luke. He had gone in to use the men's room, and while he was inside, he had decided to look in on her, but Abbie had been right where she was supposed to be.

Chapter Eighteen

The Deal with Charlie

Jake had spent most of his shift driving the area around Sal's, often getting out to look over fences or into areas that he could not see into well from his patrol car. There had been no white SUV anywhere to be found. Either Hank's theory was wrong, or they had it parked inside somewhere out of sight.

His shift was almost over, and as he drove down Ocean Drive on his way back to the police station, his mind drifted to his plans for after work. He intended to keep searching for the white SUV. However, he had a couple of stops to make before he continued the hunt. Earlier that day, when he had been searching for the SUV, he had seen Charlie Benton.

Charlie had once been a dispatcher with the CCPD and had put in almost seventeen years with the department. However, before his anniversary date, he suffered a severe nervous breakdown in the middle of a shift. He finished the call he was on, then stood up and walked out, not saying a word.

Charlie never returned to work again, and despite having money in the bank, he ceased to pay his bills and took to wandering the streets. Eventually, the bank foreclosed on his house and car, but he hadn't been using them anyway. By that point, he had taken to sleeping outside.

Within a few months, Charlie had acquired himself a large cardboard box that he slept in, which also doubled as his desk during the day. He also acquired a shopping buggy in which he kept all his prized possessions. Among his prize possessions, he kept a five-gallon bucket, some clothes, and other odds and ends, but the most prized of his possessions were his desk phones.

At some point, after Charlie had obtained his buggy, he started to collect almost every old broken desk phone he would come across as he rummaged through the trash, searching for aluminum cans or food. These days, if you spotted Charlie, you would more than likely see him seated on his five-gallon bucket behind his cardboard desk. His collection of old junk desk phones spread out before him with a huge smile from ear to ear.

The general opinion in the department had been that he had just taken one call too many. Before the incident, Charlie was a cheerful, well-liked guy, and the entire department was shocked and saddened by his situation. At first, many officers would visit or check up on him. However, over the years, most of them had either given up, moved jobs, or retired someplace else.

Every once in a while, Jake would still pick Charlie up a cheeseburger, and he would order them the same way Charlie used to order them when he worked at the department. Double meat with cheese, no veggies, no mustard, extra mayo, and a rootbeer for the drink.

When Jake had seen Charlie earlier that day, he decided that if Charlie was still in the same location when his shift ended, he would make a burger run for the both of them. Jake also thought that it wouldn't hurt to ask him about the white SUV. Charlie paid close attention to his surroundings because, in the streets, his life depended on it, and he didn't miss a thing. Charlie was crazy, but he wasn't stupid, not by a long shot.

The dispatcher's voice broke out over the patrol unit's police radio in a barrage of static. "Unit 1321, Code 3, 10-64 at 1012 Shoreline Boulevard in the parking lot of the Shoreline Motel," she said.

Jake switched on his lights and sirens for The Code 3 and responded, "Unit 1321 en route, less than a half mile away." "10-4, be advised, we received a call about two individuals holding an elderly woman at knifepoint," the dispatcher said. "10-4, pulling onto the scene now," He said as he pulled into the parking lot and turned off his sirens.

Jake got out of the patrol unit just in time to see two guys helping the lady off of the ground. "They Knocked her down and took her purse! They're going that way!" One of the guys yelled at Jake as he pointed toward the beach. The muggers had taken off running down the beach and now only appeared as tiny specks in the distance.

"Low-life Dirtbags!" Jake said as he jumped back into his patrol unit, hit the sirens, and took off down the beach in pursuit. The patrol car made it every bit of a hundred and fifty yards down the beach, where it promptly buried itself up to the axles. Jake jumped from behind the wheel to give chase, but the muggers were gone.

After he interviewed the victim and filled out the report, he had to wait with his patrol unit until a wrecker could tow it in for repairs. He shook his head as he surveyed the damage. The fenders were bent where they rested in the sand, and steam rose from under the hood. *They're not gonna like this,* he thought. Once he finally made it back to the station and finished filing his report, he took a shower and changed into his civilian clothes. He then got in his personal car and drove to his favorite Dairy Queen on Ayers Street to pick Charlie and himself up a couple of cheeseburgers.

As Jake waited in line for his and Charlie's food, Luke stood impatiently while Johnny and Stan struggled to stuff the large canvas sign into the back of his car, and he was beginning to fume. As soon as Johnny slammed the trunk closed, Luke started for the office at an impatient pace.

Johnny and Stan hurried to keep up as they followed him across the warehouse to the door that led into the hallway. Once at the door to the hallway, Luke shoved it open violently and walked through. The other two men followed behind him as the door slammed into the wall.

Abbie had slipped the loose handcuff off her wrist and was standing behind the lavatory door with it slightly cracked, listening for her captors. She had been thinking about fleeing out the front and was wondering if her captors were still in the warehouse, and if they were, would she be able to make her escape before they returned? Her questions were answered when she heard the warehouse door burst open.

As the three men began to file into the hall. Abbie sprang back to her corner, slipped the handcuff back onto her wrist, and assumed her position on the floor next to the toilet, just in case anyone decided to duck their head in and check on her. No one did. She listened to their footsteps as they passed the lavatory door on their way to the office.

In the office, Luke stood with his arms folded, and Johnny took the chair in front of the desk. Stan sat back down behind the desk, stared briefly at his meatball sub, and then absentmindedly pushed it away. The situation at hand had caused him to have a loss of appetite.

"Alright, this is what y'all are gonna do. This evening after dark, give her another injection, then when she's out, take her south out of town and drop her off out in the county somewhere. Leave her phone with her and make sure it's charged," Luke said.

Upon hearing this, Johnny gave Stan a give it here gesture with his hand. Stan reached into his pocket, pulled out Abbie's phone, and slid it across the desk. Johnny picked the phone up and put it in the pocket of his Cabana shirt. He would charge it in the SUV later.

Luke continued, "I sent him several texts giving him until the close of business Friday to bring the money by the bar, but he has not responded. I've tried to call him several times, and so far, he's a ghost. So, it's looking to me like he's not going to come through, and I don't want to keep this girl any longer than I have to. Take her south out of town just like I said, and make sure she doesn't see your faces," he said.

Abbie remained quiet in the lavatory for several minutes after she heard the footsteps pass. While in the office, Luke continued to lay out his plans for her, but after not hearing anything but silence for a while, she became anxious. After a few minutes, curiosity took hold of her, and she made her way back to the lavatory door.

Slowly, cautiously she cracked open the lavatory door and began eavesdropping in on her kidnappers' conversation just in time to hear an angry Luke scream, "Goddamn that, Harry Adams! Wait til' dark, then take the girl out to the country and do what I said!"

After hearing this, Abbie was now officially scared shitless! Now she had a pretty good idea why she had been targeted. If she had to guess, her father had once again welshed on his gambling debts.

She was pissed, but there was no time to think about that now. She had to get out of there before tonight, or she maybe never would. To the best of her knowledge, these kinds of rides out to the country hardly ever ended well.

Her imagination had begun to drift into different horrible scenarios when she was jerked back into reality by Luke's voice. "Okay, I think that about covers it. I gotta get going. I have to drop that damn sign off at the realtor's office before it closes and then get back to the bar before the evening shift starts. Come on, Johnny, let me out," he said.

She heard the scrape of Johnny's chair as he got up to let Luke out. Fearing that Luke or Johnny, as she now knew them, might check on her on their way out, she retreated to the corner next to the toilet and slipped the handcuff back over her wrist. They did not check on her on their way out. However, Johnny did check on her on his way back in, but she had been right in her corner, right where he had left her.

Abbie knew she had until after dark, but since she really didn't know how close it was to sunset, she needed to get out now. She would have to take a chance before it was too late. She gave Johnny a minute to settle in the office before slipping off the cuff. Then, slowly, she cracked the door open to listen with the intention of sneaking into the warehouse if the hallway was clear.

She was hoping that maybe someone had gotten sloppy with their keys or maybe the warehouse doors had been left open. If not, she would try to sneak back into the breakroom and climb up on top of the old shelving she had seen. She had an idea that from there, she might be able to crawl up into the ceiling and at least hide. Not an ideal situation, but she was scared and getting desperate.

She stood behind the cracked door, listening. Her mind was racing with all these thoughts as she tried to build her courage to move towards the warehouse door when, through the crack of the door, she heard the ring of a cell phone. The ring was followed by the scraping of a chair, the occupant obviously standing to take the call. Abbie let the door close slowly.

In the office, Johnny looked at Stan as his phone rang. "I better take this," he said as he stepped into the hall. It was his sometimes girlfriend Sally, and he hadn't heard from her in a while.

Abbie, not knowing the nature of the call, was even more nervous now. She wondered if the phone call was about her but couldn't hear well with the door closed. Johnny began to pace up and down the hall, as he chattered at Sally excitedly.

Abbie began to catch bits of Johnny's conversation whenever he would pace by her door and speak loudly at the same time. She could tell by the tone of the conversation that it had nothing to do with her. He was making a date. He was making plans for the rest of his evening right after he was going to end hers. That pissed Abbie off, and worse yet, as long as he walked the hallway, she was stuck.

Chapter Nineteen

Dinner with Charlie

Charlie still had his cardboard desk set up on the corner of South Alameda Street and Everhart Road, where Jake had spotted him earlier that day. He parked across the street, grabbed their burgers and drinks from the passenger seat, opened his door, and stepped out. Charlie saw him and called out across the street. "JakeJakeJake! How ya' been, Jake? How ya' been? Long time it's been Jake long time!" he said. He eyed the burger bags as Jake crossed the street towards him and smiled.

"I've been good, Charlie. Here, I brought you a burger, double meat cheese, no veggies, no mustard, extra mayo, and a rootbeer," Jake said. "You always remember how I like them, Jake, you always remember!"

Jake handed Charlie his bag and drink and then sat down on the curb next to him. They both began to unpack the contents of their bags. Jake stuck a straw through the lid of his cup and took a long drink. Charlie spread the empty burger bag out for a plate, dumped his fries out on it, opened up a ketchup packet, and began to unwrap his burger.

Jake watched as Charlie took a huge bite out of the burger and wondered if he had eaten that day. He knew that most days, Charlie would pick up trash and sweep the parking lot in front of Miss Ruby's taco stand. He would also empty the trash cans for her because she was too short to reach the dumpster. She would give him a couple of breakfast tacos and a few dollars in trade. *At least that's something,* Jake thought.

They had fallen silent, mainly concentrating on their food, but after a couple of minutes had passed, Jake broke the silence, "So Charlie, how did your day go?" he asked. "Oh, my day was wonderful Jake, wonderful, wonderful, wonderful, these phones never ring Jake, never, never, never, ever, ever, ever, ring, ring, ring!!!" Charlie said.

"Say, Charlie, that's nice... Charlie, we're looking for a car that's possibly connected to the kidnapping of a young lady, a white sports utility vehicle. Have you seen anything like that around here?" Jake asked.

"Shop Big Eddie's! For the Biggest Furniture Discounts in Town! Soccer Mom! Soccer Mom! Soccer Mom! Big Eddie's has the Biggest Savings in Town on New and Used Luxurious, Top-of-the-Line, Name-Brand Furniture!!! White SUV!!! White SUV!!! For The Biggest Discounts In Furniture, Don't Forget Big Eddie's Discount Furniture Warehouse, on the corner of Golf and South Elwood!!!" Charlie said.

After Charlie finished his rant, he went back to his cheeseburger like nothing ever happened, leaving Jake stupefied. He tried to question Charlie further, but he had gone silent and now was only paying attention to his food.

Jake decided to leave him in peace to eat. He had no idea what Charlie was talking about. Parts of it he did. For instance, apparently, Charlie felt that white SUVs were "soccer mom" vehicles... that wasn't helpful.

He was hoping for information on the white SUV and instead got snippets of an old furniture store ad. *That ad hasn't been on the radio since that store closed down two years ago,* Jake was thinking. Then the thought hit him... *That old furniture store warehouse is empty and only a few blocks from the doughnut shop!*

Jake stood up, setting his burger and drink on Charlie's cardboard desk. He had only managed a couple of bites. "Thanks, Charlie, but I have to go check something out," He said before sprinting to his car and taking off.

As Jake sped towards the vacant furniture store, he began to turn the situation over in his mind. He thought briefly about calling the precinct and then decided against it. He wasn't supposed to be working on this case and didn't want his involvement discovered for a false alarm. He decided he would have a look around first, and then, if need be, he'd call in the calvary.

While Jake was making his way to the abandoned furniture store, Harry sat in the high desert wedged in a corner between the stock tank and one of the windmill's tower legs, trying desperately to stay in the tiny sliver of shade that the tower created. He stared into the distance, and on the horizon, he could see a figure approaching. The figure was running straight for the windmill and straight for Harry.

As the figure ran closer, Harry could see that it was his wife, Lucy. She was wearing her grey Nikes with the pink swoosh along with yoga pants, a sports bra, and her Houston Astros ball cap, with her hair in a ponytail. The last hundred yards to the windmill, she broke into a sprint, pulling up short just in time to stop right in front of Harry.

Harry stared at his wife dumbfounded as she caught her breath by walking back and forth with her arms crossed above her head. After catching her breath, she placed her hands on one of the lower crossbeams of the windmill tower, locked her arms out, and began stretching her calves.

"You're dead," Harry was finally able to stammer out as his wife continued to stretch. "That's right, Hun, for a long time now, and it's time you started acting like it," She said as she switched from stretching one calf to the other.

"But it was my fault, my fault. I should have been there with you," Harry said, choking the words out through sobs as he broke into tears. Lucy changed positions, and while holding the crossbeam with one hand for balance, she began to stretch her right quad.

"We always tried to go together, you know that. Only seldom did one of us go alone, but sometimes you didn't feel up to it, and there were times that I stayed home, too. We never thought anything of it. There was no way you could have known something would happen, and I need you to stop blaming yourself and move on. We have a daughter that needs you ya' know," She said as she switched her stance in order to stretch her left quad.

"I didn't even get to say goodbye," Harry sobbed through his tears. "Oh, I know, Honey, I know, and that's not fair, but you know in your heart that I loved you, and you know in your heart that I knew that you loved me as well, and that's just going to have to be enough.

"It is time for you to move on. Our daughter needs you, and I have to go now," Lucy said as she placed her foot back on the ground. "I Love you, Lucy, I love you... goodbye," Harry sobbed to his wife and watched through his tears as she took off running. Several yards away, she turned, looked back at Harry, and waved, then took off again, disappearing into the horizon.

Meanwhile, back at the warehouse, Stan was in the middle of giving his meatball sub another try when Johnny finished his conversation with Sally and stuck his head in the office door. "I'm going out for a little bit. I'll be back after a while," he said. Stan, engrossed in his food, nodded his head in agreement.

A few minutes later, Stan finally finished off his meatball sub and then started to top it off with a few of that morning's leftover doughnuts to boot. He was feeling mostly content. *All I need now is a smoke,* he thought as he shoved another doughnut in his mouth.

While Stan was thinking about that smoke, Jake was walking to the front entrance of the vacant furniture store from the parking lot at the strip center across the street. If he had arrived a few minutes earlier, he would have seen the white SUV pull out from the side street and onto the main drag.

He peered through the glass and banged on the doors with no answer. The doors were chained and locked, so he decided to look for another way in and began to make his way around the perimeter of the building.

A couple of minutes later, he had made his way back to the front of the building and was once again standing at the front entrance. *Looks empty,* He thought as he peered through the glass of the double doors for the second time.

After walking the perimeter of the building, he discovered that there were no windows except the ones at the front of the store. However, at the back of the store, he did see an overhead door and a side door that opened out into the alley. The overhead door would be difficult to breach, but he was confident he could jimmy the side door open easily.

Abbie had heard the warehouse door at the end of the hallway close when Johnny had left earlier. She had waited a few minutes to make sure he was gone, but she now stood with the lavatory door cracked open, listening. Not hearing anyone around, she started to step into the hallway.

At that moment, Stan feeling a little better after finally finishing his lunch, leaned all the way back in his chair, reaching his arms as far back behind him as they could go. Stretching out his back, he let loose with a loud, groaning yawn, which startled Abbie. Hearing the groan, Abbie froze, holding the lavatory door open with one foot in the hallway.

Once Stan had finished stretching, he leaned forward, his elbows on the desk, forearms crossed. Bored, he surveyed the desktop until his gaze fell on his pack of mentholated cigarettes. *There's that cigarette I've been missing,* he thought as he snatched the pack off the desktop and put it in his breast pocket. "Time for an after-dinner mint," He said as he stood up.

In the hallway, Abbie heard Stan's chair slide on the floor as he stood. *I can't afford to fake being handcuffed. It might be time for that last ride out to the country,* she thought.

Stan grabbed his large to-go drink cup from the corner of the desk and started walking towards the office door. Abbie darted back into the lavatory and switched off the lights. In the dark, she retrieved the lid from the toilet tank and hid next to the lavatory door with the huge piece of gleaming white porcelain poised over her shoulder. She played a lot of softball growing up, and her batting stance was spot on.

As Abbie hid in the lavatory holding the tank's lid, she thought about how she had considered using it to break out the thick glass of the showroom entrance doors. She had decided against it. *It wasn't hard enough for that, but it's hard enough to crack Asshole's head wide open,* she thought.

She held the tank lid up as long as she could, let herself rest, and then held the lid up as long as she could again, all the while trying to listen for big Asshole's footsteps to come down the hall. All she could hear was the sound of her heart trying to beat through her chest. *He's taking too long. Something's not right,* she thought.

Jake, not seeing or hearing anything, had thought the furniture store to be empty. All the same, something in his gut told him to have a look around on the inside anyhow.

He retrieved a tire iron from the trunk of his car and walked past the storefront windows and double doors on his way to the back of the warehouse, barely missing Stan as he walked across the showroom floor approaching the double doors.

Abbie, tired of waiting, set the tank lid on the floor, leaning it against the wall, and slowly cracked open the door. It was dead quiet. She stepped out of the Ladies' Room into the hallway as quietly as possible. She checked the office. It was empty, her skateboard left leaning against the wall next to the door. Next, she checked the warehouse. It was completely empty. Unfortunately, the exit doors were locked.

She began to wonder if they had decided to just leave her. *That would be too good to be true,* she thought. She decided to go back down the hall and double-check every room to make sure she was alone, and then she would check the front entrance to see if it was still locked. If the front entrance was still locked, she would try to find something in the breakroom to smash the glass out with.

As she made her way down the hall as cautiously and quietly as possible, she checked the breakroom, lavatories, and office along the way. She wanted to make sure no one had come back in while she was in the warehouse.

Stan was standing at the showroom entrance, his drink on the floor between his feet, sorting through a ring of keys as Abbie made her way down the hall. Finding the key he needed, he removed the padlock and chain and was now in search of the key that fit the bolt lock of the large double doors, where only seconds ago Jake had walked by and only minutes earlier he had stood peering in before leaving to retrieve the tire tool from his trunk.

He finally found the right key and unlocked the door's bolt lock. Leaving the keys hanging in the lock, he shoved one of the broken double doors open and stepped out. Once outside, he took a seat on the curb in front of the store, lit a cigarette, and began to watch the traffic that was passing by on the street.

By this time, Abbie had made her way down the hall from the office and turned the corner that led to the showroom floor. As she looked across the empty showroom floor, she got some bad news and some good news.

The good news was that the showroom's double door on the left side was better than half open. The bad news was that she had found Asshole. There he was, just outside and to the right of the open door. He was sitting on the curb of the sidewalk, staring at the traffic across the parking lot and blocking her way out.

Without thinking, Abbie darted back into the office, grabbed her skateboard, and stepped back into the hall just in time to hear Jake Jimmy open the side door in the back of the warehouse. He had pried the door apart with the tire tool and put his shoulder into the door, knocking it open.

Upon hearing the door bang open, Abbie assumed the other kidnappers had returned. She had already made up her mind as to what she was going to do, but now there was no time to waste. They were closing in. She caught a glimpse of Jake out of the corner of her eye as she slid around the corner into the short hall that led to the showroom.

Still mistaking him for the other kidnapper, she took off in a desperate sprint across the showroom floor and jumped through the open door. Launching off her right foot, turning her posture slightly to the right, she sailed into the air and through the door as her hands stretched up high over her right shoulder, clutching her skateboard.

Abbie came down on Stan from out of nowhere, and she brought her skateboard down with her, swinging it down and into the back of his head, using every bit of the speed and momentum she had picked up on the way down. Stan's head and upper body whipped forward violently and then snapped back to the pavement. He was flat on his back, lost in a world of darkness.

She never saw the aftermath. Fearing the kidnapper in the hall was right on her heels. She had only taken two sprinting steps after the board made contact with Stan's head.

Her right foot hit the ground as she landed, then her left foot hit the ground. When her right foot came down again, it was on her skateboard. Never losing momentum, she had brought her board under her and skated like a flash across the parking lot, disappearing into traffic.

Quietly and cautiously, Jake had finally made his way to the entrance of the showroom floor at the end of the hall. He had missed Abbie's disappearance into the traffic by no more than fifteen seconds. Looking across the showroom, he was surprised to see one of the front-sliding doors pushed open.

That wasn't like that a few minutes ago, he thought, then he noticed what appeared to be a person lying in the parking lot, just outside the door. "What the hell now?" He said under his breath as he briskly crossed the showroom floor, half expecting to find a drunk or drugged-out vagrant. It was when he got closer to the body that he saw the blood pooling under the man's head.

Johnny's jaw literally dropped as he drove down the main drag and passed in front of the now-defunct furniture store. "What the fuck!" He mouthed as he turned on his blinker and quickly made the turn into the parking lot's side entrance instead of going around through the back alley as he had intended. While pulling up in front of the store, almost as an afterthought, He parked the SUV as strategically as possible, hoping to block as much of the view as possible from any pedestrians or traffic that might be passing by.

Johnny threw his door open as the SUV jerked to a stop and bailed out, and ran up behind Jake as he was in the process of checking Stan for a pulse. "Oh my god, is he okay," Johnny said, playing the part of the concerned bystander.

"This man is in serious trouble! Call 911 immediately!" Jake said over his shoulder as he continued to check Stan over. "I got it," Johnny said and reached in his pocket to retrieve his cell phone, except he came out with a snubnose thirty-eight revolver instead.

Johnny moved in behind Jake as he knelt over Stan and, while pretending to call 911, struck him in the back of the head with the butt of his revolver. Jake fell unconscious over Stan's body. One by one, Johnny quickly dragged them in by the backs of their shirt collars, closing and locking the double doors behind them.

Johnny had seen the man's sidearm as he knelt over Stan in the parking lot and had figured that he was a cop. After he dragged him through the door, he took the side arm and performed a hasty pat down, which produced a backup weapon and a badge. He then ran to the restroom to check on the girl. She was long gone, the empty handcuff still dangled from the handrail.

Johnny then ran back to check on Stan. He was still lying unconscious on the showroom floor. "You're still breathing," He said and then turned his attention to the cop. After a more thorough search, he had relieved the nice officer of all his belongings, dragged him into the ladies' room stall, and locked the handcuff around his wrist. With the police officer secure, Johnny went back to check on Stan.

"You don't look so good, buddy," He said as he stood over him. Stan's bleeding had not stopped, and his breathing was starting to get shallow and jerky. "Okay, it's time to take you for a ride," Johnny said. He unlocked the overhead door and pushed the up button.

While the overhead door started its slow accent, Johnny went to the front of the store, retrieved the SUV, and drove it to the alley. By the time he made it to the back alley, the overhead door was open. He quickly drove the SUV into the warehouse and then went to retrieve Stan.

He struggled to load Stan's huge frame into the SUV and then sped off in the direction of the hospital. About a block away from the hospital, He pulled over, took Stan's cell phone, dialed 911, and gave his location and emergency. He then wiped the phone down before sticking it back in Stan's breast pocket. Then, when no one was looking, he pulled Stan out onto the sidewalk and drove away.

Chapter Twenty

On the Run

Fearing that her escape would be thwarted at the last second, Abbie fled the warehouse in a terror-fueled spree, only slowing down to climb over fences that got in her way. She skated and ran for over two miles before finally calming down.

As she began to calm down, she realized that she had run toward her own neighborhood. She was now probably less than a mile from her apartment. In her fight or flight reaction, she had instinctively run to the safety of familiar surroundings.

She mulled over her situation as she walked. She thought about calling the police, but she had heard Luke curse her father's name, and since her kidnapping had to do with him, that meant that it had to do with unpaid gambling debts. If she didn't want to get her father in trouble, she would have to forgo calling the cops.

When her mother passed away, her father began a steady descent into drinking and gambling. This resulted in his and Abbie's relationship becoming strained and her eventually moving out. Whatever was going on, Abbie needed to talk to her father.

She thought of trying to make it to her father's RV, but with no money for a cab and no cell phone, she would be hard-pressed to cover the twenty-five miles or so to the RV Park in Elroy, where her father lived. She would have to make her way home and borrow her roommate's cell phone to call her father instead.

Abbie skated and walked her way back home, only to find it empty and locked. Scared, exhausted, starved, and dehydrated, she wanted inside so badly that she busted out the living room window and climbed through.

She made her way to the kitchen first and opened the icebox. Inside, there were three bottles of water, a quarter bottle of ketchup, which had a slightly ominous green tint to it, and half a carton of Chinese take-out that Liz's boyfriend Cliff had left there at least four weeks ago. Abbie grabbed a bottle of water and closed the icebox in disgust. *I'll order a pizza after I take a shower,* she thought.

As she turned away from the icebox, her eyes fell on a piece of paper on the kitchen table. It was weighed down by the pepper shaker. She moved the pepper shaker over, lifted the note, and began to read. As she read the message, her heart sank.

The message was from Liz explaining where she had gone and why. In the note, Liz said she had seen Abbie's kidnapers watching their house. *They've been here... They know where I live!* Abbie thought as she finished reading the note.

She felt stupid and scared all at the same time. She knew they had tracked her down to the skatepark but now felt foolish for not realizing that they would know where she lived. *Of course they would,* she thought as she grabbed her skateboard and looked out the window to the street. Satisfied no one was watching the apartment, she slipped out the broken living room window and ran down the stairs four at a time.

This is just perfect. I can't stay at home because they know where I live, and I can't go to the cops because even though my Dad can be a jerk, I still don't want to get him in trouble, she thought as she fled down the stairs.

When she hit the bottom of the stairs, she ran behind her garage apartment and jumped a fence into her neighbor's backyard. She then ran down their driveway and crossed the street into an alley that ran behind an apartment complex.

With only a few hours left until sunset, she decided to find a place to hide for the night. Her nerves were shot, she was not thinking straight, and she was exhausted. Tomorrow, she would find a telephone and call her father.

At the warehouse, Johnny stood watching the slow assent of the overhead door, his impatience with its pace finally getting the better of him. "Goddamn, this slow piece of shit," He said through clenched teeth as he watched the warehouse door slowly make its journey.

Patience gone, he ripped his cell phone from his pocket and initiated a call to Luke. The phone continued to ring as he got into the front seat of the SUV and violently slammed the door. There he sat, growing angrier with every unanswered ring as the overhead door continued to creep up.

"Yeah, can you hear me? Luke said, screaming into his phone. The sounds of the bar filled Johnny's ear. "Yes, I can hear you, Goddamnit! You need to get your ass back to the warehouse right fucking now! We got trouble!" Johnny said, screaming back.

"Jesus! Johnny, What the fuck is going on?" Luke asked. "I don't want to say over the phone, but you gotta get your ass over here right now!" Johnny said. "Okay, listen up, It might not be a bad idea not to say anything over the phone, but if I walk out in the middle of a shift when we're this fucking busy, that's going to look way suspicious. Don't you think?

"Especially if people were to start asking questions later. So let me ask you this. Do you think that there's any way possible that this could wait a few fucking hours until the bar closes? Now, think real hard prick," Luke said.

The phone went silent as Luke awaited his answer. "This is serious, Luke. We have a lot of work to do tonight. When that bar closes, don't fuck around. You get here right away," Johnny said before hanging up.

As soon as Johnny parked the SUV in the warehouse and got off the phone with Luke, he looked in on the cop. "Right where I left you," He said as he let the door close. He then made his way to the office, where he had thrown the cop's effects on the desk. He had been in a rush earlier and had not taken the time to examine them.

Johnny sat down behind the desk and started to sort through the items. There was a set of handcuffs, some keys, a pocket knife, two handguns, and a wallet. Johnny picked the wallet up first.

"Let's see what we got here," He said as he opened the wallet. He had noticed Jake's badge when he had briefly examined the wallet earlier. What he was more interested in now was the identification card that accompanied it.

The identification card read Patrolman, Stallard, Jacob, Badge No. 104. *Patrolman, what's a patrol officer doing snooping around here?* Johnny thought. He had made the assumption that Officer Stallard was a detective due to his not being in uniform.

Johnny turned everything over in his mind. The busted hasp he had found on the backdoor, the empty handcuff that had dangled from the handrail when he first looked for the girl, the cuff that was now occupied by patrolman Stallard.

Did the cop break in and help the girl escape? What the hell had happened to Stan, and where the hell was that girl now? Why hadn't she gone to the police? Johnny shook his head. He had no answers.

The only thing he could do now was to go try to locate the girl. They really didn't need her anymore, but he worried that she might change her mind and go to the cops. If the cops showed up at the warehouse while they had that patrol officer handcuffed in the restroom, it would be bad news.

He knew he had little chance of finding her. She would be long gone by now, but he wanted to get out of the warehouse just in case she did change her mind and decided to involve the police. If they showed up, he didn't want to be around. Besides, it was all he could do while he waited for Luke to close the bar.

After Johnny finished looking in on his unconscious guest, he grabbed the keys to the white SUV. He would go to her apartment first and watch for a while in case she showed up before he had to leave to meet Luke. On his way back, he would go by King's skatepark and look for her there.

At the windmill, Harry had sobbed all afternoon before finally passing out. Now, from deep in his sleep, he could hear a faraway sound. He tried to ignore it, but it was an agitating, repetitive sound. SQUEAK... SQUEAK...SQUEAK, every few seconds, there it was, an intolerable SQUEAK! He felt a gentle breeze blow across his face, and then something, somewhere in his mind, snapped. The squeaking was the windmill's pump laboring in the desert wind!

Using a brace of the windmill tower and the stock tank's edge as purchase, Harry quickly pulled himself to his feet, grabbed an empty canteen, and thrust it under the pipe. The late afternoon wind blew across the high desert, and with every squeak of the pump, fresh, cool water trickled into Harry's canteen.

Harry had remembered early on in his journey how Anthony Fletcher was able to use the gain bottle he had found to collect water. That's why he had made sure to keep the empty canteens, and he was thankful that he had.

The wind continued to blow. Filling one canteen while drinking from the other, Harry soon got his fill of water. He had also topped off all three of his canteens, pouring the canteen of river water out over his head and back while he filled the other two so that he could wash it out and fill it with the freshly pumped water from the windmill as well.

As he continued to drink the cool water, his mind began to clear, and once again, he began to think about his daughter. Desperate to see her again, he began to puzzle over his next move. There was something else he noticed as well. He was starting to feel the light stirrings of hunger.

Meanwhile, back in Corpus Christi, Abbie had skated to the end of the alley behind the apartment complex into the street behind Osler's Hospital. Upon seeing the hospital, she decided to try and hide in one of their waiting rooms for a while. She briefly considered that the kidnappers might check the hospitals for her but decided that it was unlikely that they would do something so risky. *There'll be security guards on duty and a lot of other people around,* she thought.

Once inside the hospital, she was thankful to be out of the Texas heat. She went straight to the Ladies' Room first. There, she took a sink bath and sorted herself out as much as possible. She had not had a shower in three nights, and if it was one thing that would get you noticed and subsequently kicked out of a hospital waiting room, looking like a vagrant would be it. After she had cleaned herself up as much as possible, she took a seat in an out-of-the-way corner and tried not to draw attention to herself.

After she sat there for a while, she began to realize that she was starving, without a penny to her name. The second thing that would get you tossed out of a public place with extreme prejudice was definitely panhandling. So she sat there quietly with her hunger. Then, she remembered the wadded-up doughnuts still in her pocket.

She pulled the wadded-up doughnuts out of her pocket, picked off a couple of pieces of lent, and ate them. Within a couple of minutes of the food hitting her stomach, Abbie began to nod off uncontrollably. She made her way to the hospital chapel, sat down in a pew, and pretended to pray as she drifted off to sleep.

Abbie awoke with a start. An older gentleman had his hand on her shoulder and was gently shaking her. He recoiled his hand when she jerked awake. "I'm very sorry, my child. I did not mean to startle you.

"I tried calling out to you several times, but you must have been in a very deep sleep, and again, my apologies for having to shake you out of your slumber," he said. Abbie started to remember where she was and realized that in her sleep, she had laid on her side and curled up in the pew.

She wiped the sleep from her eyes, and as they began to focus, she realized the gentleman in front of her was a priest. She sat up, filled with embarrassment. "Oh, I'm so sorry, Father," she said meekly. All the priest's years of experience had sharpened his intuition to a razor-like edge. He studied her with his kind eyes and knew without asking that she was not there to visit a patient, and he could also tell by the look in her eyes that she was in trouble.

"Is there anything I could do to help you?" The kindly priest asked. Abbie shook her head no. "Listen," the priest said. "I know I can not help anyone until they are ready to be helped. I serve at St. Thomas. Do you know the church?"

"It's about a mile south of here, on 18th Street, right?" she said. The priest nodded, and again he spoke. "If you need some help or a place to stay, you make your way there and find me. Do you understand?" he said. Again, Abbie nodded her head. "Good," he said.

The priest then motioned for Abbie to get up. "Now, I am very sorry about this, but visiting hours are over, and I'm afraid you'll have to go somewhere else. I recommend the church. We could go there together right now if you like," he said.

Abbie thought about the Thugs following her. *Will they check the surrounding churches for me?* She wondered. *They might,* She thought, and not wanting to put the kindly priest in danger, she declined his offer. "I'm sorry," she told the priest, but I better go.

The priest nodded and tried to hand her some cash. At first, she tried to refuse, but the priest insisted. She took the money, thanked him, tucked her skateboard under her arm, and left. On her way out, she glanced at the huge clock on the waiting room wall. It read four minutes till nine.

From the hospital, she walked to a nearby Sunoco gas station, where she got change for some of the cash Father Clements had given her and tried to call her father on a payphone, but her call went straight to his voice mail. *Probably turned it off to dodge the debt collectors. Not the first time, I'll try again tomorrow,* she thought, as she hung the receiver up back up on the pay phone.

She then thought about calling her roommate, Liz, but realized that she didn't remember her number. She only knew three numbers by heart. Her father's and her grandparents, which she had learned in childhood, and she knew her work number, but they closed at three on Saturdays and would be long gone by now. *Nobody knows anyone's number anymore. Everything's on speed dial,* she thought.

She would have to find someplace else to lay low. She had enough money for bus fare to her father's, but they had quit running at eight and wouldn't start back up again until early morning, and she didn't have enough money for cab fare. Not knowing what to do, she began to wander with no particular destination in mind.

Chapter Twenty-One

House Party

Abbie walked the streets around her neighborhood. She wanted to stay in an area where she was familiar and wouldn't draw attention. She got along well with everyone in her neighborhood. If she ran into anyone on the street, they would wave or say hello, and that would be the end of it. In other neighborhoods, her carrying a skateboard along with her baggy clothes would have the police showing up immediately.

In her neighborhood, she was well-known and liked. Some people in her neighborhood knew her from the few amateur mixed martial arts fights she had done. Others knew her as that girl with the big smile who ran the cash register and waited tables at Sugarpie's Cafe. Either way, nobody would trouble her here. She would be safe as long as she didn't get too close to her apartment or the skatepark where her kidnappers might be lurking.

She had only managed maybe an hour or so of sleep at the hospital. That had helped. However, it was starting to wear thin. As she walked along, trying to think of someplace she might be able to stay the night, she could have sworn she heard a few bars of Louie Louie.

It was so faint and short that she thought she had imagined it. She was dead tired, and her nerves were frazzled, so she chalked it up to a hallucination. *Awesome, now I'm cracking up,* she thought.

She walked another twenty feet or so, and there it was again, a little longer, a little louder. "No, I'm not cracking up. I heard that," She said under her breath. She walked another ten or fifteen feet down the sidewalk, and there was another short burst of Louie Louie.

She was beginning to think that someone was playing with a car stereo, but then the song started in earnest, even louder than before, and this time she clearly heard musical errors. *That's not a recording. That's a live band! What the hell is a live band doing playing in a subdivision at this time of night?* she wondered. With nothing better to do, she let her feet follow the music.

She had listened to the band make a few more false starts as she walked toward the music before they finally got together. *Not bad once they get warmed up.* She thought as she continued to follow the music down the street to the intersection.

At the intersection, she made a left and walked on the sidewalk to the driveway of the large two-story house from where the music was emanating. She had walked past it many times but had never met the owners.

The house was a two-story Spanish-style house with white stucco walls and a red clay tile roof. The house boasted four huge columns in the front that held up a very spacious portico, the top of which was made into a large balcony area. There was also a huge swimming pool with a beautiful mosaic dragonfly inlaid on the bottom.

The pool was surrounded by animal statuary of all kinds, some real and some fantastical, everything from Lions and Unicorns to Dragons of Asian and European mythology. There were also metallic dragonflies worked into the wrought iron of the storm doors and the driveway gates, which now stood open.

Through the gates, at the end of the long drive, Abbie could see inside the open door of the garage beside the house. Inside, the band was playing on. Some people were dancing. Others were swimming or floating around on inflatable lounges in the mosaic dragonfly-inlaid swimming pool, while some took turns plunging in from the diving board. The majority of the remainder seemed to be entertaining themselves by talking, enjoying a nice beverage, or eating some barbecue.

Abbie had walked past this house on Ocean Drive many times. She had always been fond of it and had wanted to see the inside, but right now, she was more interested in the barbeque. *Maybe I can get myself invited to the party, get a plate and see the inside of the house.* She thought as she walked toward the open gate.

There were two guys at the end of the driveway, close by the gate. One was standing next to the gate, and the other was sitting on an Igloo cooler. The one that was standing looked like he could have been two guys all by himself if he wanted to. Three guys, if they were as skinny as his buddy, sitting next to him.

Abbie was too hungry to be timid. She walked up and stood right in front of the two guys at the gate. *Damn, that barbecue smells good,* she thought. She had caught the aroma of real Texas Pit Barbeque on the wind as she stood there in front of the two guys at the gate.

Before she could say hello, the big guy beat her to it, "Howdy, want a beer?" He said, in a thick East Texas accent. "Sure," Abbie said. "Get off the damn cooler, Billy Bob! Lady wants a beer," The big guy said as he grabbed his slightly intoxicated friend by the back of his bib-overalls, lifting him into the air. Abbie snickered. That was the first time she had laughed in days, and it felt good.

The big guy held his friend up with one arm while he fished a beer out of the cooler. He then kicked the lid down with his foot, replaced Billy Bob back in his seated position, opened the beer, and offered it to Abbie. This he did all in one smooth motion.

As he handed Abbie the beer, he said, "I'm Max. This here is Billy Bob. May I ask your name, ma'am?" he said. Abbie blushed. *Did he just call me Ma'am? I like this fella already,* she thought.

"My name's Abbie, and it's very nice to meet you," she answered as she took a sip of her beer. "Well, what brings you here this evening, ma'am?" Max asked. "Well, I heard the music a ways off and didn't have anything better to do, so I just kind of followed it," she said.

"Well, now you have something better to do. Go help yourself to some barbecue. Spare swimsuits are in the pool house. Help yourself if you want to swim. If anyone asks, you're my guest," Max said. "Thank you! I don't know what to say," Abbie said.

"Don't mention it, little lady. I've seen you around the neighborhood plenty. You're good with the kids and people around here like you, and besides us, neighbors got to stick together, right? You just come on in and make yourself at home!" Max said with a big grin.

By this time, the party was on fire. People undulated back and forth from inside the house and balcony area to the portico and pool area. The band had got their timing down and was sounding pretty good, their music overtaking the roar of the party guests' conversations, only being outdone by occasional whoops and screams of excitement from people as they danced around or played in the pool.

The party looked great, but Abbie wasn't exactly in the mood. She was happy to be somewhere she could feel safe for the moment, but she had other plans besides enjoying the party. The first part of her plan was to wrangle herself a big plate of barbecue, which she did. The next thing she did was wait in line for twenty minutes to use the restroom.

While in the restroom, she stared at the shower and wished she had time to use it. However, people were already knocking on the door. As she sat there trying to figure out a way to use the shower, she had a thought.

She remembered Max's offer to use the pool and realized that if she took him up on his hospitality, she would be able to inconspicuously use the pool's shower in front of the pool house. She didn't feel much like swimming, but she desperately needed a shower. Plus, this would have the added benefit of Max seeing her seem to enjoy the party as if everything was normal. She did want to blend in, after all.

Abbie walked into the sparsely furnished pool house. There was a sleeper sofa along the left wall. Along the right wall was a door to a small half bath, a washing machine, and a dryer. In the center of the room stood a poker table with a set of chairs. A small tiki-style bar stood behind the poker table along the center of the back wall.

She located the rack of loaner suits next to the washing machine and dryer. She grabbed a bikini from the rack and looked at it. *That's no good. I've seen tree pollen floating through the air bigger than that,* she thought and quickly hung the suit back up.

She began to slide the hangers from left to right, looking for something more suitable. From left to right, the bikinis got even skimpier from one to the next. She looked through them all till she hit the empty hangers all the way to the right side of the rack. She stared at the empty hangers. *They're probably not empty. The bikinis are probably just too small to see,* she thought.

She grabbed the first too-small bikini she had bypassed and waited until the half-bath was unoccupied. Inside the half-bath, she stripped down, put on the bikini, and stood in front of the full-length mirror on the back of the door. "Oh my, Jesus doesn't like that," she sighed. It didn't cover everything, that was for sure. *Oh well,* She thought and mentally braced herself to go outside. She noticed the washer as she left the half bath. *Don't mind if I do,* she thought, as she put her clothes into the washing machine and grabbed a towel. *Well, Max did say to make myself at home.*

Outside the pool house, she took that much-needed shower. At that point, her plan to blend in and not be noticed went incredibly awry. Eyes fell on her immediately as she showered in front of the pool house. Then, she drew even more attention as she made her way from the pool house to the pool.

By the time Abbie had retrieved her clothes from the dryer, she had made all kinds of new friends. However, fortunately, as the party wore on, she was finally able to sneak away to an upstairs closet. Inside the closet, she wadded up some t-shirts for a pillow and covered herself up with an extremely large coat that she had found hanging. Almost immediately, her exhaustion overtook her, and she fell into a deep sleep.

Chapter Twenty-Two

The Most Important Meal of the Day

The pain in Jake's wrist and arm, along with the throbbing in his head, brought him to consciousness. His wrist hung in the handcuffs from the handrail in the same fashion as Abbie's had. *Fucking low-life dirtbags,* Jake thought as he sat there on the floor. He had come there to be the hero but had only succeeded in getting himself into some kind of trouble.

There was a bag or some type of hood over his head. It was hot, and he wanted to pull it off, but he knew the hood was the only thing standing between him and death. The moment he saw anyone's face, he knew it would be over.

Outside, Luke parked his car in the alley behind the former furniture store and glanced at the time on his cell phone as he dialed Johnny's number. "Yeah," Johnny said, answering his phone. "I'm here. Come let me in the side door," he said. "It's busted. Just push it open," Johnny said. "What the hell? What happened?" Luke asked. "Not sure come in, and I'll tell you what I know."

In the office, Luke sat across the desk from Johnny, staring at Jake's Police Identification and badge. "Jesus Christ," He said with a deep sigh after Johnny had explained the situation. "He saw your face?" he asked. "No, he just told me to dial 911 over his shoulder. He never looked me in the face. He was concentrating on Stan the whole time. After I knocked him out, I bagged his head," Johnny said.

"We got two choices as far as I can see," Luke said, "One, we take a chance and let him go and hope he didn't get a good look at you, or two, we kill him." Johnny sighed loudly as he rubbed his face with his hands. Then dropping his hands to his knees, he drew in a deep breath, "Dammit, Luke, this is too much," He said as he exhaled.

"Yeah, this thing has gone sideways for sure, but since you say he didn't see your face, I'm gonna leave it up to you. If you want to cut him loose, we'll work out a plan. Of course, if we do that I think it would be a good idea if you left town for a while. Don't you?" Luke said. "Definitely," Johnny agreed.

"Personally, I'd kill him. If you decide to do that, I'd suggest you take his car keys there and start walking the parking lots to see if you can locate his car with the panic button. Once you find his car, you can shoot him up with a hot load of heroin. Then just stick him in his car, put the keys in the ignition, and walk away," Luke said.

All the blood drained from Johnny's face. "No, I don't want to kill him. We'll do a version of your plan. I'll inject him like we did the girl. Then I'll drive him to his car in the SUV and load him in when no one is looking," Johnny said. "Maybe, I tell you what, the sun is going to be up in a few hours. You go locate the car before that happens, then come back. We'll decide what to do from there," Luke said.

"What about the girl?" Johnny asked. "Good riddance. She wasn't any good to us anyway. I rather she had not seen Stan's face or had known the location of where she was held, but even if she does go to the cops, she could only identify Stan, and he's not talking to anyone right now. When he does wake up, he knows enough to keep his mouth shut. She didn't see either one of us. All we have to do is get rid of the cop, and we're home free.

"If the cops do show up, we'll deny any involvement. Yes, I lease this building, but that doesn't mean I knew that someone broke in and was using it unbeknownst to me. Catch my drift. Besides, if she were gonna call the cops, I think she would have done it by now," Luke said.

Johnny nodded his head as he picked up Jake's keys, "I'll go look for the car," he said. "I'm gonna catch a nap. I've been up all damn day and night. Wake me up when you get back," Luke said. "Yeah, no problem," Johnny said over his shoulder as he walked out.

Johnny had located the cop's car in less than twenty minutes. He had simply walked up and down the street, pressing the panic button on the key chain until the car's alarm system began to wail. With the cop's car located, he walked back to the warehouse.

The office was dark. Luke had switched the lights off, stretched out on the floor, and was asleep. *How the Hell did he fall asleep so fast?* Johnny wondered. The answer was alcohol and exhaustion. Luke had not slept in over eighteen hours and had drunk way too much. They were shots purchased by friendly bar patrons, and he had not wanted anything to seem out of the ordinary, so he had accepted them.

Johnny himself had not slept in well over thirty hours and was starting to feel the effects. Luke had said to wake him up after he found the cop's car, and then they would decide what to do, but Johnny knew that there was an excellent chance that Luke might insist on killing the cop. He wanted no part of that when he could just as easily drug him up and drop him off at his car.

Leaving Luke asleep on the floor where he would not interfere, Johnny went to prepare a syringe for the cop. With the syringe in hand, Johnny opened the door to the restroom and looked under the partition of the stall. He could see the cop's lower body seated on the floor with his legs straight out in front of him.

Johnny carefully looked through a crack in the stall's door and saw that the cop still had the pillow case that he had tied over his head in place. Seeing that the cop was still hooded, he opened the stall's door. The cop sat with his head slumped down on his chest, and Johnny wondered briefly if he was still alive until he saw the rise and fall of his chest as he took a breath. *Must still be loopy from that whack to the head I gave him,* Johnny thought.

After watching his chest rise and fall a couple of more times, Johnny stepped over the incapacitated cop and bent over to give him the injection in his upper thigh. Jake threw a wild blind punch that connected somewhere, which was followed by a scuffle. In the exchange, Johnny somehow fell, smacking his head on the toilet.

The dreadful hour of two in the morning had come and gone. Tinker had performed the morning ritual of dragging his half-zombified friend out of bed and hauling him to work. As usual, Hank sleepwalked his way through the doughnut shop's morning setup, but after a couple of cups of coffee, he began to wake up.

Less than three and a half miles north of the doughnut shop, Abbie was waking up as well. She was in no way ready to wake up, but she hadn't much choice. She had a few beers at the party the night before, and they were ready to leave.

She opened the closet door slowly, trying to be as quiet as possible. Just as the opening was getting big enough for her to slide through, the hinges reverberated with a bone-scraping squeak. Abbie froze in her tracks and held her breath.

The man who was passed out in the bed responded to the noise with loud, heavy breathing followed by a tossing fit. He then rolled over and curled up on his side. She stepped out of the closet and looked toward the bed. She could see by the blue glow of the alarm clock on the nightstand that it was Max and that his blanket had fallen to the floor. She picked up the blanket, covered him up, and quietly slipped out of his bedroom door.

Abbie then managed to use the restroom and sneak out of Max's house unnoticed, saving herself the embarrassment of him finding out she had spent the night uninvited. It was a quarter after six in the morning when she left his house and started walking to the bus stop on Sante Fe and Delmar. Ten minutes later, as she waited for the bus, she decided she would call her grandparents later that morning to make arrangements to go to their house in Alice for a little while.

Since Sugarpie's was closed, she would ask the bus driver to drop her off someplace that would be open early. Someplace where she could use some of the money that the kindly Father Clements had given her to get some breakfast and, hopefully, be able to use a phone.

As she continued to wait for the bus, she began to think about Max. She felt a little guilty about spending the night uninvited. He more than likely would have let her stay had she asked, but Abbie had not wanted to risk it. *I'll have to tell him what I did and apologize when I get back from Alice,* she thought.

While Abbie waited for the bus on the corner of Sante Fe and Delmar, Hank stood behind the cash register at Sal's. They just had a wave of customers come through that had kept him and Tinker swamped for a while, but now they were back to the regular Sunday lull.

Hank wondered how people always managed to show up in waves. He and Tinker had joked many times that they all met around the corner till there was at least a crowd of twenty before they would proceed to the doughnut shop. Hank checked the clock on the wall, and his face went from smiling to serious. He knew that Jake would be working that day. *He should've been here by now,* he thought.

Meanwhile, in the Chihuahuan Desert, Harry was up early as well. He had elected to stay at the windmill that evening and throughout the night, sipping water and resting. He still suffered tremors that woke him up at intervals throughout the night and had to get up once to perform a battery swap to deactivate the low-battery alarm, but even so, he still managed to get a few hours of sleep before waking in the early morning darkness.

As the pre-dawn light began to encroach upon the darkness, Harry turned his plan over in his mind. It wasn't much of a plan as far as he was concerned. He had thought it over and could still see no better option than to head back east to the dirt road. However, there was one caveat. He had decided not to head back directly to the east. Instead, he would veer off course slightly to the south toward a rather large mesa he had seen in the distance.

The windmill sat in the middle of a huge desert prairie of creosote, yucca, and cactus. It was lower in elevation than the hills and mountains that surrounded it. Harry hoped that from the mesa top, he would be able to see over the undulating plains and hills that now blocked his view to the dirt road in the east and, if he was lucky, the bend in the road that marked the location of the third cairn as well.

As he waited for the morning light, he added up a rough estimate of his travel time back to the third cairn at the dirt road. He had a rough idea about how long it had taken him to get to the windmill. Taking that and his estimate of the distance to the mesa into consideration, he estimated that it could be well after midday before he made it back to the third cairn.

He thought about the rock overhang he had seen on his way down from the mountains to the dirt road. He had not needed to shelter there before, as the sun was setting, but he now hoped that he would not have to hike in the heat of the desert afternoon for too long before he made it there.

As Harry speculated on the rock overhang, the morning light grew in intensity until he could finally begin to see his surroundings. He stared at his rucksack with the camera positioned on top, facing directly at him for a moment, then stood up, grabbed it, slung it on, and sorted out his POV camera.

Once his equipment was sorted, he walked over to the stock tank and looked in. He had broken off a yucca stalk the day before and fished the dead rat out. If he hadn't known any better, he would have thought the water clean.

As he turned to leave, something on the ground next to the bottom of the stock tank moved and caught his eye. It was a small grayish-brown grasshopper. It was a little over an inch and a quarter long, with two dark horizontal bands across its wings. Its mottled grayish-brown color made it all but disappear into the pebbles and sand next to the stock tank. To Harry, the fact that he had seen the grasshopper at all was incredible.

He dropped to his knees, swatted his hand down over the grasshopper, and caught it. The memory of childhood summers spent catching grasshoppers beside the lake to use as bait for sun perch flashed through his mind. He then stood up and, holding the grasshopper between his thumb and index finger, blew the sand off of it and ate it.

Like her father, Abbie was having thoughts of breakfast as well. She had been waiting for the bus for what seemed to her like forever when, finally, she saw it making its way down the block. As the bus approached, she stood up and walked to the curb to let the driver know that she wanted to board. The bus came to a stop and opened its doors. Seeing that there were only a couple of passengers disembarking from the rear doors, she went up the steps to the ticket machine and purchased a ticket.

As Abbie pulled her ticket free from the machine, she asked the bus driver if he knew someplace that would be open for breakfast. When he turned to face her, his eyes went wide, and his mouth hung agape with what seemed to her to be either surprise or fear.

The bus driver also seemed to be having some difficulty catching his breath. "Are you okay?" She asked the bus driver. The bus driver began to nod, slowly at first, but then, as he regained his composure, his mouth closed, and he began to nod more enthusiastically, and then he exclaimed, "You're the girl on the missing poster!"

"What are you talking about? Abbie asked. The bus driver tried to answer but started to get excited again. "Calm down, and tell me what you're talking about," she said. "Okay, okay, I'm sorry, but You've been missing for at least three days now. I kinda figured you might, you know, be dead by now. It's kinda like seeing a ghost," the bus driver said.

"What missing poster you're talking about?" Abbie asked. "There's one up at Sal's Doughnut Shop. I've seen it the past three mornings in a row," the bus driver answered. "Sal's Doughnut Shop?" Abbie asked. "Yeah, it's the only place open early enough for me to grab some coffee and breakfast before I have to start my route, and breakfast is the most important meal of the day, ya' know," the bus driver said.

"Are they open on Sundays?" Abbie asked. "Yes, Ma'am, but you're gonna need a transfer ticket. It's on Bakner Street. This is route six. It goes all the way down Airline Avenue, but you'll want to get off on Bakner Street. Then, use the transfer ticket to get on the Route Five bus. You'll get off the Route Five at the Center Street stop. Sal's will be across the street to your right."

Shit, that doesn't sound too far from that warehouse, Abbie thought as she purchased the transfer ticket. "Thanks," she said as the ticket issued from the ticket machine. "No problem, Ma'am, good luck!" the bus driver said as she took her seat.

Chapter Twenty-Three

Welcome to Sal's

Abbie saw her missing poster in the window of the doughnut shop as she crossed the parking lot. She was appreciative that people would care enough to go to the trouble, but she hated her driver's license photo. She pulled the poster down and walked up to the counter.

"I'm pretty sure he would have been here by now," Hank had just finished saying to Tinker, speaking of Officer Jake, when he heard the entrance bell over the door ring as Abbie walked in. "Welcome to Sal's Doughnuts!" Hank said as he turned and came face to face with Miss Abigail Reese Adams.

"Someone here looking for me?" She asked, holding her missing poster up next to her face. "You might say so!" Hank said as Tinker flew from the back to stand by his side at the counter. "For starters, the Corpus Christi Police Department, myself and Tinker here, also our friend Jake, and your roommate.

177

"I'm Hank, by the way, and this is Mister Walter Wade Danville," Hank said, nodding his head in Tinker's direction. "You can call me Tinker," he said. "Nice to meet you two. Y'all can both call me Abbie." Hank nodded. "We're very pleased to meet you, Abbie. You look hungry. What will you have? It's on the house," he said.

"I'll take a BOB and some coffee," she said. "Coming right up. Tinker, could you please give Jake a call and Let him know that Abbie is okay while I get her some food," Hank said to Tinker as he made Abbie's order. "Yessir, no problem," he answered.

Hank seated Abbie at a booth with some coffee and the BOB (breakfast on the bun) that she had ordered. He then retrieved her wallet from the back and gave it to her as he took the seat across from her in the booth.

Within a few minutes, Abbie had caught Hank up on everything she had been through in the past four days. She told him about her abduction, her escape, why she hadn't gone to the police, and how she now planned to go hide at her grandparent's house in Alice.

After learning that she had her cell phone taken away, Hank offered to let her use his. She tried her father again with no answer. Then, not forgetting his promise to Abbie's roommate Hank, asked Abbie to call Liz next using the number he had saved to his phone. While Abbie spoke to Liz, Hank mulled her story over, and by the time they finished their conversation, he had a couple of questions.

"So, the guys that abducted you are still out there, and your father is in hiding?" Hank asked Abbie after she ended her call with her roommate. "As far as I know, yes," She said after taking another sip of her coffee. "And, you think that you're still in danger and that it might be best if you got out of town?" he asked. "Yes, until I can find out what's going on with my Dad and try to get it straightened out. I also told Liz not to come back to the apartment until I call her," She said as she rested her coffee cup back on the table.

Hank was considering what Abbie had said when the silence was cracked by Tinker slamming the doughnut shop's phone down in its cradle. "Jake was a no-show at work today. They sent someone to his residence to do a welfare check, but no one was home," he said.

"He could be in danger!" Hank said as he jumped from the booth, "He may have stumbled into trouble while looking for you. If he ran into those three thugs you told me about, we better get to that warehouse quick! Watch the counter, Tink!" He said as he motioned for Abbie to follow him. "You got it, Buddy!" Tinker said as Hank ran for the back door with Abbie right on his heels.

Hank quickly unlocked the Impala's driver's side door, jumped behind the wheel, leaned over, and threw the passenger side door open for Abbie. Skateboard in hand, she jumped in, slamming her door shut. With her giving Hank directions, they sped toward the abandoned furniture warehouse.

Hank and Abbie made it to the warehouse in minutes. Not wanting to draw attention, Hank elected to park across the street. As he pulled into the parking lot at the strip center, he saw Jake's car sitting where he had parked it the night before.

"Abbie, that's Jake's car!" he said. Abbie grabbed Hank's cell phone from the cup holder where he had thrown it while getting in. Now that someone was definitely in danger, not calling the police was no longer a priority for her.

"No, I can't. I'm sorry, I have to go," Abbie said and then placed Hank's phone back in the cup holder. "The dispatcher wanted me to stay on the line, but I hung up. The cops are on their way, but we're already pretty sure that Jake's in there, right!" She said, her voice a mixture of worry and frustration.

"Yeah, and it might take the cops a while to get here too," Hank said as he took the keys from the ignition and stepped out of the Impala. "We better head in," Abbie said as she opened the passenger door and stepped out as well. "Yep," Hank said as he walked to the back of the Impala *and* opened the trunk.

Inside the warehouse, Johnny began to gain consciousness. As the fog began to clear, his mind began to puzzle together the events of the day before. Slowly, realization began to creep in and answer some of the questions that were being posed by his groggy, half-asleep mind. Questions like, *Where the hell am I? Why the fuck am I on the restroom floor? What time is it?* And are *those Sirens?*

Johnny's eyes popped open as the answers started to come to him one by one. *I'm at the warehouse. I'm on the restroom floor because I got knocked out, and yes, those are fucking sirens!"* He thought as he jumped to his feet.

He ran to the office and shook Luke awake violently. "I got knocked out, and I hear sirens!" he said. Luke, still hungover, groggily pushed himself to his feet. "What the fuck are you talking about?" He asked, yawning while rubbing the sleep from his eyes.

"Listen, they're getting closer," Johnny said, jerking his thumb over his right shoulder in the direction of the approaching sirens. "Shit, we better get outta here just in case they're coming this way," Luke said, finally waking up to their situation. "If they are coming this way, there's no time to get the SUV out. That overhead door is too fuck'in slow," Johnny said. "We'll take my car. It's already in the back alley," Luke said, grabbing his keys from the desk.

Keys in hand, Luke hit the office door with Johnny right behind him. They ran past the Ladies' Room, where Jake was still handcuffed, to the end of the hall and yanked the door to the warehouse open.

In the warehouse, Luke and Johnny sprinted past the SUV to the side door. Luke through the broken door open and, trying not to draw attention to himself, started walking in the direction of his car, with Johnny following. Just then, Hank and Abbie, who were trying to find a way into the building, came around the corner and ran right into them.

Abbie, coming face to face with Luke as he exited the building, drew her skateboard back over her shoulder and swung it at his head in a baseball-bat-like fashion. Luke ducked low, coming in under the skateboard and driving his left shoulder into Abbie's midsection. Wrapping his arms around her waist, he tackled her to the ground.

As Luke and Abbie hit the ground, Johnny swung an overhand right at Hank with everything he had. Hank ducked under Johnny's swing, lunged forward, covering his head with his left arm, and caught Johnny around his waist with his right arm. Using his momentum, Hank swung around to Johnny's back, like a small child swings around a pole when playing.

Once on Johnny's back, Hank locked both his arms around Johnny's waist and glued his head to the center of Johnny's back to avoid any elbow strikes. He then placed his right instep behind Johnny's right heel, blocking it, and sat down with his arms still locked tightly around Johnny's waist.

Hank's weight pulled Johnny back. Johnny tried to move his foot back to catch his balance, but Hank still had it blocked. Unable to balance himself, Johnny started falling to his right side. Hank, still controlling him from the back, positioned himself to control Johnny's top left arm as they fell to the ground.

As Johnny crashed to the ground on his right side, Hank applied an arm lock to his left arm and glanced over in Abbie's direction. Abbie and Luke had landed with Abbie on her back. She had wrapped her legs around Luke's midsection, locking her ankles behind his back. Her right arm was clenching Luke's neck, pinning his head to her chest. Her left arm encircled Luke's right arm above the elbow, pinning it to her side.

Luke tried to strike Abbie with his free left arm, but with Abbie holding him in tight, he could not extend his arm enough to deliver an effective punch. Abbie continued to clinch Luke's head, arm, and midsection, hanging all her weight on him while he struck at her repeatedly with his left arm until he was exhausted.

Seeing that his subdued strikes were not effective, he pushed himself up with his left arm, raising Abbie off of the ground. Abbie felt this and knew that he was about to slam her to the ground. To keep from getting the wind knocked out of her, she would use a secret breathing technique called Ushing, which had been taught to her by her Sensei.

Luke slammed her into the ground, but to his dismay, she held on. He pushed himself up with his left arm a few more times, lifting Abbie up and then slamming her to the ground. Each time, Abbie would start ushing just before she hit the ground. Using the secret breathing technique, she was able to hang on while Luke had exhausted himself, lifting her weight.

A few feet away, Johnny bucked back and forth, but Hank's Kimura lock kept him from rolling forward, and his right shin planted firmly in Johnny's back prevented him from rolling back. Hank switched his Kimura grip to a wrist-lock, and holding the wrist-lock with his right hand, he used his left to push Johnny's shoulder to the ground, placing Johnny face down with his right arm behind his back.

In the meantime, Luke, completely exhausted, was unable to lift Abbie's body weight any longer and tried the only thing he could while still stuck in her clinch. With the last of his energy, he threw a few weak punches with his one free arm, but they were in vain. Abbie's clench still kept him from creating the distance he needed to punch effectively, and on top of that, he was now muscle fatigued.

Hank pinned Johnny's right arm between his knees, grabbed his left arm, and brought it behind his back. He then reached into his back pocket, retrieved one of the two pairs of handcuffs that he had taken from the trunk of the Impala earlier, and placed them on Johnny's wrists. With Johnny no longer a threat, Hank looked up to check on Abbie and saw a *Channel Two Live Action News* crew filming Abbie from a news van on the other side of the parking lot.

Hank looked from the news van to Abbie just in time to see her move with incredible speed and agility. With Luke now exhausted, she unlocked her ankles from behind his back, scooted her waist out to the left, and scissored her legs, bringing her right knee and shin across his chest.

She then released her clinch and simultaneously pushed him back with her hands and the shin she had brought across his chest. This created the space she needed to throw a violent mule kick right up into Luke's jaw.

Hank watched as Abbie sprung to her feet in a combat stance before Luke could even hit the ground. When he did hit the ground, he fell flat on his face with a loud smack on the asphalt. Abbie placed her knee on his back to hold him down while she dug his right arm out from underneath his limp body and placed it behind his back.

She then grabbed his left arm by the wrist and brought it behind his back as well, then retrieved the handcuffs that Hank had loaned her earlier and locked Luke's wrist behind his back just as several CCPD patrol cars came screeching to a halt in the parking lot with their red and blue lights flashing and sirens blaring.

Chapter Twenty-Four

The Party's Over

By midmorning, Harry's eyes were following the dirt road all the way down to the bend where he knew the third checkpoint cairn stood. From the top of the mesa, he could also see the distinctive hilltop with the pinnacled rock outcrop that he had previously chosen for his reference point.

Wish I could go straight to the hilltop and carry on from there, he thought. However, he knew that it was at least twice as far away. If he tried to hike straight to the hill, he'd not even make it halfway by midday, and he would be caught out in the high desert with no shelter from the sun. In his condition, it would be better to hike to the third checkpoint, where he knew he could find shelter not far up the mountain under a rock overhang he had seen earlier.

He began to pick his way down the trail. One of Alejandro's Camera drones buzzed from side to side as the gamblers at Hacienda Ramierez watched him make his descent to the bottom of the mesa, gambling on his every move.

Joy, who was watching from Belyy's guest room, had wagered by house phone that Harry would make it up and down the mesa without breaking any bones. She was holding her breath and intently watching Harry's final steps down the mesa when Belyy entered the room.

"Joy... Joy!" Belyy Russky said, calling out loudly, trying in vain to draw her attention away from the monitor. "Oh, Daddy! You missed it! A couple of hours ago, he pounced on this bug. He snatched it right up and crunched it down like a fuck'in Dorrito!" she said.

"Yes, yes, we heard," Belyy said with a hearty laugh, "One of Esperanza's runners bring Ricky "Aces" and Belyy news to tennis courts, where Belyy and Ricky "Aces" teach girls tennis. Esperanza's runners do okay job of keeping us updated.

"Anyways, the other guests, they have all gone. The last group they leave little after ten. So, this evening, I have poker game with other gamblers of desert gauntlet who stay behind, "Blackjack" Smith, Mister Kujira, Ricky "Aces", Waldwolf Hiedler, and also Joey "Two Cards" if we can pry him from monitor.

"Joey "Two Cards" is very much invested in Mister Adams's trek across desert. He stay in bedroom glued to monitor like you. Anyways, the other girls go to lay by pool with Belyy until poker game. You want to go with group?" Belyy asked. "No thanks, Daddy, I want to stay and see what happens next," Joy said, never taking her eyes from the screen.

"Very good, you invest your own money in jackpot like big girl. You watch all you want. Tonight at midnight, we find out if Belyy win or if Belyy lose on 72-hour expiration wager Belyy place on Mister Adams. This is very exciting, No?

"If you are watching and he dies before midnight, let me know, huh? In case Esperanza's messenger is slow again. Anyways, Belyy wants to be first to know.

"If you change your mind, we'll be at pool, wear new white bikini Belyy, buy you last month in Italy, okay? It is very thin, very sexy, Belyy, like very much on you, okay? Goodbye for now, little Medovik," Bely said before leaving Miss Joy Ride to her monitor.

As Belyy and his ladies lounged next to Enrique's pool, Hank and Abbie were pulling into the parking lot at Sal's. It had taken a while to finish their interviews with the CCPD, not to mention the Press. The local news media had been listening in on police scanners and, because of the close proximity of the warehouse to the news station, their mobile satellite van and news crew had arrived at the scene ahead of the CCPD.

They had gotten there in time to record Hank and Abbie subduing Luke and Johnny, placing them in handcuffs, and turning them over to the police. They also recorded Luke and Johnny being placed in the back of the patrol cars and Jake's rescue. Afterwhich they interviewed Abbie, Hank, and the CCPD Detectives.

Later on, as Abbie and Hank entered Sal's, they were greeted by a very nervous Tinker, "Where have you been? Y'all've been gone over an hour! I called the police, but they said that they already had you on the other line! Where's Jake? Is he okay? Was he at that warehouse?" Tinker asked, rambling.

"Calm down, Tink! Jake's okay. They just took him to the hospital for a routine physical, but he should be out real soon," Hank said over Tinker's incessant questioning. He and Abbie then told him the whole story in between helping customers.

"Well, all's well that ends well, I guess," Tinker had said in a celebratory tone after Hank and Abbie had finished telling him about their adventure at the warehouse. "All's well for the most part," Abbie said, "Except I still get no answer when I try to call my Dad, and I'm starting to get a little worried.

"He's probably still hiding out from these guys that we just got arrested. He's probably in his RV with his phone turned off. He's done it in the past with the bill collectors, but with everything that's been going on, I'd like to go check on him just to be sure. Do you think you could give me a ride," she asked Hank.

"Of course," He said and then turned to Tinker. "Sorry, Buddy, I'll need you to cover. It's possible that our two new friends in the clink might still have some other partners out there roaming around. We better go make sure her dad is okay." "No worries, it's slow, and we close in a couple of hours anyway," Tinker said with a shrug.

As Hank drove Abbie to the trailer park, the gamblers at Hacienda Ramirez watched a few more insects fall prey to Harry as he made his way back to the third checkpoint. He had also gathered a few beans from some mesquite trees that had tasted somewhat like honey to him.

He was trying his best to ration his water, but the sun beat down on him without mercy. As he began to stagger in the heat, the gamblers began to make their wagers on whether or not he would make it to the checkpoint. Harry continued pushing through the desert heat, telling himself that once he cleared the fallen rocks from the opening of the rock overhang, he could rest in the cool shade.

It was late afternoon by the time Harry had finally made it back to the third checkpoint at the dirt road, the drone flying overhead and gamblers watching and wagering on his every step along the way. Completely overheated and exhausted, he desperately began to make his way up the mountainside to the rock overhang. The gamblers, discerning his intentions to shelter under the rock overhang, began to wager on whether or not he would make it there.

As he approached the rock overhang, to his relief, he saw that the fallen rocks in front of the entrance had actually been stacked there. They had been stacked intentionally to build a rock wall to block out the wind and hold in the heat from the campfire. As he struggled to the entrance of the rock overhang, he became dizzy. Completely overheated and exhausted, he fell to his knees yards from the opening.

The gamblers jumped to their feet like they were watching a racehorse approach the finish line. Harry had pushed himself too hard for the poor condition his body was in. He pulled himself closer to the rock wall's opening. He knew that he needed to get into the shade before he had a heat stroke and died.

My daughter, I need to make it back to my daughter, he thought as he gathered what little will he had left and pulled himself the last few feet to the rock wall entrance. With the last of his strength, he dragged a thorny dead bush aside from the opening and pulled himself into the small shallow cave under the rock overhang. Some of the gamblers cheered while others cursed.

Harry had laid facedown in the coolness of the cave for several minutes until he had rested enough to roll over and push his back up against the cave wall. As he did so, Joy Ride gasped, and the other gamblers stood in astonishment as his POV camera came into focus. He was not alone. On the other side of the cave opposite of Harry was the mummified remains of a man.

The mummy sat back against the wall with his legs out in front of him, much in the same posture as Harry, the only difference being that the mummy had blankets under him. His empty, wide eyesockets stared back at Harry, and his teeth were exposed in a huge skeletal grin as if he were happy to finally have company.

At first, Harry jumped a little at the sight of his new friend, but he quickly settled. He had been through a lot in the last few days, and now a skeleton staring back at him didn't quite seem to be the end of the world.

Harry reached into his ruck, removed a canteen, and took a rationed drink While he looked his new friend over. The canteen was almost empty. *At least the other two are still full,* he thought. To the mummy's left side lay a cowboy hat and a backpack with a machete strapped to its side. At his right hand lay a large fixed-blade knife, and next to that lay the knife's sheath.

The mummy wore a long-sleeve, button-down work shirt, blue jeans, and cowboy boots. One boot was off and lay at the skeleton's feet. Harry leaned forward to get a better look and began to puzzle out his friend's situation. The skeleton had used the knife to split his right pant leg clear up over the knee. Just under the knee, the mummy's leather belt had been fashioned into a tourniquet. It hadn't been difficult for Harry to deduce that his poor friend had been snake-bit. He had crawled under the rock overhang to recover, and with no medical attention, he had passed away.

As Harry began to realize his situation, his eyes darted back to the mummy's backpack. *There couldn't be anything in there to eat.* He thought as he scrambled to his knees, reaching past his new friend to grab the backpack. When he hefted the bag, he felt there was weight to it. *That's good,* he thought as sat back on his side of the cave and began to work the zipper.

Harry's eyes grew almost as wide as his new friends as the contents of the backpack spilled out between his knees. He took mental note of several key items. Those being two cans of fruit cocktail, a tin of sardines, a twelve-ounce bottle of hot sauce, and a can opener.

He was starved but thought it best to take things slow. He opened a can of fruit cocktail and began to sip the syrup. It was hard not to chug the whole can. However, he held back because he did not want a repeat performance of what had happened at the river checkpoint with the first canteen of water.

Harry let his eyes wander over the rest of the backpack's contents as he nursed the syrup from the can of fruit cocktail. He could feel the sugar entering his system as he picked through the items and tossed some aside.

"These are kinda sketchy," He said to his new friend as he tossed some bagged chips and a sleeve of crackers covered with evidence of mouse activity. "And I'll leave these for you," He said as he tossed a pair of underwear and some socks to the side.

He began to move the things he could use into a separate pile. For instance, a large, stainless steel water bottle that showed obvious signs of being placed directly into many campfires, a stainless steel skillet with a lid, a set of tongs, and a small box of plastic eating utensils. Harry opened the latter and retrieved a spoon. There was also a pair of leather gloves, three disposable cigarette lighters, and his new friend's wallet.

In between shoveling spoonfuls of fruit cocktails into his mouth, Harry thumbed through his new friend's wallet. He was surprised to find one thousand six- hundred and eighty dollars in U.S. currency but then quickly realized its purpose. "Good idea, you would have needed some cash on you had you made it across the border," Harry said to his new friend as he spooned more fruit cocktail into his mouth.

As Harry finished the fruit cocktail, he began to feel much better. The fog seemed to lift from his brain, and his appetite was now tremendous. He thought of eating more of the canned food but thought it best if he rationed it. He went back to investigating the wallet to distract himself from the can of sardines.

The next thing he found in his new friend's wallet was his identification card. In all capital letters, in the upper left corner were three lines that read, "GOBIERNO DE JALISCO, PODER EJECUTIVO, SECRETARIA DE VIALIDAD Y TRANSPORTE." Below that, more to the center of the card in gold capital letters were the words "LICENCIA DE CONDUCIR," and below that was Harry's new friend's name.

Harry held the Jalisco State driver's license up at arm's length as he looked back and forth from the skeleton's wide grin to the same wide grin in the driver's license photo. "Dario, Ignacio, Agerico, Cholula," Harry read his new friend's name aloud.

"Well, Dario, my name is Harry Adams, and I owe you a big one. This evening, when it cools down a little, we'll see what we can do about giving you a decent burial, my friend," He said as he leaned back against the cave wall and closed his eyes.

Chapter Twenty-Five

Catfish's Bait Shop and Trailer Park

Hank had made the half-hour drive from Sal's to Catfish's Bait Shop and Trailer Park in Elroy, Texas, in 23 minutes, and Abbie was currently knocking on the door of her father's thirty-three foot, two thousand and eight Winnebago Vista, with no answer. Hank walked back to the Impala and fished something out of the glove box. "Nice RV," He said as he walked back to Abbie, who was still standing at the door.

"My father bought it a couple of years before my mom died. It needs a few repairs mechanically, but all the utilities work. He lost the house a few months after I moved out and wound up moving into it," She said as she turned away from the door. "That's tough. I'm sorry to hear that," Hank said. "Don't be, he and my mom had some of their best times in this RV I think that's why he held onto it. You know, for the memories," she said.

After a moment passed, Hank held up the object he had retrieved from the *Imapla's* glove box. "Mind if I give it a try?" he asked. Abbie looked at the small black leather lock-pick's tool pouch in Cobin's hand, "Yeah, sure, give it a try." she said. Hank unzipped the small tool pouch, removed a tension bar and pick, and went to work on the RV's door lock.

In less than a minute, Hank and Abbie were inside the cool air conditioning of Harry's RV. Abbie went straight to the rear of the RV and checked the bedroom and bathroom. "Nobody here," she said. "There's no note anywhere, only this stack of mail," Hank said as he let the stack of overdue bills fall back to the kitchen table. "Let me borrow your phone to call my grandparents' house. There is a chance he might have gone there," Abbie said. Hank handed Abbie his phone and then continued his examination of the RV.

Abbie had not wanted to worry her grandparents, and had put off calling them for as long as possible, but now she had no alternative. After a long conversation, she finally hung up. Harry had not been there, and it had taken Abbie a little while to assure her grandparents that everything was okay.

"He's not at my grandparents. I think it's time to call the sheriff's department and report him missing," she said. "Yeah, that's probably a good idea," Hank said as Abbie dialed the sheriff's department. After Abbie made her phone call to the sheriff's department, she found Hank in her father's bedroom, looking at a framed photo of her mother and father.

"On their way?" he asked. "Yes, they said they are sending a patrol unit out," Abbie answered. "Good," Hank said and then held up the framed photo. "They look very happy here," he said. "Oh yes, they were, extremely. That was the day my dad brought home the Caddy. He bought it brand new in '04," Abbie said.

Hank studied the photo. In the photo, Harry and his wife were posed in front of their new car. Harry had his left arm around his wife's shoulders and was hugging her close to him. The couple was all smiles. "I'd figure this photo would be pretty important to your father," Hank said. "Definitely," Abbie said. "So, I'm guessing he wouldn't leave without it," Hank said. "Definitely not," Abbie agreed.

Hank pulled the wardrobe door open, "How about his clothes? Does it look like he packed a bag before he left?" he asked. Abbie stared briefly into the wardrobe, "Nope, he's wearing his brown suit and loafers. Everything else is here as far as I can tell," she said.

"There's food in the ice box, the trash hasn't been taken out, and the air conditioning was also left on. I don't think your father expected to be gone that long," Hank said as he took a picture of the framed photo with his cell phone before setting it back down on the nightstand.

"I think it's good you notified the sheriff's department, but I think we better take a look around ourselves after you're done making your report to the deputy," Hank said as he walked to the table and began to leaf through Harry's unpaid bills as he waited.

After the sheriff's deputy had finished his interview, Hank and Abbie thanked him for his time, and he exited the RV. "I'm exhausted," Abbie said after she closed the RV's door behind the sheriff's deputy. By the time the sheriff's deputy finished his interview with Abbie, it was already late afternoon. "Me too. I've been up since two in the morning," Hank said.

"I don't think it's safe for me to stay here or at my apartment," Abbie said. "No, I don't think so either, but you could stay the night in my Uncle Dan's guest room if you like," Hank said. "Thanks," Abbie said, relieved to have a place to stay for the night.

Meanwhile, at Hacienda de Ramirez in Enrique's private casino, Belyy Russkiy, Mister Oki Kujira, "Blackjack" Smith, Waldwolf Heidler, and Ricky "Aces" sat at a card table, embroiled in a high-stakes poker game. The monitors in the casino still carried Harry's POV and the camera drone's live feeds. However, the gamblers at the table were doggedly focused on their cards.

Only Joy Ride and Joey "Two-Cards" Lombardi still watched attentively, with Joey watching on the monitor behind the bar of the casino and Joy Ride watching from the privacy of Belyy's guest room. After the excitement at the cave, they both had become all the more obsessed with Harry's adventure and were now afraid to take their eyes away from the monitor for even a second. They had even watched him sleep.

For a while, Harry had slept almost as well as his new friend Dario. That was until the low battery alarm on his POV camera rousted him from his sleep. "First things first, Dario," He said as he changed the POV camera's battery, "I have a little bit of work to do, and while I do need to make sure this camera stays on, I see no harm in lightening my load while I do it," Harry said, as he then placed the battery pack into Dario's smaller lighter backpack.

When Harry emerged from the cave, on his right side hung Dario's Machette, and on his left side hung Dario's hunting knife. "Okay, let's see if we can find you a decent resting place," He said as he looked back at his new friend lying in the cave.

Harry had Dario's driver's license in his pocket and intended to report his whereabouts to the authorities in case the man had family. However, something told him that this mountain would probably be Dario's final resting place.

With this in mind, Harry walked up the mountain trail from the rock overhang until he found the perfect spot. The view from there was spectacular, and that area would stay dry during the summer months. They were in the middle of a drought at the moment. However, summer monsoons in the Chihuahuan deserts could be sudden and fierce.

The rocky surface of the mountainside would be too hard to dig. Harry would have to do an above-ground burial. He would have to clear the gravesite of any rocks before laying Dario to rest. He would then have to cover him with a pile of stones large enough to protect him from the desert wildlife.

Harry knelt at the gravesite and began to toss the larger rocks into a pile off to the side. The camera drone buzzed in and hovered above him about fifteen feet off the ground. *Been gone awhile must have needed a battery swap,* he thought as he continued to work.

The boulders he could not lift easily he had to roll off to the side. As he worked to move one particularly large boulder, the one that he intended to use as Dario's head marker, some movement in his peripheral caught his attention. He turned his head to look, and no more than three feet away sat a rattlesnake, coiled and ready to strike.

Startled, Harry jumped back on his feet and grabbed for Dario's machete but then decided against it. Instead, he retrieved one of the larger rocks he had moved earlier, held it high above his head, and sent it crashing down. The rock hit the rattlesnake, wounding it.

The angry rattler struck at the air as he sent another large stone crashing down. The wounded rattler turned and desperately started to slither away, trying to escape to the underside of a huge boulder.

In fear of losing the rattler, Harry drew Dario's machete. Now that the rattler was on the move, wounded and not coiled to strike, he felt more confident to approach it. Three swings of Dario's machete and the rattler lay headless and writhing in the sand. Harry stood over the dead rattler with his heart racing. In the casino, Joy Ride and Joey "Two Cards" Lombardi's hearts were racing as well, but the gamblers at the card table had missed the whole show.

When Harry regained his composure, he gathered some fuel for a fire and returned to the cave under the rock overhang. As he went through the entrance, his eyes happened to fall upon the thorn bush he had been forced to pull out of the way when he had first entered the cave. He stared at the heavily thorned bush with scorn.

The bush had been hell to get out of the way, and he had almost died trying. He still had the wounds on his hands from its long, thick thorns. *How the hell did it even get wedged in there,* he wondered as he entered the cave. Then, in a flash of comprehension, he realized its purpose. "Very smart, good idea, you wedged it in there to keep out the critters," He said to Dario as he entered the cave.

Once he had the fire going, he went out and collected a few paddles of prickle pear cactus, or nopales as they are called in Spanish. He collected the younger, more tender paddles using Dario's machete to cut the base of each paddle of cactus while using his tongs to hold the paddle while he worked so as not to get his hands riddled with painful stickers. He was no survivalist, but growing up in West Texas, he had seen nopalitos, which were nopales cut into strips on the menu many times.

He used the long tongs to flip the cactus paddles over a few times in the fire, making sure to burn the glochids off both sides. With the glochids burned away, he was able to cut the nopales up into nopalitos without getting stickers in his hands.

The nopalitos then went into the stainless steel skillet along with the rattlesnake that he had cleaned and cut into small pieces earlier. He then placed the skillet into the fire and went back to preparing Dario's final resting place.

Watching carefully for rattlers, Harry finished clearing the gravesite and then moved the largest boulder, the one that would serve as Dario's headstone, into place. Then, after cutting down a creosote bush to use as a broom, he swept the gravesite clean. After sweeping the gravesite clean, he went into the cave, wrapped Dario in his blankets, and carried him to his new resting place.

He was partially done stacking the stones on Dario's grave when he began to smell the cooking rattlesnake meat and nopalitos in the wind. "I'm sorry, my friend, but even a gravedigger has to eat," He said, apologizing as he left to retrieve the skillet from the fire. After a large helping of nopalitos and rattlesnake, with a generous application of hot sauce, he returned to his task of stacking rocks.

In his endeavor to make Dario's grave as secure as possible from the desert animals, he had stacked far more rocks than necessary, and by the time he finished, it had grown late. He said a few words of prayer over his new friend's grave, and then, exhausted from his labor, he proceeded back down the mountain trail toward the rock overhang.

As Harry walked down the mountainside, he noticed that he could see the trail under the moonlight. He looked at the moon as he walked along and saw that it was almost half full. *If I wake up early, I will leave right away. There'll be enough light to see, especially down a trail I already know,* he thought as he continued down the path to Dario's cave.

At the cave, he went through the entrance, then pulled the thorn bush into place behind him. He then packed the stainless steel water bottle, skillet, tongs, plastic eating utensils, leather gloves, and cigarette lighters into his ruck. He also folded up and packed Dario's smaller backpack, the tin of sardines, and the other can of fruit cocktail along with the can opener and, most importantly, the twelve-ounce bottle of hot sauce.

Once his rucksack was packed, Harry set his POV camera up on top of it, facing the camera toward himself, and then went to sleep. He later awoke in the early morning hours. What time it was, he could not be sure, but he was anxious to get moving. He slung on his ruck, positioned his camera, and walked up the mountain trail to Dario's grave. At the grave, Harry laid his hand upon Dario's headstone. "Thank you once again, my friend," he said.

After Harry had paid his respects, he began to follow the mountain trail back down to the dirt road. After negotiating the trail, he easily located the third cairn and reshot the 243-degree azimuth for the two-lane blacktop CHIH-76 checkpoint. *I'll have to keep a close eye on the compass until sunrise when I can either search for the hilltop with the rock outcrop or shoot another reference point altogether,* he thought. Then, once again, Harry Adams walked out into the high desert.

Chapter Twenty-Six

Back to the Trailer Park

Monday morning, Abbie borrowed Hank's cell phone and called Sugarpie's Cafe. Her boss had already heard about her abduction on the news and was upset. He told her that he would have a check for her to pick up Tuesday morning when they opened. He also said that there would be a little extra added to her normal wages to help hold her over and that she could come back to work whenever she was ready.

Later that morning, Hank drove her back to the trailer park in Elroy, where they continued to interview Harry's neighbors in hopes of finding a clue as to where he might have gone. By late morning, with the exception of the one empty site directly across Harry's, they had questioned all of his immediate neighbors, and none of them had seen or heard anything.

"Now what?" Abbie asked after they had questioned all the neighbors to no avail. "Now we branch out. We'll go to the bait shop first and ask around there. If they don't know anything in the bait shop, we'll ask the people fishing from the pier, and if we strike out there, we'll inquire along the lake beach," Hank said as they walked back to the Impala.

The bait shop was nestled on the bank of a small cove on the south side of the 22,000-acre Lake Mathis. "Catfish's Bait Shop and Trailer Park," Hank said as he read the sign that was mounted to the roof of the bait shop through the Impala's windshield.

Abbie pushed open the passenger door and stepped one foot out, "I guess we better go in and see if Mister Catfish knows anything about where my father could have gone," she said. "Yep, sounds like a plan," Hank said as he opened the driver's side door and stepped out as well.

Inside the bait shop, Hank saw an older man with a bushy, white beard, wearing a captain's cap, standing behind the counter. He had on rectangular gold-framed glasses and wore a short-sleeved, thin white linen embroidered guayabera shirt over khaki shorts. "What can I help you, folks, with today," He said in a friendly voice.

"Hello, Sir, my name is Hank, and this is my friend, Abbie," Hank said and thrust his hand out. "Nice to meet you. I'm Catfish. The owner of this here establishment," He said as he shook hands hartley with Hank first and then Abbie.

"Now then, what can I do for you two?" he asked. "Well, you see, Catfish, Abbie here is Mister Harry Adams's daughter. He rents a campsite from you," Hank said. "Yes sir, he sure does, campsite number Seventeen. The sheriff's deputy was by here earlier to question me, and he filled me in on the situation.

"I'm sorry, ma'am. I didn't know you were his daughter. Harry's a good guy. I hope he turns up safe," Catfish said. "Thank you," Abbie said in reply.

"Did you have any helpful information for the sheriff's deputy?" Hank asked. "No, I didn't have anything to tell him other than I was pretty sure that Harry was here as late as Wednesday afternoon and that I didn't notice his car was gone till sometime Friday. The deputy left his card and said to call him if I think of anything else," Catfish said.

"I see…Tell me, Catfish, has the site across from Harry's been vacant long?" Hank asked. "Oh, it's not vacant. That's Skillet's site. He left out sometime Thursday morning to go fish at the bay, but he'll be back Wednesday morning sometime," Catfish answered.

"Wednesday morning sometime, how do you know?" Hank asked. "Well, he told me, he stops by the bait house every morning for coffee and checks in. If he's gonna be gone, he always lets me know where and for how long," Catfish answered.

"I see…Well if he didn't leave until Thursday morning sometime, then it's possible he could have seen something. Do you think we could get his cellphone number from you?" Hank asked. "I could, but it wouldn't do you any good," Catfish answered. "And just why not?" Abbie asked, somewhat perturbed. "He doesn't have any service," Catfish said with a shrug.

"How do you know?" Abbie asked. "Because he doesn't pay for it," Catfish said. "What would he do in an emergency?" Abbie asked. "He has a phone, and he keeps it charged. He can dial 911, but that's it," Catfish said.

"Oh, I see. That's sad that he doesn't have enough money to keep his phone turned on," Abbie said remorsefully. At that, Catfish began to laugh hysterically. Finally catching his breath, he said, "Oh, Honey, he can afford it. He doesn't look it, but he has more money than he can spend."

"I don't get it," Abbie said, "If he can afford it, then why wouldn't he get his phone turned on?" She asked, somewhat confused. With that, Catfish grinned, and with a wink, he said, "He's recently divorced." "Right..." Hank said, realizing at that point that there would be no contacting Skillet by telephone or any other means, "Wednesday it is then. You might want to call the sheriff's office and let them know about Skillet's return as well," he said.

"Sure thing, wish I would have mentioned it earlier," Catfish said. "No worries, we appreciate your help," Abbie said. "One more question, Mister Catfish. Do you mind if Abbie and I walk the pier to see if anyone else might have some information on Harrry's whereabouts?" Hank asked. "No, not at all. You two look around as much as you like!"

Abbie and Hank thanked Catfish once more as they exited the bait shop onto the deck outside the door. The covered deck wrapped from the front of the bait shop around to the backside, which faced Lake Mathis. There were stairs from the covered deck that led down to a huge t-shaped pier that extended 150 feet out into the lake.

On his way out, Hank stopped and looked at the people that were fishing from the pier. He then looked out across the water. He watched as people fished from boats and played along the shore of the beautiful Lake. "There's a lot of people out today. I guess we better get started," He said to Abbie. She nodded, and they both headed down the steps to the pier.

As Abbie and Hank busied themselves questioning the people on the pier, a very excited Belyy Russkiy, accompanied by his ladies, came bursting into his guest room. "Joy, can you believe this Harry guy?" He said as the other girls hurried about, giggling excitedly as they changed their clothes and gathered their things.

"Belyy never think in million years he live past alcohol withdrawal in desert!" He said laughing, "Anyways, very exciting news. Belyy invited to disco party in Prague. I charter jet we go now, ok!" He said excitedly.

"No, Daddy, it's not ok. You know, I bought into the desert jackpot with my own money. I want to see how it ends," Joy Ride said through pouting lips. "Yes, but Belyy lose bet on alcoholic dying in 72 hours and lose interest already…how many checkpoints did you wager alcoholic make anyways?" "All the way, Daddy, all the way," she said.

"What, no way alcoholic make it all the way!" Belyy said, laughing hysterically. "But you are right, you wager your own money so you stay and watch… but Belyy cannot miss disco in Prague. It's disco, baby! Disco!! There is going to be so much cocaine!!!

"So, Belyy and other girls go to Prague… Belyy, tell Enrique you stay and watch desert gauntlet to end…When desert gauntlet over, you call, and Belyy send car for you, okay, goodbye, for now, my little *Kiska-Koshka* goodbye!" Belyy said as he left the room, with the other girls giggling as they followed behind.

After Belyy had left, Joy continued to watch Harry's trek across the Chihuahuan desert. By later that morning, he was well on the other side of his hilltop reference point. He had found a well-used shelter site on the west side of that hill and had stopped there to replace his camera's battery and eat the other can of fruit cocktail from Dario's pack. However, it had been too early in the day to shelter there, so he decided to push on, hoping to find shelter in the mountains before midday.

The mountains lay far in the distance, but when Harry crested hilltops, he could see the heat shimmering off of the two-lane blacktop that ran along the foothills at the mountain's base, and occasionally, he would catch glimpses of sunlight flashing off of chrome and glass as vehicles made their way down the highway. He would have to be careful crossing CHIH-76, especially on the way back, when he would be carrying 20 kilos of cocaine. He had no desire to rot in a Mexican jail for drug smuggling.

The desert sun rose steadily over the course of Harry's trek toward the two-lane black-top. He arrived at the cairn in the heat of midday to the chagrin of many of the gamblers who had wagered that he would perish in the desert before making it to the fourth checkpoint.

He had drunk most of his second canteen of water while working on Dario's grave, and now, after the brutal desert hike, he had very little left in his third and final canteen. Thankful to finally make it to the fourth checkpoint, he flipped over the rock that marked the canteen's location at the prescribed three feet to the west of the cairn and dug out the canteen.

Just like always, there were instructions, along with new coordinates. The instructions read, "Use coordinates to identify the correct trailhead. The fifth checkpoint is on the other side of the mountains at the trail's end, on this side of the canyon."

Harry looked to the mountains across the highway. He could pick out what looked to be several different trailheads in the foothills. Nevertheless, he sighted through the compass and turned his body until the new azimuth fell under the indicator line on the bezel, and the correct trailhead fell under the sighting wire of the compass.

Similar to the trail through the smaller mountain range he had crossed over before, this trail also appeared to lead through a low saddle between two large mountain peaks. It made sense to Harry. It would take days to go around, so although the trails that led through the ravines and gorges to the saddles were meandering, they were still the fastest by far.

"First things first, I need to find someplace to shelter out of the sun for a while," Harry said as he crossed the two-lane blacktop and started hiking to the trailhead at the bottom of the mountains. As he got closer to the trailhead, he scanned the mountainside, in vain, looking for someplace to shelter from the heat of the midday sun, and began to realize that he had made a mistake.

Leaving Dario's cave that early in the morning had thrown him off schedule. The well-used shelter at the hilltop, which he had bypassed, was well-used for a reason. It would do no good to return to the hilltop now. It was too far back. By the time he made it back to the shelter, the hottest part of the day would already be over.

His only choice now was to proceed forward. He followed the meandering mountain pass through rock formations, up draws, and along shoulders and ledges as it wound its way up, and by late afternoon, Harry had made it to the top of the mountain pass.

The sun was no longer as high, and the terrain had changed considerably. There was sparse vegetation at the top of the mountains that culminated into thick scrub brush and trees that Harry could see at the bottom of the mountains on the canyon side.

As he continued to walk the trail, he came upon a spot under a rock ledge that partially blocked the sun. He sat down and opened the tin of sardines from Dario's pack. The camera drone made one more fly-by as Harry drank the oil from the sardine tin and then disappeared. *Probable needs a fresh battery,* he thought as he drained as much of the oil as he could into his mouth. He then refilled the tin with some of Dario's hot sauce and ate slowly with a plastic spoon, occasionally adding more hot sauce from the bottle.

The Impala had been thundering down I-37 toward Corpus Christi for ten minutes when Abbie finally spoke. "I can't believe we spent all day at the trailer park only to come up empty-handed," she said. They had spent the entire day questioning every camper and tourist they could find to no avail. "Nothing but dead ends. I guess our best shot is to come back Wednesday and talk to this Skillet character," Hank said.

"I thought tomorrow, I'd go to a couple of the bars where my dad hangs out and ask around to see if anyone knows anything. Wanna go?" Abbie asked. "Naw, I better show up at work tomorrow, or Sal will have my hide.

"I'll ask him if I can take Wednesday off as soon as he comes in from the beach. He'll say yes. He's always in an agreeable mood when he gets some surfing in before work. That way, Wednesday, I can drive you back to the trailer park so we can talk to this Skillet guy," Hank said.

"Yeah, that sounds like a good plan to me…Thank you, Hank. I really do appreciate it," Abbie said. "Don't mention it. However, I will expect a free meal at Sugarpie's once you get back to work," Hank said with a smile as he drove into the city.

Chapter Twenty-Seven

Rattlesnake Cave

After Harry had finished the tin of sardines, he dozed off in the shade under the rock ledge. He woke up later that evening and continued down the mountain pass until he lost the unfamiliar trail in the darkness. Not wanting to stray too far from the trail, he decided to make camp for the night.

He fell asleep only to be awoken in the early morning hours, once again by the low battery alarm of his POV camera. He was getting sick of that sound, but he dutifully changed the battery. *I'll need that ten grand to pay off that thug bartender if I somehow manage to live through this hell,* he thought.

He had no idea how long he had slept, but he had slept hard and was now wide awake. He took a seat with his back against a small pine tree and waited for light. The trail had gone over an area of rocky, barren ground that was still difficult to see in the dark of the night before, but as the morning's first light steadily intensified, he was finally able to pick the trail out.

A few minutes later, he was better than halfway down the mountainside and could see the canyon that cut through the middle of the mountain range in the distance. As he made his way down the mountainside, it became increasingly more wooded as the trail led him down into a gorge. Not being able to see past the trees at the top of the gorge, Harry was resigned to follow the trail.

The trail finally ended at a well-used campsite under a stand of oaks and pines no more than 20 yards from the edge of the canyon. In the center of the campsite, Harry could see a large ring of stacked rocks where others had made their campfires. The ground all around the campsite had been beaten down to bare, packed dirt. Past the tree line of the campsite, the ground turned into wind-swept rock for about ten yards before terminating at the canyon's edge.

The fifth checkpoint cairn sat in plain sight at the canyon's edge, directly across the campsite from the trail's entrance. Harry walked across the campsite to the cairn, stood next to it, and looked down into the canyon.

He estimated that in some areas, the canyon walls might be as high as a thousand feet in elevation. From where he stood now, next to the cairn, down to the river bank at the bottom of the canyon, was at least 600 feet or more.

His eyes followed the cliff faces, ledges, and rock formations from the top of the canyon walls down to the river that ran through the bottom of the canyon. The riverside was bordered by thick underbrush and trees, which then gave way to its sandy banks. The sandy banks of the river then terminated at the base of the canyon walls.

The camera drone buzzed by Harry and then swooped down into the canyon. *Must be giving the gamblers a bird's eye view of the canyon,* Harry thought. He didn't blame them. The canyon was definitely a captivating sight.

He stood for a moment, transfixed by the beauty of the canyon, as he took in the breathtaking colors that were filtered in through the early morning light. Under different circumstances, he might have sat there and soaked everything in for a good while, but that was not a luxury he could afford at the moment.

Next to the cairn was a pile of rocks. Harry squatted and moved the largest rock from the top and retrieved a single canteen. The instructions on the canteen read, "262-degrees, Rattlesnake Cave in canyon wall on the west side of the river."

Harry looked down the canyon wall and decided that it would be best if he left most of his gear behind. He would only take his partial canteen of water, the three empty canteens to gather water at the river, the hunting knife, and, of course, the POV camera.

Before he got started, he transferred the bulk of his gear that he wasn't taking into Dario's smaller pack and hid it just outside the campsite. *At least this will make the climb down easier, not to mention the climb back up with 45 pounds of cocaine on my back,* he thought.

He then prepared to shoot his new azimuth. Knowing that the compass would do him no good once he started winding his way down the face of the canyon wall, he resolved to find the best landmark possible. Standing directly behind the cairn, he shot the new azimuth and searched for his new reference point.

Halfway down the opposite canyon wall, in line with the compass's sighting wire, he spied a rather large distinctive ledge. Satisfied with his new reference point, he put on the leather gloves from Dario's pack and began the dangerous descent. The camera drone hovered close. The gamblers watched its feed along with the feed from Harry's POV camera in anticipation as they wagered on whether or not he would fall from the canyon wall and what his injuries would be if he did.

Harry slowly picked his way down the canyon wall, sometimes easily along shoulders and ledges and sometimes with more difficulty, having to search out scarce hand and toe holds. At the bottom of the canyon wall, he walked about 200 yards across the sand of the east bank to the river. He then walked downstream until he found a section that was no more than twenty feet across and waded to the other side.

On the other side of the river, Harry began walking toward the ledge he had chosen for his reference point. As he walked along in the sand, he glanced down, and there in front of him was a baby rattlesnake less than ten inches long. He thought briefly of eating it, but it was way too small. He sidestepped the snake and kept moving.

They don't call it Rattlesnake Cave for nothing. Better be careful, he thought as he continued toward his reference point. It was then that he saw another baby rattler. He sidestepped that one as well, only to almost step on yet another baby rattler.

He gave up on counting the baby rattlers somewhere in the forties and had probably seen twice that many by the time he located Rattlesnake Cave. The cave was about fifteen feet up the canyon wall from where the river took a hard bend.

The trail to the cave wound up the canyon wall through large boulders and rocks that littered the area from the cave all the way down to the river bank. Harry wondered briefly if the huge boulders had fallen from above or if they had washed up in the bend of the river during some huge flood in the past.

His eyes nervously traced the path up to the cave's entrance. He wondered how Enrique's men managed to traverse the path so regularly without getting snake-bit. What he didn't know was that whenever Enrique's men entered Rattlesnake Cave, they wore special gear for protection and were armed with eight-foot-long professional snake-handling tongs.

Harry did not have any of that. All he had was a small sapling pine that he had cut down with Dario's machete to use as a staff and to clear the trail of the baby rattlers. Using the staff for protection and as a probe to clear the trail ahead, he began to make his way up through the boulders and rocks to the entrance of the cave, killing three large rattlers along the way and two more at the entrance of the cave.

The entrance of the cave was just tall enough for Harry's Five-foot-ten-inch frame to stand comfortably, and there was no mistaking that he had found the correct cave.

As he stood at the entrance, the morning sun flooded the eastern-facing cave, and bathed in the morning light, sitting in a heap on the ground surrounded by rattlers was a skeleton. Harry and the gamblers watching through his live POV camera feed all knew at once that it was Lester Hunckle from Montclair, Louisianna.

Past Lester, in the back of the cave, Harry saw a pile of stones, where he assumed the bundle of cocaine had been stashed. He looked back at Lester momentarily. He was chained at his feet, and his hands were bound behind his back with wire.

Locked around his neck was a thick metal collar. The metal collar was anchored to the cave wall with a heavy piece of four-foot chain. Lester's bottom jaw had fallen off into his lap. Despite that, his top right gold tooth was still in place and gleaming in the morning sun.

Harry watched transfixed as a giant black centipede with a red head and orange legs began to crawl its eight-inch-long body from one empty eyesocket into the other. The centipede was more than likely in the process of hunting down some poor spider. As he stood there transfixed, he caught a small movement in his peripheral and looked down from the centipede and Lester's gold tooth just in time to dodge a striking rattlesnake at his feet.

Harry jumped as high as a Texas A&M cheerleader, getting the carelessness scared right out of him. "No more staring at gold teeth, I better pay attention, these fuck'in rattlers are everywhere, and "Bill Haast" I ain't," He gasped under his breath after beating the snake to death with his pine staff. After he had caught his breath, he carefully ventured to the back of the cave and retrieved the cocaine.

Chapter Twenty-Eight

The Drunken Shark

"Good morning, Hank!" Jake said as he entered Sal's Doughnuts. "Morning," Hank said cheerfully from behind the counter. However, he was a little confused by the huge grin on Jake's face. "Good morning, Jake!" Tinker called from the back. "Good morning, Mister Tinker," Jake said happily. Hank had expected Jake to be in a more somber mood. He and Tinker had called to check on him, and from what they had gathered from their conversation with him over the phone, Jake had more than likely lost his job.

"Well, someone's in a good mood," Hank said to Jake from behind the counter. "You mean someone's in a good mood for having just lost their job," Jake said. "So they fired you all the way, no suspension?" Hank asked. "Nope, no suspension. They fired me fired me all the way. Get me my usual and join me in a booth, and I'll tell you why I'm in such a good mood," Jake said.

Hank grabbed Jake two Boston creams and a large coffee and went to join him in their accustomed booth. "I'm sorry they let you go," Hank said as he placed Jake's order on the table and sat down across from him. "Well, it's not your fault. You didn't twist my arm and make me look for Miss Adams, and believe me, there were other factors at play as well.

"Sure, my supervisors were not pleased that a "patrol officer" had been snooping around a missing persons case and then managed to get himself captured in the process on top of it. Plus, I also managed to total yet another patrol unit earlier that day. Not to mention that this was not the first time that I've broken the rules a little.

"Let's just say my previous record was not all bright and shiny, to say the least. At any rate, fuck'em and feed'em fish heads, I say! I'm hanging out my own shingle, and it's gonna read "Bayside Private Investigations," Jake said, grinning from ear to ear as he pantomimed the imagery of the words in the air with his hands.

"That sounds like a good plan to me. When are you going into business?" Hank asked. "I have my license in my pocket now. I've been getting things in order for a while now. I guess you could say I was reading the writing on the wall," Jake said. Just then, the entrance bell over the door rang.

"Good morning, Abbie. Can I get you some coffee," Tinker called from behind the counter. "Good morning TInker. Yes Sir, please, that would be great," she said. "Good morning, Abbie," Hank called as he and Jake stepped from the booth. "This is Mister Jake Stallard," Hank said to Abbie by way of introduction. He then turned to Jake and said. "Jake, this is Miss Abigale Adams."

"Miss Adams, I was hoping that I would get to meet you. I wanted to thank you for your help at the warehouse. I don't think it would have ended too well for me otherwise," Jake said. "You're welcome. You were there looking for me in the first place, and no, Miss Adams, Abbie will do just fine," she said, smiling back at Jake.

"Would y'all like to have a seat," Hank said, waving a hand at the booth. "Sure, but only for a minute," Abbie said as the three of them slid into the booth. "I can't stay long. I need to go by Sugarpie's to pick up my paycheck. Then, after I get it cashed, I need to go pick up a new phone. After that, I was thinking about going to check out some of my father's favorite bars to see if anyone knows where he might've gone," Abbie said.

"Is that right? Which bars is it that your old man likes to frequent? If you don't mind me asking?" Jake asked Abbie over the top of his coffee cup before taking a sip. "I Don't mind at all," Abbie said. "He sometimes goes to the Drunk Monk Tavern on Airline and sometimes to Bernie's on Third Street. I thought I'd check those first just to make sure, but his usual spot is The Drunken Shark on North Shoreline Boulevard. He has some friends there, and I was thinking that he might've mentioned something to one of them."

A look of concern crossed over Jake's face, but he shrugged it away. "That's a rough place, but I know you can handle yourself. Still, I don't have anything going on today, so if you wanted, I could give you a ride," he said. "Well, if you aren't too busy, that would be great. Plus, it'll save me from public transit," Abbie said. "Don't mind at all. We'll leave after coffee," Jake said as he took a bite out of his Boston cream doughnut.

Later that day, Jake could hear Lynard Skynard's "Gimme Three Steps" issuing from inside the bar as he and Abbie walked up the ramp to the entrance door of the wood frame building that sat just off the beach. To the right of the entrance ramp was some outdoor seating, consisting of some picnic tables under a simple corrugated tin roof that had been added onto the side of the building.

Right now, it was too early and too hot, but Jake knew that later, these tables in the front of the bar would be packed with party-going beach revelers. The inside of the bar would be packed as well, along with all the tables under the thatched umbrellas that sat on the back deck of the bar facing the bay. Jake knew this bar well, and one of the things that he would not miss about working for the CCPD was all the late-night calls to The Drunken Shark.

"Abbie!" the bartender called out with excitement. He recognized her as soon as she and Jake had come through the door. "Huey," she called back as she ran to give him a hug over the bar. "Well, well, well, looks who's here," a voice called from a table to Jake's left. Jake turned and seated at the table were three men.

The man seated in the middle definitely showed signs that he was running powder-assisted. Jake had seen it many times before while working patrol. He could see his dilated pupils and his runny nose, which he repetitively wiped with the back of his hand before quickly placing it back under the table each time.

As Jake stood there, he identified some of the other symptoms of cocaine use in the man as well. Including excitability, boost in confidence, risky behavior, and especially running of the mouth.

"And without his tin star," the cokehead continued, "Or his taser, or his gun, or his back-up. Why it's Officer Stallard, Oops, I mean mister Stallard, since they canned your ass, ain't that right?" the cokehead said. "You're partially right," Jake answered. "I don't have my tin star, They asked for it back, and that's a damn shame because I really wish that I had it right now so that I could shove all six points of it up your ass.

"You're also right about the taser, but I never liked it anyhow, but you're wrong about my gun," Jake said as he pulled his short-sleeved button-down shirt open. On his left side in a shoulder rig, Jake's 1911 Colt .45 lay resting on top of his white tank top.

"I like my gun. I liked it so much that I went ahead and got my Private Investigators License just so that I could carry it everywhere, even in establishments such as this one, which earns over 51 percent of its annual revenue from alcohol sales.

"That means that if I put a bullet through your low-life dirtbag forehead, my old friend and fishing buddy John, or Detective Kilgore, I should say, is gonna come down here, and after I show him whatever weapon that is your fingers have been caressing under the table there, he's gonna rule the whole thing as a justifiable homicide.

"Hell, I won't even have to do any paperwork like I used to, so either you get both of your hands out on the table where I can see them, or you hurry up and pull that weapon." Jake watched as the sweat ran down the crazed addict's face. His buddies slowly placed their hands on the table, but his pride had been hurt.

Jake watched in slow motion as the coke-fueled junkie's whole body stiffened as he held his breath and yanked at the revolver in his waistband, but he had been too slow. The sweat running down his face had told Jake something. The fact that he had gone a whole twenty seconds without wiping his nose with the back of his hand had told him even more.

The instant the cokehead held his breath, Jake's Colt 1911 was in his hand so fast it seemed to Abbie as if it had appeared there magically. The moment the cokehead's revolver's barrel cleared his waistband, Jake sent a .45 slug right through the center of his forehead just like he said he would. The cokehead stared blankly for a moment. Then his revolver clattered to the floor as he fell face-first into the table.

"So, is this what I can expect on a regular basis now that you're out on your own?" Detective John Kilgore of the CCPD homicide division asked Jake with a smile. Just like Jake had said, Detective Kilgore, who Jake knew worked days, had been called in to investigate the scene. "I sure as hell hope not," Jake said.

"Well, I've interviewed the other two witnesses," Detective Kilgore said, referring to the cokehead's two buddies. "All I need now is a statement from each one of you," he said as he indicated to Huey, Abbie, and Jake with a sweeping motion of his right hand, in which he held his pen. He questioned each one privately in turn and took their statements down on the pad, which he held in his left hand.

"Jake, you already know there'll be an investigation by the licensing commission, but it looks like a justifiable homicide to me, a simple case of self-defense, so I'm gonna head on back to the precinct so that I can get the paperwork filled out," Detective Kilgore said.

"Sounds good, John. Are we still gonna hit Lake Mathis this weekend?" Jake asked. "You bet! Those bass don't stand a chance," Detective Kilgore said over his shoulder as he walked out the door.

After the detective's departure, Jake turned around and walked up to the bar. "Sorry about the mess," He said to Huey as he slid one of his freshly printed brand-new business cards across the bar. "Money's kinda tight right now. I'm just getting started, but if you ever need my services, I owe you one on the house," he said. Behind him, the coroner was placing the cokehead's body in a bag while the EMTs waited.

"Bayside Private Investigations, huh," Huey said as he read Jake's card, "Well, thanks for the card. I'll hold onto it. You never know, but don't worry about the mess. That guy had it coming. Besides, I've known Abbie here a long time, and any friend of hers is a friend of mine," he said as he shoved Jake's card into his shirt pocket.

"My dad's been coming in here since I was in grade school," Abbie said to Jake in explanation. "Well, he used to," Huey said, "but I haven't seen him in over a year. He ran his bar tab up sky high and then disappeared."

Chapter Twenty-Nine

Camping

The gamblers that wagered Harry would not leave Rattle Snake Cave had lost their money. He had made it back to the canyon campsite a little after midday. It had taken him a little longer to scale the canyon wall with the added weight on his back. In addition to the 45 pounds of cocaine, there was also the weight of four large rattlesnakes that he had killed in the cave, the smallest of which was at least three and a half feet long.

He also the weight of the water that he had gathered from the river along with the fresh canteen of water that had been left with the bundle of cocaine. The instructions on the canteen left with the cocaine had read, "Go back to cairn at canyon campsite."

Back at the top of the canyon wall, Harry went outside of the campsite to where he had stashed Dario's pack with his extra gear. He emptied his gear from the pack and quickly replaced it with the cocaine, then he stashed the pack back in the rocks. Next, he went to the cairn at the edge of the canyon wall and retrieved the single canteen that had been left there by Enrique's horsemen while he was in the bottom of the canyon.

The instructions on the canteen read, "Follow trail back to CHIH-76 checkpoint." *Pretty straightforward. They seem to be taking me back the same way I came,* he thought. He took a long drink from the canteen, then set about building a fire in the camp's firepit. Once he had a good fire going, he put some of the river water he had collected into Dario's large stainless steel water bottle and set it in the fire to boil.

Next, he found a large flat rock to work on and butchered all four of the rattlesnakes that he had killed at the cave. He then gathered nopales, prepared nopalitos, and placed them in the skillet with some of the rattlesnake meat. He placed the skillet in the coals of the campfire and checked on the river water he had set to boil water. As each bottle of water came to a boil and was purified, he would transfer it to a canteen and set another bottle of river water into the campfire to boil. Dehydration was no longer an issue.

The rattlesnake meat that didn't go into the skillet he shoved onto sticks that he propped up on rocks in the smoke of the fire. When the nopalitos and rattlesnake meat in the skillet was done, he doused it liberally with hot sauce and ate heartily.

He was done with his dinner by early afternoon. The river water had been purified, and his gear packed. With everything ready, he positioned his camera so that it would stay on him as he slept and settled in to get some rest.

Again, Harry was awakened by the sound of the low battery alarm on his POV camera. How long it had been going off, he had no idea, but it was now sunset. He estimated that he had slept somewhere around six hours. He changed the battery, put on his gear, and made his way to the campfire. Luckily, his rattlesnake meat had remained undisturbed as he slept and was now well-smoked on the sticks.

As Harry was removing the chunks of meat from the sticks and putting them into Dario's stainless water bottle, he began to think about how that night's moon would be waxing well over half-full. Visibility the night before had been good, and tonight's would be even better.

I could make a push for Dario's cave now in the cool of the night and make it there by nine or ten in the morning, he thought. Anxious to see his daughter, he collected the cocaine, packed it and his gear, and started to hike back up the mountain pass.

The sun had completely set by the time Harry left the campsite, but as predicted, visibility was fairly good thanks to the moonlight. He picked his way along the familiar trail through the mountain pass without incident, and within a few hours, he was standing by the cairn at the CHIH-76 checkpoint. There, he retrieved the canteen from next to the cairn, and with the help of one of Dario's disposable lighters, he was able to see that the instructions simply read, "63 degrees."

Harry set the compass up as Carlos had shown him to do for use in nighttime or low-visibility situations. He would have to check it periodically until there was enough daylight to shoot a reference point. He turned his body until the compass's indicator line fell at 63 degrees on the compass's dial and then preset the bezel for easier nighttime reference. *180 degrees opposite of the direction I took to get here,* he thought as he walked out into the desert.

Later that morning, Hank and Abbie arrived at Catfish's Bait Shop and Trailer Park to find Catfish and Skillet on the covered deck behind the bait shop having their morning coffee. They were seated at a picnic-style table that overlooked the beautiful Lake Mathis.

Catfish noticed Hank and Abbie as they rounded the corner to the back of the bait shop and greeted them. "Hey, good morning! I see you two made it back," he said. "Good morning, Yes sir, we did," Hank said. "This here is the gentleman I told you about," Catfish said as he pointed across the table.

"Is that right? Well, good morning to you as well then, Mister Skillet," Hank said. Skillet replied with an enthusiastic, "Good morning!" and raised his coffee cup in salute.

"I'm Hank, and this, here is Harry's daughter Abbie. I suppose Catfish told you why we're here," Hank said. "Yes, he sure did, and I'm sure sorry, your dad's missing, ma'am. He's sure enough a friendly sort of fella, was always nice to folks around here. I hope he turns up okay," Skillet said to Abbie. "Me too. We were wondering if maybe he said something to you about where he was going or if maybe you saw or heard something that might give us a clue to his whereabouts. Any little thing might be helpful," she said.

"No, Ma'am, like I was telling Catfish here. I didn't get to talk to him beforehand. I was gonna let him know that I was going to go stay down at Lake Texana for a while, you know, southwest of Ganado, but he was already gone in the morning when I got up and ta' movin' around," Skillet said. "Was he here the day before?" Abbie asked. "Sure was. I saw him that evening, but when I got up the next morning, he was gone."

As Abbie was questioning Skillet, Hank stood and watched the people fishing from the pier as he listened to the waves crashing along the shore. "Night anglers!" He suddenly exclaimed." The sound of the waves had reminded him of the last time he had gone to King's Beach and the night anglers that had been wade fishing there.

"Catfish, do y'all have many people fishing here at night?" he asked. "Sure do. I leave the lights on the pier on all night, and it's usually very busy, especially in the summer months, and there are always quite a few boats out on the water as well," he said. "I see... I think we've been questioning the wrong people," Hank said.

"Sorry, I didn't think to tell you that earlier," Catfish apologized. "Yeah, me too. I didn't think of that either," Skillet said. "No worries, gentleman. Catfish, would you mind if we questioned some of your guests tonight?" Hank asked. "Not at all," Catfish said with a smile. "I wish y'all luck," Skillet added. "Well, we better get some rest," Hank said to Abbie, "It may be a long night."

While Hank and Abbie rested in preparation for their night of investigation at Catfish's Bait Shop and Trailer Park, Harry continued to slowly make his trek across the desert. Under the weight of the cocaine, his progress had been much slower than he had estimated.

Finally, a little after midday, he made it to the dirt road checkpoint below Dario's cave. Wary of unexpected vehicles coming down the road, he opted to stash the cocaine in the cave before returning to retrieve the canteen from beside the cairn.

The heat of the day was fierce, and he was fatigued from his trek under the weight of the cocaine. He worked quickly to dig up the canteen buried next to the cairn so that he could hurry back to the shelter of the cave. On his way back up the trail, the low-battery alarm on his POV camera began to buzz annoyingly.

In the cave, Harry pulled the thorn bush in behind himself to block the entrance and then swapped out the dying battery for a fresh one to get rid of the incessant low-battery alarm. He then made a meal of smoked rattlesnake meat doused with hot sauce. After he finished his meal, he set up his camera so that it would face him, and then he laid down to rest until after the heat of the midday had passed.

Several hours later, at Catfish's Bait Shop and Trailer Park, Abbie woke up to the sound of her father's alarm clock blaring. She reached over, turned it off, and checked the time. *Seven-thirty,* she thought groggily. As the sleep left her brain, she began to realize that it was seven-thirty in the afternoon, not seven-thirty in the morning, and then she remembered that they had elected to use her father's RV to catch up on some sleep before going out to question the night anglers.

She jumped out of bed, opened her father's bedroom door, stepped into the living room section of the RV, and called Hank's name to wake him up. Hank, asleep on the sofa, paid her no mind.

"Hank!" She finally yelled loud enough to get his attention. "Huh, what," he muttered, still half asleep. "The night anglers, we have to go interview the night anglers," she said. "Oh, yeah, that's right," He said as he swung his feet to the floor and stared at them momentarily until he was awake enough to move.

"I guess we need to start at the pier," he said. "I hope it's not, but like you said, It could be a long night. We better take some coffee to go," Abbie said as she fished through her father's kitchen cabinets for the makings. "Sounds good," Hank said.

They approached the pier a little after dark. At the very end, an angler sitting in a lawn chair had one line in the water and was busy baiting his second hook when Hank and Abbie approached him.

"Any luck?" Hank asked casually. "Not yet, but I'm just gettin' started," the angler said. "I'm Hank, and this is Abbie," Hank said in an easygoing manner. "Howdy, y'all can call me Tommy. Nice to meet you folks," he said.

"Abbie's father lives here in the trailer park. His name is Harry. Do you know him?" Hank asked. "Can't say as that I do," Tommy the angler said as he cast his second line into the water.

"Well, he went missing sometime late last Wednesday night or early Thursday morning. Do you remember if you were on the pier that night?" Hank asked. "I'm out on the pier every night, but I don't remember that particular evening," Tommy said.

"Well, anything that you might have seen or heard could be useful," Hank said. "No, sorry, that was a week ago. That's a little far back for me," Tommy said. "Yes, Sir, I understand," Hank said sympathetically, "Last question, Harry would have been driving a dark blue 2004 Cadilac Coupe Deville. Notice anything like that coming or going?" he asked.

"No, no, besides, I wouldn't have been able to see much from out here on the end of the pier anyway," Tommy said as he pointed back up the pier. Hank followed his finger in the direction he was pointing to see that visibility from the pier to the road was mostly blocked by camper trailers and trees.

"You'll probably want to talk to Floyd," Tommy said. "He fishes up there closer to the road. He might have seen something," Tommy, the night angler, said as he recast his line out into Lake Mathis. "Yes, definitely, we would like to speak with Floyd. Will he be here later?" Abbie asked. "He's fishin' from a boat tonight with friends. They left here earlier, but yeah, they always drop him off back here at the pier," Tommy said.

"About what time is that usually?" Abbie asked. "Depends on how the fish are bitin'," Tommy said with a shrug. "You wouldn't happen to have a phone number for Floyd, would you?" Hank asked. "Sure do, but he keeps it turned off when he's fishin', says it scares the fish, but I think he just doesn't like to be bothered when he's out fishin'," Tommy said.

After Tommy, the night angler, attempted to call Floyd a few times, Hank and Abbie thanked him for his help, left their phone numbers, and went on to look for more possible witnesses. As the night dragged on, they continued to interview people at the pier, along the lake banks, and in the other common areas of the trailer park to no avail.

A little after midnight, Hank's cell rang, "Hello," he answered. "Hello, this is Tommy," the voice on the other end replied. "The fish just weren't bitten', and Floyd's already back. He's waiting here at the pier to talk to you guys, and he says he saw Harry leave." "We'll be there immediately," Hank said. A few minutes later, as Hank and Abbie made their way back to the pier, they could see that Tommy and Floyd, the anglers, were still under the lights, fishing off the end of the pier.

"So, Floyd, Tommy mentioned that you saw Harry leave the trailer park. Is that right?" Hank asked Floyd after Tommy had made the introductions. "That's right, I live just a couple of spaces down from Harry. Sometimes, we'll bring stuff back from town for one another. Save a trip, you know.

"Anyways, I was fishing, and I recognized the headlights of his car coming through the trees. So, I hot-footed it up to the road and stood under the streetlights next to the bait shop entrance to flag him down. I was gonna see if I could get him to pick me up a sixer on his way back from wherever he was going. Only he didn't even pay me any mind. He drove right past and never saw me. I just figured he was in a hurry or something," Floyd said.

"Could you tell if anyone was with him?" Hank asked. "No, he was alone. It was dark, but I got a good look inside the car when he drove under the streetlights. I mean, if someone was in there, they would've had to be lying down on the floorboard or something for me to miss them," Floyd answered.

"About what time would you say this all happened?" Hank asked. "Mmmm, It was around ten o'clock, I reckon," Floyd answered. "Did you see which way he went?" Hank asked. "Sure," Floyd said, "He went north toward Mathis."

Chapter Thirty

Texas Interstate Thirty-Seven

Hank and Abbie had thanked Tommy and Floyd and were walking their way back to Harry's RV. Hank was deep in thought as they walked, but finally, he spoke. "There aren't any major intersections between here and Mathis, are there?" he asked. "Don't think so," Abbie said. "Well, it might be a long shot, but I think we should take a ride. I want to check something out."

A little after one in the morning, Hank pulled the Impala out onto Interstate 37 and headed north. Less than twenty minutes later, he and Abbie pulled into Mathis, "The Small town on the Big Lake," as the locals were fond of saying.

Hank drove to the intersection in the middle of town and pulled into the Alamo fuel station on the corner. "I think we should ask about your dad in here, just on the off chance that he stopped for fuel," he said.

234

"Okay, then will check the others," Abbie said as they exited the Impala. "Not likely, if he stopped in Mathis for fuel, he stopped here," Hank said.

"There's a gas station on every corner of this intersection. Why this one?" Abbie asked. "Because I went through your father's bills on the table. This was the only fuel company that he had a credit card for, and he made a good deal of his charges at this particular station," Hank said.

"Why didn't we check here earlier?" Abbie asked. "I didn't think of it till we talked to Floyd. Your father could have gone in any number of directions from the trailer park. I really didn't know which way to look, but if he went this way like Floyd said he did, then there is a good chance he stopped here," Hank said as he opened the door to the gas station's convenience store.

The cashier's counter was to their left as they entered. To their right, in a row along the wall, were four eight-liner gambling machines, only one of which was in use. Hank pulled his cell phone from his pocket and approached the cashier.

"Excuse me, my name is Hank, and this is Abbie," he said as he showed the cashier Harry's image on his cell phone, "We were wondering if you might recognize the gentleman in this picture. He is missing, and his daughter here is very worried about him," Hank said as he gestured toward Abbie, "There is a chance that he may have come through here a week ago. It would have been Wednesday evening, sometime after ten," He said, still holding the phone up for the cashier to see.

The cashier gingerly took Hank's phone and scrutinized the image for a few seconds, then shook her head no. "Sorry, I don't recognize him, but I may not have been here. Let me check the schedule," She said as she walked to a desk behind the counter.

"Yeah, I was working that night. Sorry, I didn't see anything," The cashier said to Hank from behind the counter. "What about the security cameras," Abbie asked. "A week is too long ago. They would have been deleted by now," The cashier answered Abbie apologetically.

Just then, the man at the eight-liner machine must have won something. Hank heard him jump up and cheer his good fortune. *At least someone's having some luck,* he thought.

Feeling like they had reached a dead end, Hank and Abbie thanked the cashier for her help, left their contact information, and started to walk out. As they walked to the door, the guy's luck at the eight-liner machine ran out. "Dang-it!" He shouted and then stamped his foot, drawing Hank's attention just as he and Abbie were walking past.

Hank glanced at the gentleman briefly as he opened the door for Abbie. He then walked through the door behind her but stopped dead in his tracks on the other side as it swung shut behind him. "What's up?" Abbie asked, confused by his sudden stop. Hank retrieved his cell phone from his pocket and pulled up the image of Harry and his wife. He then zoomed in on Harry's wristwatch in the photo and showed it to Abbie.

"Yeah, so what? It's my dad's wristwatch. Actually, it was my grandfather's 1965 Seiko Diver's watch, to be exact, so what?" Abbie said. "Well, without drawing too much attention to yourself, why don't you peek in through the window there and look at the watch on that fella's wrist that's sitting in there playing that eight-liner machine," Hank said. Abbie covertly moved to the window, cupped her hands to the glass, and peeked through at the man's wrist.

"Hey, that's my Popo's watch," She screamed as she reached for the handle on the convenience store's front door in a fit of rage. Hank reached out, grabbed her collar, pulled her back, and stood in her way. "Whoa, easy there, missy," he whispered, "Sad to say, but he might have come by your grandfather's watch, honestly. Also, if you kick his ass and take his watch, I don't think he'll be willing to give us much information about how he came by it. Just stay here and let me handle this," Hank said as he turned to enter the convenience store's door.

Hank entered the convenience store, turned left, and walked past the man playing the eight-liner machine. "Hey, how's it going," He said to the player as he walked by on his way to the drink coolers at the back of the store. He had chosen this route intentionally so that he would have the opportunity to speak to the man.

"It's going like a self-cleaning oven, baby," The player answered as he continued playing the eight-liner. Hank grabbed a couple of Dr. Peppers from the cooler and turned around. "How's that? I don't follow," He said as he moved to one of the center aisles.

"Do you have a self-cleaning oven at your house?" The eight-liner player asked. "We do," Hank said. "When was the last time you worried about cleaning it?" "Never," Hank said with a laugh. "Exactly, no worries," The player said. "Well, that's what I like to hear," Hank said as he walked up the aisle, grabbed a couple of moon pies from a shelf, and set them on the counter along with the sodas.

The cashier added up the items on the counter, and Hank handed her some cash. After he had paid the total and collected his change, he walked toward the door where the player sat at the eight-liner machine, "I'm Hank," He said as he stuck out his hand.

The player turned from his favorite eight-liner machine, grabbed Hank's hand, and began to pump it up and down vigorously. "Nice to meet you there, Hank! I'm Slick Willie, and any hair you see on the top of my head is purely your imagination," He said as he laughed and then pretended to run his fingers through the imaginary hair on the top of his head.

"Say, you haven't seen this fella around here, have you?" Hank asked, holding up his cell phone with Harry's image on the screen. "He went missing about a week ago. That's his daughter out there, and she's very worried about him," Hank said as he pointed outside the window to Abbie, who was still standing out in the parking lot.

"Hey, that's my boy Harry. Yeah, he came by here last week. Me and some of the fellas was shootin' dice on the side of the building here. He said he needed to raise some cash if he could. He didn't have the buy-in, so we let him put up his watch," Slick-Willie said as he lifted his arm to show Hank the 1965 Seiko Diver's watch.

"Looks like he didn't do too well that night," Hank said. "No, he didn't, but he'll be back. I told him I'd sell it back to him or give him a chance to win it," Slick Willie said with a laugh.

"He didn't mention where he was headed, did he?" Hank asked. "Sure he did. Said he was headed to some town called Perdido," Slick Willie said. "Are you sure?" Hank asked. "Yeah, I'm sure. When he lost his watch, he stood up, cursed, and said, "I hope my luck is better in Perdido," Slick Willie said.

"Where the hell is Perdido, Texas," Hank asked. "You got me. I never heard of it, but when he took off, he left that way towards San Antone if that helps," Slick Willie said as he pointed to North Interstate Thirty-Seven.

"It sure does help. It helps a lot," Hank said as he quickly grabbed a Texas road map and paid for it at the counter. "Thanks, buddy," He said to Slick Willie as he hit the door.

Outside the convenience store, Abbie was waiting with her arms crossed, "What's up with my dad's watch," She asked impatiently. "Your father lost his watch in a dice game, but Slick Willie's just holding it till we can come back with the money, but that's not important. What is important is that he told me that your father said that he was headed to Perdido, Texas," Hank said as he quickly walked to the Impala.

"Slick Willie, who's that, and where the hell is Perdido, Texas?" Abbie shouted at Hank over the roof of the Impala before getting in. "Slick Willie is the gentleman in the convenience store that is holding your grandfather's watch, and I don't know where the hell Perdido, Texas is, but you're gonna find it on that map inside that bag," Hank said as he pulled the Impala out of the gas station and onto Interstate-37.

Hank and Abbie hadn't made it very far before Abbie realized that there was no such place as Perdido listed on the Rand Mcnally Texas road map. As a last-ditch effort, Hank continued driving north on Thirty-Seven till he found a large truck stop about twenty minutes outside of Mathis where Interstate Thirty-Seven and Texas Highway Fifty-Nine intersected.

At the truck stop, Hank walked in and approached several truck drivers who were seated in a group and engaged in conversation. "Does anyone know the directions to Perdido, Texas?" he asked. Only one truck driver, a driver for a fuel delivery service, had ever heard of it. "Yes, Sir, I can tell you how to get there. Ain't much out there, but I deliver to their one and only fuel station occasionally," he said.

Hank asked the truck driver to mark it on his road map. When the driver saw the road map, he laughed and said, "That's your problem right there. You won't find it on that map. Perdido isn't on any map, but if it were, it would be right here," He said, marking an X on the map. "I'm gonna need some fuel," Hank said as he looked at where the driver marked the X on the map.

Chapter Thirty-One

Smuggler's Run

Harry awoke to the sound of the low-battery alarm on his POV camera. "What? I just changed that," He said as he groggily rose up to one elbow. It was then that he realized that he had slept through the entire night. He had intended to head out that afternoon when it had cooled down and make a push for Hacienda Ramirez. *Oh well, it cannot be helped now,* He thought as he changed the POV camera's battery.

After he swapped out the low battery for a fresh one and had repacked the cocaine into his rucksack, he hiked up the trail to where Dario lay in his rock crypt. The camera drone made its first pass of the day as Harry stood next to Dario's grave.

As the morning light broke, Harry thought about how much he owed Dario Ignacio Agerico Cholula, the poor man who had packed everything he needed but luck. "Your misfortune saved my life, so at least you didn't die for nothin'," Harry whispered.

After he had said goodbye to Dario, he continued up the mountain pass. When he began to hike down the mountain pass on the other side, he made sure to stop at vantage points along the trail to rest and watch for any human activity, especially along the river's banks below. With the cargo he was now carrying, it was crucial that he avoid all contact with people, whether they be Cartel members, federales, or civilians.

He carefully made his way down the trail and collected the canteen at the checkpoint next to the dry creek bed. The instructions read, "Cross the river at the same location, follow instructions left at river checkpoint," A coordinate of 70 degrees was included, but Harry didn't need it. The river crossing was less than half a mile away, and he could already hear the water rushing over the rocks at the shallow river crossing from where he stood.

In less than half an hour, Harry was retrieving the canteen from beside the cairn at the river checkpoint on the U.S. side of the border. The instructions on the canteen read, "98 degrees cairn off trail at gap." *Gap, what the hell are they talking about?* He thought as he grabbed the compass that hung around his neck.

Harry stood directly behind the cairn, flipped the compass open, brought it up to his cheek, and shot the 98-degree azimuth. The sighting wire of the compass fell on a small gap between a large mesa and a mountain. "Oh, I see," he said. The gap was to the south of the same large mesa that he had used as a vantage point earlier when searching for the best path to the river.

The land between the river checkpoint and the small gap to the south of the mesa appeared to be mostly sand dunes and small hills. This would be challenging terrain with the added weight of his cargo but nowhere near as difficult as the route he had previously taken to the north of the mesa. He walked toward the gap until he crested the top of a large hill.

At the bottom of the hill was a two-lane road. He quickly laid down and took cover behind the hilltop. He followed the road with his eyes to the north until it disappeared into the mountains, where he previously had the misfortune of crossing the road through a rock cut.

Here, the road was open, and he would be able to cross it without having to climb down one side and up the other of a rock cut. The only inconvenience here would be getting spotted by the border patrol or state troopers. He looked across the road and noticed the small hills on the other side. *I better get across this road and out of sight on the other side of those hills as quickly as possible,* he thought.

He lay on the hillside and surveyed the road for a few moments. A truck passed by and continued on its way south until it disappeared over a hill. As soon as the truck was out of sight, Harry struggled to his feet under the weight of the cocaine as the camera drone buzzed in close, tracking him from above as he scrambled down the hill and then sprinted across the road, his legs burning under the weight of the cocaine.

On the other side of the road, he ran up and over a hill, collapsing on the other side. There he lay, panting, his lungs starved for oxygen. No one had seen him on the road, and the gamblers who had wagered otherwise groaned at their loss while those who bet otherwise cheered.

After Harry caught his breath, he crossed through a ravine at the bottom of the hill and started walking toward the gap on the south side of the mesa. Once he finally made it through the gap, he looked to the far north and could see the Chiso Mountain range with its foothills spilling out into the desert. To the east, he could see the small mountain with his "Lone Ranger" rock formation that he had used as a reference point earlier. Beyond that, on a mountaintop in the far distance, he could see Hacienda Ramirez.

He found the cairn marking the checkpoint just off the trail on the other side of the gap. The instructions on the canteen read, "102 degrees, Mesa de Angelita two miles south of Hacienda Ramirez, cairn on top of mesa." *Mesa de Angelita, that's the mesa where I'll drop the coke off!* Harry thought as he grabbed the compass hanging from his neck.

From the vantage of his current elevation, Harry could see a small mesa to the south of the Hacienda Ramirez compound and highly suspected it to be the one. He shot the 102-degree azimuth to be certain. The sight wire of his compass fell directly on the small mesa that he had suspected. *That's it, the last mesa...* Harry thought as he stared at it in the distance.

There were really no highly recognizable land features between his current location and the mesa, and it was quite possible that he could lose sight of it as he traversed up and down the ravines, hills, and sand dunes that lay between him and his last checkpoint. *I'll just have to keep an eye on my compass when I can't see it,* Harry thought as he struck out for Mesa de Angelita.

Mesa de Angelita was an extremely small mesa on the outskirts of Enrique's ranch. At about five hundred feet in elevation and named for Erique's Grandmother, it sat about two miles south of the Hacienda Ramirez compound and about three-quarters of a mile north of Texas Farm to Market 170.

The cairn had been easy enough to spot, and Harry retrieved the canteen. Exhausted and dehydrated by his cocaine-laden trek to the top of the mesa, he drained it in one long drink. The instructions written on the side in the now familiar script of permanent marker read, "Locate rock formation at south edge of mesa, place product in bottom of crevice, return to fountain in courtyard."

Harry found the rock formation at the south edge of the mesa. He removed the cocaine from his rucksack and placed it deep down inside the crevice and was relieved beyond comprehension to finally be rid of it. He looked down from the top of the mesa to the barbwire fence that separated Enrique's ranch from FM 170 and figured someone would be coming down the farm-to-market road shortly to retrieve the cocaine.

He then looked to the southwest toward Big Bend State Park and remembered the family vacations he had taken at the stunningly beautiful park as a child and the ones he had later taken there with his own family with much sentimentality. He resolved that if he survived this ordeal, he would somehow get the old RV running again and bring his daughter back there for another vacation as soon as possible.

He then turned his attention to Hacienda Ramirez in the west. He had been able to see the mountain-top hacienda in the far distance ever since he had crested over the mountain pass and had wanted nothing more than to get there and settle with Enrique. Once he had settled with Enrique, he could be on his way to reconcile things with his daughter. Now that he had rid himself of the rucksack full of cocaine and wouldn't be getting killed or going to federal prison, that might be possible. He took one last look at the horizon from the top of the last mesa before he made his way down and headed off in the direction of Hacienda Ramirez.

The trek from Mesa de Angelita to Hacienda Ramirez had seemed to take forever, but the Spanish-style mansion was now less than a mile away. As Harry got closer, he could see the trail that he had missed in the darkness that would have taken him safely down the mountain instead of over the cliff face. He could also see the open gates of the west courtyard wall from where he had started his journey.

Less than a half-hour later, Harry walked through those open gates at the west wall of the Hacienda Ramirez courtyard to be welcomed by the sound of a live mariachi band and much fanfare. Enrique's entire family had become Harry's endeared fans early on in his struggle, especially Enrique's grandmother. The family had even gone so far as to start having all their meals in the casino so that they could watch Harry's adventure while they ate and drank at the bar. Also in the crowd applauding Harry's return were Joey "Two Cards" Lombardi and Joy Ride. Joey "Two Cards" Whistling loudly and screaming, "Bravo, Bravo!" While clapping his hands loudly.

"Okay, Okay, everybody quiet, please. We still have business to discuss," Enrique said cheerfully through his microphone as he took center stage next to the doctor's scale that stood in front of the now somewhat subdued mariachis, who continued to play albeit quietly in the background.

At that point, Alejandro and Carlos escorted Harry to the stage. Alejandro helped him to remove the camera equipment and set it aside. Harry was then ordered to strip down to his underwear for the scale once more. This time, however, they held a large towel up in front of him for modesty.

Enrique and the crowd watched patiently as Carlos balanced the scale. He gave the small balance weight on the triple beam a final little bump, and the scale slowly zeroed. Enrique read the weight and turned to face the crowd.

"174 and a half pounds," He exclaimed into his microphone. Enrique then covered his microphone with his hand and consulted privately with his little sister Esperanza, who was also his head cashier and turf accountant. While Enrique conferred with his little sister, Carlos gave Harry the box containing his belongings, and he got dressed behind the towel.

Enrique, obviously very excited by what his little sister had told him, turned to the crowd. "Ladies and Gentlemen, you are not going to believe this, but the winner of the Desert Gauntlet, Weight Pool, as well as the Winner of the Desert Gauntlet Jackpot, is the one and the same, Miss Joy Ride!" Enrique said excitedly into his microphone in a manner that put Harry in mind of a baseball announcer, exclaiming the winner of the World Series.

"She bet on you to make it all the way, Harry. Can you believe that shit?" Enrique whispered into Harry's ear as he covered the microphone once again for privacy. Enrique then gestured for his little sister, Esperanza, who had been counting out the money, to come on stage. "How much did she win altogether there, Esperanza?" Enrique asked his little sister as she took the stage with a small black bag over her shoulder.

"I just finished adding it up, and minus the Casino's cut, of course, counting the weight pool plus the Desert Gauntlet Jackpot, Miss Joy Ride won a total of 68,648 dollars and 32 cents!" Esperanza exclaimed into the microphone.

The crowd cheered as Joy jumped up and down with excitement. "Whoa! 68 large, nice! Come on up here and get your money, Miss Ride!" Enrique said as he gave Joy a gesture to come up on stage. Joy ran up on stage excitedly as everyone applauded. On stage, Esperanza handed her the bag of money as Enrique placed his arm over her shoulders.

"So how does it feel to win over 68 thousand dollars, Miss Ride?" Enrique asked Joy through the microphone and then held it down in front of her face as he waited for an answer. "Feels fucking awesome," She exclaimed into the microphone as she held the money up over her head in victory.

"So tell me, now that you have all that cash, what are you going to do with it?" Enrique asked next. "I'm going to go back to school and start a new life," Joy answered with tears in her eyes. "Awe, That's very nice. I wish you all the luck, Miss Ride, last question. What made you risk taking the long shot that this man would make it out of the desert when everyone else bet on him to die out there?" Once again, Enrique held the microphone in front of Joy and waited for an answer.

"I don't know, I just saw something in him, I guess. I don't know what or why, but something just made me feel like I could believe in him," Joy said into the microphone. "Believe in me, you don't even know me," Harry said in a state of bewilderment. "No, no, I don't, but I'd like to, and I got 68 thousand dollars in this bag, so why don't you let me buy you a cup of coffee down the road somewhere, and we can work on that," Joy said into the microphone.

Enrique moved the microphone to Harry for his answer. Harry was completely dumbfounded. He had not expected this and was unprepared. Slowly, he leaned toward the microphone and stammered out, "Yes…yes, Ma'am…I think I'd like that very much." After hearing Harry's answer, the crowd roared with approval, completely overwhelmed by the surprise happy ending.

Off stage, Joy stood next to Harry as Enrique's niece Maria, the family doctor, took his blood pressure and gave him a quick exam. "You're a little dehydrated, but I don't think you'll need an IV. If we were in a hospital, I would probably give you one just because, however, we're not, so drink this," She said, handing him a sports drink and two large bottles of water.

"You probably would have been in really bad shape if you hadn't gotten the sodium from the hot sauce and the canned goods. The body needs some electrolytes to stay hydrated, and I'm sure you were low," The doctor said as she listened to his chest with a stethoscope. Harry thought once again of his friend Dario.

"You lost almost thirty pounds in a week, but you have been eating occasionally, so you're not at risk for refeeding syndrome. However, you do have sun and wind exposure, so you'll need to use this," She said as she handed him a salve.

"Also, you can take acetaminophen or Ibuprhen for any soreness or pain if allowed by your personal physician. Other than that, stay cool, hydrate, and rest for a few days, and you should be fine," She said as she stood up and waved for Uncle Enrique to come over.

Enrique walked over and handed Harry back his car keys. "Your cash is in the trunk, and Grandmother Angelita says for you to be sure to come back next year for the barbeque," He said to Harry with a smile and then turned to face Miss Joy Ride. "And that goes for you too, Miss Ride. We hope to see you at next year's barbeque as well."

As Harry and Joy said their goodbyes, Hank and Abbie were traveling on Farm to Market 170, not far from Hacienda Ramirez. After leaving the truck stop, they had taken turns driving for eight and a half hours and were just now arriving in Perdido, Texas.

It was a little after ten in the morning, and they were in need of some coffee and something to eat. "Well, I guess we know where we're stopping for coffee and gas," Hank joked as he pulled into the only gas station for miles around.

At the pump, Hank turned the Impala's ignition off as he turned to Abbie, "After I top off, we'll go in and get a couple of cups of coffee and something to eat. While we're in there, we'll see if the cashier has any information on your father's whereabouts." "Coffee sounds great. I'm running on fumes," Abbie said as she opened the passenger-side door to get out.

The gas station was a small mom-and-pop operation without much of an inventory. Hank and Abbie selected a couple of honey buns from a shelf, poured two coffees to go, and made their way to the cash register.

At the cash register, Hank paid for the gas, coffee, and honey buns. After the transaction, he retrieved his cell phone from his pocket and addressed the cashier, "Excuse me, Ma'am," He said, holding up his phone and showing her Harry's image. We're looking for this man. Have you seen him around?" he asked.

The cashier stared at the image on the phone and then stared off into the distance as if deep in thought. Then she stared back at the phone, then back off into the distance again, and then she nodded her head yes.

"Really?" Hank asked, surprised. "Where about's did you see him?" he asked. The cashier raised her arm and pointed to where she had been staring. Hank and Abbie turned around and looked through the storefront window. There outside at the pumps was Abbie's father, Harry Adams.

Harry and his daughter's reunion had been an awkward one. Her father was thirty pounds thinner than he had been, looked like he had been through hell, and was in the company of an attractive girl who was not much older than Abbie. Also, there was the matter of the almost eighty-thousand dollars in the trunk of his Cadillac.

Harry had told them the short version of what had happened, which explained his absence and appearance. Harry then told his daughter about how Joy had been the only one to believe in him and how she had bet on him to win against all odds when everyone else had bet on him to die out in the desert. Afterwhich, Abbie developed an immediate fondness for her father's new friend.

Once all the introductions had been made and everything had been sorted out, Hank's thoughts turned to the money. "If you get pulled over by a state trooper with that much cash, they'll seize it for sure, and Abbie had to report you and your car missing. That means they're looking for you right now," he said.

"Great, now what do we do?" Joy asked. "Well, we could take my car. However, there's the chance that we could still get pulled over," Hank said, "and this close to the border, they'll want to go through the car. I think that instead of just leaving Harry's car here, a better plan would be for him to drive ahead while we three trailed behind with the money in the Impala.

"Presidio is the closest town to here with a bank, hotel, and clothing store. Harry would travel ahead of us at a few miles per hour over the speed limit, stopping occasionally so that we could catch up. Between Harry traveling over the speed limit and the fact that the cops are already looking for his car anyway, he would make an excellent blocker for the money car.

"We'd stay in communication by cellphone. If he got pulled over for some reason, we'd just stop until he got it straightened out. They won't detain an adult missing person, especially once he tells them that he was just out "camping." I'll throw some camping gear in your trunk that will back up your story unless I miss my guess they'll look.

"Once in Presidio, we'd get a hotel room and some clothes for Harry, and then once he was all cleaned up, he could go to the police station and let them know that he's okay. After that, I could escort the two of you to the bank, making sure nothing happens along the way. At the bank, y'all would get a couple of safety deposit boxes to stash your cash in until you're able to move it later," Hank said.

Harry looked at Joy, who eagerly nodded her approval. "That would be very generous of you," Harry said. "Well, I'm not exactly that generous. It is a federal crime to transport unlawful money, and since I would be risking the Impala getting seized and possible jail time, I was thinking ten percent would be fair," Hank said. "Sounds good to me. How about you, Joy?" Harry said. "Sounds good to me. It's cheaper than taxes!"

Chapter Thirty-Two

The Trial

Two weeks before the trial of Luke Harrison, Johnny Merle, and Stanley Richard, a well-known Corpus Christi lawyer recognized Abbie's photo as he read about her case in the *Corpus Christi Wave*. Although the lawyer recognized Abbie's photo in the newspaper, she did not recognize him when he showed up to offer his services pro bono, nor did his name ring any bells, not at first.

The gentleman had walked up to her in his Brooks Brothers suit and Florsheim Castellano wing-tip shoes held out his business card, and said, "Hi, I'm William Robert Nash, Attorney at law. We met once before."

Abbie had stared at him blankly until he had said, "At the house party on Ocean Drive. I am Maximus Aaran Robinson's personnel attorney. He owns Dragonfly Helicopter Services." It was then that she was able to put it together and finally recognized William Robert Nash, who was known to his friends as "Billy Bob."

After listening to their whole story, Billy Bob advised Jake to tell one small lie in court. He advised Jake that in order to keep Charlie off the witness stand while avoiding an illegal search and seizure wrap, it would be necessary for him to say that he heard a woman screaming in the warehouse. This would invoke exigent circumstances, giving Jake a legal reason to have broken into the warehouse without a warrant.

Abbie, for her part, was advised to tell mostly the truth, except she would collaborate with Jake's story by testifying that she had indeed screamed at some point. Also, she would omit the reason she had been kidnapped in the first place so as not to bring her father's illegal gambling to light.

The trial had been a long process, but Jake and Abbie both gave their testimonies and answered all questions just as Billy Bob had coached them, and everything went smoothly. Luke, Johnny, and Stan were found guilty on two counts of aggravated kidnapping, assaulting a police officer, and various other charges. Charlie taking the stand was avoided, and Abbie's father was never mentioned.

As for Abbie's father, he and Joy had made it to that bank in Presidio, where they opened new accounts and rented safety deposit boxes and succeeded in getting all their cash locked away. All the cash, that is, except for the money that had belonged to Dario.

Harry had told Abbie the story of Dario, and they both had tears in their eyes by the time he was done, "I took so much from the man I can't take anymore," Harry said as he shoved the cash into Abbie's hands. Three days later, Father Clements at St. Thomas was rather shocked to find an envelope containing one-thousand-six-hundred and eighty dollars in the poor box along with the money he had loaned Abbie in a separate envelope with his name on it that read, Thanks for the loan.

After Harry and Joy's money was safe in the bank, they made their way to Catfish's trailer park. With Luke and his crew locked up, Harry had no one to pay his ten grand to, so he used the money to make the much-needed repairs to his RV. He then took Abbie and Joy on a trip to Big Bend State Park, where he and Abbie were able to make a fresh start.

When Abbie returned to Corpus Christi, Harry and Joy continued on an extended vacation. They had been on the road for three weeks and were relaxing at "Chain-O-Lakes," northeast of Cleveland, Texas when Harry's cell phone rang.

"Harry, this is Joey, Joey "Two-Cards" Lombardi, You remember me?" The voice on the other end had said. Shocked and somewhat worried, Harry answered, "Yeah, Joey, I remember you. What can I do for you?"

"Well, I never left Perdido, Harry. Alejandro and I have been here in the control room the whole time, editing all the video that was shot of you crossing the border. Harry, we've been editing day and night, and I think we've come up with something special here, sorta've an illegal border crossing survivalist show.

"The only problem is we need to shoot a few more scenes and reshoot some of the other scenes from different angles so that we can get this thing complete. So what you say, you come on back down here and help us out, huh? It won't be like before, Harry. I promise we'll take care of you.

"I had my people obtain the proper permits to cross the river legally and everything. Enrique will provide security, and you'll stay in an air-conditioned camper until it's time to shoot your scenes. You come back and do this for me, and I'll make you a rich man. Come on, Harry, what do you say?" Joey, "Two-Cards," asked.

After discussing it briefly with Joy, she and Harry decided to go on what wound up being a vacation in West Texas and Mexico. Joey joked over the next few weeks that they would have to hurry up and finish filming before Harry got too fat. They ate, they drank, and they filmed what was needed to complete the documentary, which Joey decided to call "Harry Adams, Border Survivor!"

The show was hugely popular, and Harry started to make good money by teaching survivalist seminars, which was something that always made him laugh. The money from the seminars, coupled with the residuals he received from "Harry Adams, Boarder Survivor!," was enough to make his and Joy's vacation on the road permanent.

Harry and Joy weren't the only ones to come out ahead. While the media coverage of Jake's rescue from the warehouse had not been good for the CCPD, it had been good for Hank. He became a local hero overnight, and supporters flocked to Sal's, causing the doughnut shop to be packed and Hank's and Tinker's tips to be quite considerable for a few months.

The news coverage had been the most lucrative for Abbie, as she had become the media's sweetheart immediately. The news crew had arrived in time to record all of Jake's rescue and had waited to interview Abbie after she had finished speaking to the police.

The clip they aired of Abbie on the news before her interview showed her taking Luke down, turning him over to the police, and then walking nonchalantly across the parking lot to retrieve her skateboard, which she held by her side during the entire interview.

This, coupled with her court testimony of how she escaped, using her skateboard to knock one of her kidnappers unconscious, gained the interest of Grinder Street magazine, which later interviewed Abbie. The interview with the popular skateboard magazine had two positive benefits for Abbie. One, she got a sponsorship with the company that made the brand of skateboard that she had cracked Stan's head open with, and two, she received a college sponsorship.

Abbie mentioned during her interview with the magazine that her ultimate goal was to obtain a college degree. Many generous people had read Abbie's interview, and a fund was created and gifted to her that would pay for up to one hundred and twenty credit hours at a college of her choice. Abbie began taking classes the semester after the trial was over.

In the weeks following the trial, Hank and Tinker continued working at Sal's, and Abbie busied herself with work, school, her occasional sponsorship requirements for Grinder Street Skateboard Company, and getting reacquainted with her father, but this didn't last long.

While Jake had worked at getting his new private investigation business off the ground, he continued to make Sal's his morning coffee stop, and Abbie had started joining her friends there in the mornings as well. Soon, Jake fell into the habit of seeking their help on some of his more difficult cases. Hank turned out to be a great asset to Jake, which led to him insisting that he pay Hank on a case-by-case basis as a consultant.

Hank started working for Jake under his license and began to make better money working for him than he did working for Sal, and he slowly transitioned from one job to the other.

Abbie had done the occasional odd job for Jake as well and had found that she liked it. She liked it so much that she switched from nursing school to criminal justice and became a licensed private investigator in a little over two years.

Hank eventually earned a license as well. It had taken him a little longer because, unlike Abbie, he did not have sponsors. However, the money he earned helping Harry and Joy get out of the desert gave him a good start.

He was able to pay for the rest of his school with his paychecks and tips from Sal's and the extra money he made working for Jake on the side, and a little over a year after Abbie had earned her license, Hank received his as well, with both he and Abbie continuing to work for Jake's private investigation firm, Bayside Private Investigations.

Epilogue

Two years have passed since I started working full-time for Jake at Bayside Private Investigations. These days, I watch the sunrise before I go to Sal's in the morning. No more getting up at two in the morning to sling doughnuts for me. These days, I prefer to be asleep at that hour. If you're outside in the morning and you don't hear the birds chirping, that's because they have enough sense to know that it's too damn early to be up.

There has been zero mention of looking for any sort of office space for Bayside Private Investigations. We still meet at Sal's every morning, have coffee, and make our plans for the day. Sal doesn't mind since I sometimes watch the shop for a couple of hours while he goes to the beach to catch a few waves.

Speaking of the beach, this morning, I watched another spectacular sunrise over South Bay before leaving for Sal's. As I pulled the Impala out onto Ocean Drive, the newly rebuilt *four-fifty-four turbo-jet* roared to life with a raw power that the next generations would never know.

Tinker had lovingly kept the Impala going through the lean years, but eventually, I bought a used truck to drive while he rebuilt the Impala. He's now in the process of rebuilding the truck and has it broken down into little pieces all over his shop, with plans to build some kind of high-tech paddy wagon out of it.

All this mechanic work is starting to get a little pricey, I thought as I turned right onto Airline Avenue. I was hoping Jake had something with a nice payday lined up for me. What I needed was a case like that Remington sculpture that had been stolen from that rich Houston oil baron's mansion out in River Oaks.

That had been a good payday, I thought as I waited at the red light. The light turned green, and I made the right-hand turn onto Bakner Street. In less than a minute, I was pulling into Sal's.

The greeting bell chimed as I walked through the doughnut shop's front door. Jake looked up from a pile of paperwork, "Good morning!" he said. "And good morning to you, Sir," I said as I walked behind the counter and helped myself to some coffee. "I have a job here. I think you and Abbie could work together while I wrap up the loose ends on the McCafferty case."

"Oh yeah, what you got?" "I've got two bail skippers, a couple of real lowlife-dirtbags, you interested?" he asked. Before I could answer, the greeting bell chimed again as Abbie walked through Sal's front door. "Abbie, you're just in time... Jake has a couple of bail jumpers for us," I said. "Excellent, what do you have on them?"

"Betty, the Bond Agent tells me that these guys are known cohorts and will likely be found together," Jake said as he slid two files across the table. I could hardly believe my eyes. There, in one of the files, was a mugshot of Mister Dirty Shirt himself, and in the other was his yellow gap-toothed cohort. "Well, now I don't think these two will be hard to find," I said.

Since the bail skippers and I already had a run-in, I figured they were likely to recognize me. Therefore, Abbie and I both agreed that it would make more sense for her to be the bait while I watched from somewhere close by.

She had read the files on Kyle Leslie Harlen, also known as Dirty Shirt, and his buddy, Mister Robert Lee Booth, also known as Yellow Gap Tooth, and had learned that their pattern was to attack younger, smaller men.

Harlow had admitted when questioned, that this was because they preferred to overpower their victims while not having to worry about interference from some good samaritans answering calls for help. "Females have a tendency to scream, whereas guys, unless they're smart, usually have the tendency to clam up," Harlow had said in an interview conducted by a Corpus Christi police detective.

As a result of what she had learned in their files, Abbie disguised herself to look like a young male. Her head was already shaved around the sides and back, so she just tucked the rest of her hair under a ball cap. Her loose-fitting carpenter pants and oversized t-shirt that she wore to have room to move in when she skated also worked well to hide her figure, and she stood at five foot seven, which was a convincing height for a young male.

On our fourth night out, I was wearing a…we'll say, borrowed valet jacket and was watching Abbie from under the drive-thru portico of the hotel across the street from the Selena Memorial Statue on Shoreline Boulevard when. After three nights of nothing, I finally spotted the two thugs walking in Abbie's direction.

"Coming your way from the north," I said through her earpiece as I crossed the street to the side, where she was sitting on a bench that was facing the bay. As the thugs approached, she stood and began to walk past them. Dirty Shirt stepped in front of her, blocking her path, and began to speak. As Abbie distracted them, I came up behind Yellow Gap-tooth and forcibly jerked him back to the sidewalk by his shirt collar. In the same instant, Abbie violently threw Dirty Shirt to the ground with an outside leg reap.

The next morning, as I made the right-hand turn from Airline Avenue onto Bakner Street, a huge grin creased my face as I thought about the look on those thugs' faces when they hit the ground. That had been a good day. *But today's a new day, and there's no telling what kind of case Jake might have,* I thought as the Impala rumbled to a stop in the parking lot of Sal's Doughnuts.

About The Author:

J.D. Cody was born at Rosewood General Hospital, which once stood on the Corner of Westheimer and Fondren in Houston, Texas. His childhood was divided between his parents' and paternal grandparents' homes on the outskirts of Houston in Sugarland, Texas, and his maternal grandparents' home on the R.E. Bob Smith Ranch between Orchard and Rosenberg, Texas.

Mr. R.E. Bob Smith was an oil baron, cattle rancher, and one of the founders of the Houston Astros. J.D. Cody's grandfather, H.T., worked for R.E. Bob Smith Ranch as a horse trainer and was well known for winning the Houston Livestock Show and Rodeo, cutting horse championship multiple times.

R.E. Bob Smith's ranches sprawled some 6,000 acres along the Brazos River, and J.D. Cody's grandfather's employment there gifted him the opportunity to wander the entirety of the ranch. Thus, his childhood was split between two different worlds, one of inner-city living and one of the fields, lakes, and deep woods along the Brazos River bottom.

At eighteen years of age, J.D. Cody enlisted in the U.S. Army and went through basic training at Fort Jackson, South Carolina, before continuing on to Fort Gordon, Georgia, for his advanced individual training. The remainder of his enlistment was spent in the U.S. Army Signal Core as a telecommunications technician specializing in encryption/decryption equipment.

His first year of active duty was spent at the U.S. Army Garrison, Yongsa, Seoul, Korea. Upon his return to the United States, he married his high school sweetheart, and the two of them moved to Waynesboro, Pennsylvania, where he reported to his new duty station at Raven Rock Mountain Complex, Site-R, near Blue Ridge Summit, Pennsylvania.

After finishing his enlistment at Raven Rock Mountain, J.D. Cody returned to civilian life with an Army equivalent of a bachelor's degree in digital communications and multimedia exchange and could have gotten a well-paying job. Only he was too stupid to know that at the time.

Instead, he moved back to Texas, where he worked in construction, truck driving, janitorial services, farming, and martial arts. He has also worked as a furniture delivery man, correctional officer, kennel worker, cowboy, and many other jobs, too numerous to mention.

J.D. Cody currently resides in very rural Texas, where he lives a very happy life with his high school sweetheart, Missis J.D. Cody, and his son. They share their home with their three beloved dogs (one small Buddy, one medium Rocky, and one large Roscoe), one pine snake that goes by the name Mister Fink Sneakerton, and the three laying hens Bubbles, Crystal, and No'Ma'am.

Made in the USA
Columbia, SC
16 May 2024